Last Licks

Cynthia Baxter

KENSINGTON BOOKS
www.kensingtonbooks.com

KENSINGTON BOOKS are published by

Kensington Publishing Corp.
119 West 40th Street
New York, NY 10018

All Kensington titles, imprints, and distributed lines are available at special quantity discounts for bulk purchases for sales promotion, premiums, fund-raising, educational, or institutional use.

Special book excerpts or customized printings can also be created to fit specific needs. For details, write or phone the office of the Kensington Sales Manager: Attn.: Sales Department. Kensington Publishing Corp., 119 West 40th Street, New York, NY 10018. Phone: 1-800-221-2647.

Kensington and the K logo Reg. U.S. Pat. & TM Off.

First Kensington Hardcover Edition: January 2020

ISBN-13: 978-1-4967-1420-6 (ebook)
ISBN-10: 1-4967-1420-2 (ebook)

ISBN-13: 978-1-4967-1419-0
ISBN-10: 1-4967-1419-9
First Kensington Trade Paperback Edition: September 2020

10 9 8 7 6 5 4 3 2 1

Printed in the United States of America

Last
Licks

Chapter 1

Next to cookies, ice cream stands as the
best-selling treat in America.

—*www.icecream.com/icecreaminfo*

"How does this sound? Green ice cream—pistachio
would be perfect—that's mixed with chocolate chips,
nuts, crushed chocolate cookies, and—here's the best part—
tiny eyeballs made of sugar!"

"It sounds amazing," I told my eighteen-year-old niece
Emma, whose big brown eyes were lit up with excitement.
"And I bet you have a great name for it."

"I do!" she replied gleefully. "Monster Mash!"

"I love it," I told her. "I'm adding it to the list. Of course,
we'd have to find someone who actually *makes* sugar eyeballs."

Halloween was less than three weeks away, and Emma
and I were sitting at one of the round marble tables at my ice
cream store, the Lickety Splits Ice Cream Shoppe, trying to
come up with fun flavors that had a spooky theme. We had
just finished our usual breakfast of Cappuccino Crunch ice
cream, which I consider a perfectly respectable substitute for
a more normal breakfast since it contains coffee, cream, and
protein-rich nuts.

But so far, our enthusiasm had greatly outweighed our

productivity. In fact, Monster Mash was only the second fla-vor I'd written on the list. The other was Smashed Pumpkins, which was pumpkin ice cream with pecans and pralines—both smashed into little pieces, of course.

Yet while we were still at the brainstorming stage for cre-ative new flavors, thanks to my artistic niece, my shop al-ready looked like Halloween Central. I had given her free reign with decorating, and the results had astounded me. Just looking around was enough to put me in a Halloween mood.

Emma had begun by hanging fake spiderwebs all around the shop. She'd made them by draping strips of gauzy fabric from the shiny tin ceiling and along the exposed brick wall. She had even put them on the huge, cartoon-like paintings of ice cream treats that my best friend, Willow, had painted for the shop. One was a picture of a huge ice cream cone, one was a banana split, and the third was an ice cream sandwich. The webs were anything but eerie, especially because of the furry stuffed spiders she had added here and there. In fact, the huge smiles she'd embroidered on their faces made them look positively cute.

Intertwined in the spiderwebs were strings of tiny orange lights. They nicely complemented the string of orange jack-o'-lantern lights that Emma had hung across the front display window that overlooked Hudson Street, Wolfert's Roost's main thoroughfare. To me, those grinning pumpkins cap-tured all the fun of what had always been one of my favorite holidays. A second string of jack-o'-lantern lights festooned the glass display case that contained the giant tubs of ice cream.

But the best part of Lickety Splits' Halloween décor were the life-size creatures my clever niece had made out of papier-mâché, paint, fabric, and glue. At the moment, Count Drac-ula was sitting at the table behind me, his mitten-like hand holding a plastic spoon. In front of him was a ceramic coffin the size of a dinner plate piled high with fake ice cream made from balls of fabric. Emma had done an incredible job of replicating one of Lickety Splits' signature dishes, the Bananafana Split. And customers were more than welcome to share the Count's table while they ate their own ice cream.

Emma had also constructed a life-size witch, complete with a tall, pointed hat and a long, crooked nose. She stood at the front door, greeting customers. Well, scowling at them, actually. But when you're dealing with Halloween clichés, mean-looking witches are so much more effective than friendly ones.

Outside the shop, on the pink-and-lime-green bench I'd placed underneath the display window, sat Frankenstein. His face and hands were made from nubby green burlap. He even had bolts in his neck. He was grinning at the ice cream cone he held, which was piled high with three humongous scoops. Definitely a monster-size portion by anyone's standards.

To make these creatures, Emma had enlisted Grams's help. Night after night, my niece and my grandmother had sat up at the dining room table long after I'd gone to bed, bent over their sewing like pioneer women. But instead of quilts or gingham prairie dresses, they were creating these wonderful, lovable monsters.

True, I'd had to say no to Emma's idea about dripping fake blood over Count Dracula's banana split. After all, I was in the business of selling ice cream, not freaking out potential customers. But I'd said yes to the fuzzy black-felt bats she had wanted to sew onto his shoulders. The way I saw it, you could never have too many vampire touches.

I was astounded that Emma had found the time to work on such an ambitious project. A few weeks earlier, she had begun taking two classes at the local community college. One was Life Drawing, meant to feed her outstanding artistic talents. The other was some computer thing I never did understand. All this was in addition to working part-time at my ice cream shop. Since I hadn't been eighteen myself for a decade and a half, I didn't know if all young women her age had that much energy or if she just happened to be exceptional.

"How about ice cream concoctions that are based on popular costumes?" Emma suggested. "Like . . ." Her eyes traveled around the shop, taking in the characters she had created. "Like pirates and clowns and maybe even ghosts.

"We could make clowns whose heads are a scoop of ice cream and faces are made from pieces of candy," she went on. "And ice cream cone hats! We can put frosting on the cones and then stick on colored sprinkles—"

"Or pearls," I interjected. "We could decorate the hats with pearls. The candy variety, not the jewelry kind."

"What on earth are pearls?" Emma demanded.

"They're tiny round balls made of sugar," I explained. "They're also called dragées. They come in all colors, but my personal favorite is the shiny silver variety."

"Like miniature disco balls?" Emma asked, blinking.

I laughed. "Exactly," I said, adding ice cream clowns to the list. "How about ghost ice cream cones? A scoop of vanilla ice cream in a cone that's been dipped in white chocolate."

"And witches!" Emma cried. "Ice cream cones make perfect witches' hats! We can cover them with something smooth and black—fondant would work great. And we can make little brims . . ."

"Wonderful," I said, scribbling away.

"But we still need more Halloween-inspired flavors," Emma said, frowning. And then her face lit up. "How about Creepy Crawlers? We could start with chocolate, since it's brown like dirt, and mix in gummy centipedes and spiders." Excitedly, she added, "We could put in powdered cocoa, too, so it *really* looks like dirt. And maybe there's something we could use for pebbles . . ."

I grimaced. "I'll have to think about that one. It sounds fun, but I'm not sure anyone would actually want to eat it."

"I bet it'd be a real hit with ten-year-old boys," my niece countered.

"True," I replied. "Probably with forty-year-old boys, too."

I was in the midst of making notes about the Creepy Crawler flavor when the door to my shop opened. I glanced up, surprised to see a young woman striding inside confidently. Even though I'd unlocked the door when I'd come in that morning, the CLOSED sign was still hanging on it.

Yet even as the woman glanced around and saw that Emma and I were the only ones in the shop and that neither of us was standing behind the counter selling ice cream, she looked perfectly at ease as she surveyed my store.

She appeared to be in her late twenties or early thirties and was dressed in fashionable-looking jeans, a baggy, oatmeal-colored sweater, and brown-suede ankle boots. Her thick, flyaway red hair was pulled back into a messy bun, with lots of loose ends falling around her face and neck.

"I'm sorry, but we're not open yet," I told her.

"So I see," she said, still looking around. Her tone crisp and businesslike, she asked, "How big is this space?"

"About nine hundred square feet," I told her. "That includes the work area in back."

"Are you the manager here?" she asked.

My stomach suddenly tightened. I wondered if she was an inspector of some kind. I instantly felt guilty, even though I was pretty confident that I had nothing to feel guilty about.

"Yes," I replied, growing increasingly wary. "I'm also the owner. My name is Kate McKay."

"And I'm Chelsea Atkins," she said.

I glanced over at Emma, who looked as if she was just as puzzled as I was. "Is there something I can help you with?" I asked.

"I hope so," she said. "I'm the assistant director on a

movie that's being filmed here in the Hudson Valley. Which means that my job is basically to make sure that everything runs as smoothly as possible."

Once again, I looked over at Emma. Her expression had changed completely. Her eyes had grown wide, and her cheeks were now the color of my Strawberry Rhubarb Pie ice cream.

"A film? You mean like a big Hollywood movie?" she half-whispered.

"That's right," Chelsea said, her tone still brusque. "It's being made by a production company called Palm Frond Productions. It's based in Los Angeles, which is also where I live."

"Who's in it?" my star-struck niece asked.

"No one you're likely to have heard of," Chelsea replied. "At least, not yet. But this movie, *The Best Ten Days of My Life*, is going to make its star famous. Savannah Crane is destined to be the next big thing. Some people are even saying that she's about to become the new Jennifer Jordan."

Thoughtfully, she added, "Ironically, Jennifer Jordan tried out for this role. She really, really wanted it, too." She shrugged. "But that's Hollywood."

"I love Jennifer Jordan!" Emma cried. She reached into the purple backpack lying on the floor beside her and pulled out a tattered magazine. "Look! She's on the cover of this week's issue of *People*! I even follow her on Twitter and Instagram!"

I glanced at the actress pictured on the cover of the magazine. Jennifer Jordan was beautiful, with long, straight, jet-black hair and huge eyes the color of dark chocolate. Her cheekbones were so sharp that they practically stuck out of the page. I vaguely remembered seeing her in a movie, but I couldn't remember which one.

"But I've got a problem," Chelsea went on, "and I wondered if you might be able to help."

"We can help!" Emma cried. She began fluffing her mane

of wildly curly dark hair, not quite as black as Jennifer Jordan's but much more distinctive because of the blue streaks running through it. You'd have thought she was auditioning for a role in this movie herself.

I was much more cautious. "What exactly is the problem?" I asked.

"Tomorrow morning, we were scheduled to shoot a key scene at a diner that's a few miles from here, over in Woodstock," Chelsea explained. "But the owner called me late last night and said there'd been a small fire in the kitchen. The fire department has closed the restaurant, and no one is allowed on the premises until it's finished its investigation. So we suddenly find ourselves with no place to film the scene."

I could see where this was going. "But this isn't a diner," I said, pointing out the obvious.

"No, but the diner part isn't important," Chelsea said. "What we need is an eatery of some kind. A place that has some charm. Some style. And it just so happens that the main character, the role of Suzi Hamilton that Savannah Crane is playing, is eating ice cream in this scene. That's why I went online to look for ice cream shops in the Hudson Valley and found yours."

"I see," I said.

So did Emma. She looked as if she was about to burst.

"You want to film a scene for a big Hollywood movie *here*?" she cried. "At Lickety Splits?"

"It would sure be a quick fix for a disaster we didn't see coming," Chelsea said. "Normally, the location scout on a project like this spends a long time finding the spots where each scene will be filmed. But we don't have much time. Basically, we're stuck. And, well, you can help." She looked at me expectantly.

"What would I have to do?" I asked uneasily.

"Basically nothing," Chelsea said. "That is, aside from

closing your shop for whatever length of time we need to finish filming. Probably just a few hours, starting first thing tomorrow morning. Another thing is that the crew would have
to come in beforehand to set up. Ideally, we'd show up late
tonight, ideally around nine o'clock."

"But what about all these wonderful Halloween decorations my niece put up?" I asked, still doubtful.

"I promise you that by the time we leave, this place will
look exactly the way it does now," Chelsea assured me. "The
first thing we'll do is take plenty of photos. Once we're finished, we'll put everything back."

Glancing around, she added, "And if there's any damage,
which hardly ever happens, we'll fix it. I can guarantee that
at the end of the shoot you won't even know we were here."

I thought for a few seconds, then thought of something
else. "What exactly happens in the scene?" I had visions of
chaotic shoot-outs, ceilings caving in, and bad guys being
pushed through windows.

"The scene opens with Savannah Crane's character sitting
at a table by herself, eating ice cream," Chelsea explained.
"Her boyfriend comes in and sits down. They have an argument, and then he gets up and leaves. End of scene."

"That's it?" I asked.

"That's it," she said.

Do it! Emma was mouthing, practically jumping out of
her chair.

"Would it be okay if I was here during the shoot?" I asked,
trying to sound casual. "With a few members of my staff, of
course," I added, nodding toward Emma. "I'd feel much more
comfortable if we could stick around to keep an eye on things."

"As long as you understand that you have to stay out of
the way," Chelsea replied. "And that you have to remain absolutely silent while we're filming."

I was about to say yes when she reached into her bag and
pulled out some papers.

"Here's a contract that outlines the terms," she said as she handed it to me.

I read through it quickly and found that it pretty much spelled out everything she'd just said. There was a bit of legal mumbo jumbo, too, wording I couldn't come close to understanding.

I should have Jake take a look at it, I thought. He *is* a lawyer, after all. And I want to be perfectly certain that—

And then I caught sight of a number at the bottom. With a dollar sign next to it.

"What's this number?" I asked, blinking. "This dollar amount?"

"That's what we'll pay you for the shoot," Chelsea explained patiently. "It's our normal fee. I'm afraid it's non-negotiable, but it is pretty standard."

I literally had to stop myself from letting my jaw drop. I was that flabbergasted.

It was a very large number.

"I'm sure all this is fine," I finally managed to say, "but I'll have to run it by my lawyer."

Out of the corner of my eye, I could see Emma's face fall. She started making histrionic gestures that were so distracting that I turned away.

"But that shouldn't take long," I added. "He can probably look at it this morning."

Chelsea nodded. "I'm sure he'll be fine with it. As I said, this is our standard contract, and we're offering the usual amount. How about if somebody stops by to pick up the contract later today?"

"That's fine," I said, still reeling. "I'll let you know when it's signed."

"So we're set," Chelsea said.

"I guess so," I replied, feeling a bit dazed. Emma was pumping her fist in the air in victory.

"Great. Here's my contact info," Chelsea said, handing me

a business card. I, in turn, grabbed one of the flyers I keep on the display counter, jotted down my cell phone number, and gave it to her. In addition to the shop's phone number and address, the flyer lists Lickety Splits' hours and a few of our most popular flavors. Emma designed it, of course. After all, she's my marketing department and my art department as well as my best employee.

"I'm so glad this is working out," Chelsea said, reaching over and shaking my hand. "And don't hesitate to get in touch if you have any more questions."

"I do have one more," I said. "Will anyone actually be eating any ice cream during the shoot? I just want to know what to have on hand."

"We will need ice cream," she replied. "We could supply it ourselves, but given how fast all this is happening, it would be great if you could do it."

"I'd be happy to," I told her. "I also have dishes and spoons, of course."

"Perfect," Chelsea said. "Sometimes the props people make a big deal about what they want to use, but the prop master on this shoot is pretty mellow."

As soon as she left, Emma exploded.

"O-M-G, this is the most exciting thing that's ever happened in this town!" she shrieked. "A real Hollywood movie, being filmed here—right in your shop!"

"It *is* pretty cool," I admitted. I was already busy with my phone, texting Jake about the movie shoot and asking him to stop by to look at the contract as soon as it was convenient. "I just hope that—"

"A Hollywood director! Real cameras! Movie stars!" Emma cried, waving her arms in the air excitedly.

"The actress playing the lead role isn't exactly a star," I pointed out. "At least not yet. And—"

"Just think, Kate, you can hang framed photos of the actors and the director on the wall!" she continued. "Auto-graphed!"

"Emma, that's a nice idea, but—"

I was about to tell her about my lingering concerns. One was the possibility of things getting broken and never really fixed correctly, no matter how well intentioned the film crew was. Another was disappointing my regular customers when they showed up to buy ice cream and found that my shop was closed.

But before I had a chance, the door opened once again.

Emma snapped her head around. I got the feeling she was expecting a famous movie star to walk in. Instead, Grams was coming into the shop.

When I was five years old, my father died. Soon afterward, my mother, my two older sisters, and I moved to the Hudson Valley to live with my grandmother. Then, when I was ten, my mom died. Grams became our mother then.

In fact, Grams was the reason I was living back in my hometown. She had fallen on the stairs back in March, seven months earlier. It immediately became clear that now that she was getting older, she needed help running the house. So I came up with the obvious solution: I left my job working for a public relations firm in New York and moved back to Wolfert's Roost.

My grandmother wasn't alone. There was a man with her. A tall, attractive man who appeared to be about her age.

Which I found at least as interesting as a movie star walking into Lickety Splits.

As usual, Grams was dressed comfortably. But over the last several weeks, as she'd gotten more and more involved with volunteer activities at the local senior center, she'd started wearing spiffier outfits. Today, for example, along with her beige pants and the black blazer she wore over a cream-colored blouse, she had draped a mint-green silk scarf around her neck. She had recently gotten a haircut at Lotsa Locks, the hair salon a few doors down from Lickety Splits. As a result, her gray, blunt-cut pageboy was doing an exceptional job of falling into place.

But there was something else I noticed. Today, she looked prettier than usual. More animated. Her eyes were bright, and her face seemed to be glowing, an effect that had nothing to do with makeup. I had a hunch that the good-looking man she was with was the reason.

He, too, was nicely dressed, wearing crisply-ironed khaki pants, a black knit golf shirt, and shiny black loafers. His silver hair was almost the same color as Grams's, and his eyes were a distinctive shade of hazel.

I had to admit that they made a cute couple.

"Hi, Grams!" I greeted her. "This is a nice surprise. What brings you into town this morning?"

"I have someone I'd like you both to meet," she replied, smiling. "A new friend I made at the senior center. Emma, Kate, this is George Vernon. George, this is my great-granddaughter, Emma, who's an amazingly talented artist as well as a computer genius. And this is my favorite granddaughter—although I guess I shouldn't admit that. Anyway, this is Kate."

"Pleased to meet you," George said, giving me a firm handshake. "And I'm afraid I have to add that old cliché about having heard so much about you. All of it positive, of course. Your grandmother raves about you both constantly. Emma, I've heard all about your creativity. As for you, Kate, it's pretty clear that you really are her favorite granddaughter."

"Grams is definitely at the top of my list of favorite people, too," I assured him, laughing.

"Mine, too," Emma piped up.

"Both of these young women deserve every bit of praise they get," Grams insisted. "Kate here isn't only a former public relations star who's made a great success of her new ice cream empire. She's also the sweetest, most considerate, strongest, cleverest—"

"You can see I wasn't exaggerating," George interrupted, his tone teasing.

"But Grams has been quite secretive about you," I told him, casting my grandmother a sly look. "In fact, I'm afraid I don't know a thing about you."

He shrugged. "There's not much to tell. I'm just one more retired businessman. And a widower who's still getting used to being on my own. Frankly, I was getting a little tired of playing golf every day, so I decided to check out the local senior center. I met your grandmother the first time I walked in. And the next thing I knew, she'd signed me up for the Halloween Hollow committee." Looking over at her fondly, he added, "The woman wouldn't take no for an answer. Which makes her my kind of gal."

"I didn't exactly have to twist your arm!" Grams exclaimed. But the flush of her cheeks told me she didn't mind his ribbing in the least.

"At least not after you agreed that I could still sneak off to play golf a few times a week!" George shot back.

"What's the Halloween Hollow committee?" Emma asked.

Grams pulled out a black wrought-iron chair and sat down on its pink-vinyl seat. "You know that I've gotten the folks at the senior center involved in volunteering, mainly working with kids in the community."

Emma and I both nodded.

"You also know that in recent years, trick or treating has pretty much gone out of style," Grams went on.

I did know that—and it made me sad. When I was growing up, Halloween was one of my favorite holidays. And trick or treating was what it was all about. I still remembered all the fun my two sisters and I had had planning our costumes weeks in advance, as well as agonizing over which shopping bag or pillowcase to carry to maximize the number of treats we could stash away. Then came the thrill of the big day itself, going house to house collecting candy. Even the final step was exhilarating: sorting through the day's haul that night, gleefully exclaiming over each Snickers bar or peanut-butter cup as if there was no other way in the world to acquire them.

"So I came up with an idea," Grams continued, her voice reflecting her growing excitement. "We're going to build a haunted house in the high school gym so all the kids in Wolfert's Roost can celebrate there—safely. And one of the women at the senior center came up with the perfect name for it: Halloween Hollow."

"What a great idea!" I exclaimed.

Grams was beaming. "It's going to be sensational. A few of the regulars at the senior center used to work in construction, and they're already drawing up plans. The house will be wonderfully creepy, with creaking doors and cobwebs and strange noises . . . and all the seniors who volunteer will dress up as ghosts and monsters and ghouls."

"Don't forget to tell her about the foam pit the kids can jump into," George interjected.

"A foam pit?" Emma exclaimed. "That sounds awesome!"

"There'll be plenty of candy, too," Grams said. "And we thought that you might be willing to donate some ice cream, Kate."

"Of course!" I exclaimed. "We can set up a do-it-yourself ice cream sundae station where kids can decorate a scoop of ice cream with all kinds of goodies. Not only syrups and whipped cream, but also rainbow sprinkles and sugar pearls in a lot of different colors and pieces of Halloween candy."

"I'll help!" Emma cried. "Can I dress up like a witch? I love wearing costumes, and I hardly ever get a chance. I could make them for all of us—"

"Actually, I kind of like what you're wearing," George commented, nodding at the shirts Emma and I had on.

The knit polo shirts were bubble-gum pink, their breast pockets embroidered in white with the words LICKETY SPLITS ICE CREAM SHOPPE. While I'd ordered them online for my staff members and me to wear whenever we catered events off-site, we'd also started wearing them at the shop sometimes. And if we weren't wearing the shirts, we put on cute black-and-white-checked aprons with LICKETY SPLITS ICE CREAM SHOPPE written on them in pink.

"Those matching shirts make you look very professional," George noted. "Wearing them at Halloween Hollow would give your shop some good exposure, too, since a lot of the parents would see them."

"That's true," Emma said. "But I can wear this shirt anytime. Wearing a witch costume would be much more fun!"

"Then witch costumes it is," Grams said with a nod.

"What about you, George?" I asked. "What's your role in all this?" Jokingly, I added, "I suspect that my hard-driving grandmother is putting you to work big-time."

"You got that right," he replied. "As soon as I mentioned that I'm handy with woodworking, Caroline here put me in charge of overseeing construction. The haunted house, the foam pit . . . I'm overseeing all of it." With a wink, he said, "Good thing I hung on to my tools when I retired."

"Our goal is to make it fun for kids of all ages," Grams noted. "The little ones will come to the gym right after school lets out. Then, in the late afternoon, the middle school kids will get a turn. In the evening, it will be open to high school students."

Beaming, she added, "It's the perfect way to give the children something fun to do without running around the streets of Wolfert's Roost throwing eggs and smashing pumpkins."

"Frankly, when I was a kid, I had a great time throwing

eggs and smashing pumpkins," George said with a grin. "It was what Halloween was all about!"

Grams swatted his arm playfully. "I have no doubt that you got into your share of trouble when you were young."

Feigning surprise, he asked, "What makes you think that's changed?"

"It all sounds wonderful," I said sincerely. "And I'll be happy to help as much as I can."

"Me, too," Emma offered. "Hey, how about if I build some more of these papier-mâché monsters, like Count Dracula here and Frankenstein out in front? Mummies or ghosts or funny monsters with purple faces and orange hair . . .

"And I can make posters advertising Haunted Hollow!" she went on, as full of good ideas as usual. "Bright orange poster board with those scary-looking letters that look like blood dripping . . . We can put them up on the schools' bulletin boards. We can even put some up around town, including in the window of this shop."

"These are all great ideas!" Grams said enthusiastically. "Thank you both so much for agreeing to be part of this. We've put together a marvelous crew, but we can still use every pair of hands we can get."

"You're not the only one with big news, Grams," Emma suddenly said. "Kate has some of her own!"

I'd been so absorbed in Grams's plans that I'd completely forgotten about what had happened right before she and George had shown up.

But before I had a chance to tell them, Emma exploded with, "A Hollywood crew is filming a scene for a movie here at Lickety Splits! *Tomorrow*!"

"My goodness," Grams cried. "That *is* big news."

"Who's in it?" George asked. "Anyone famous?"

"Well, no," Emma replied, her enthusiasm deflating just a little. "But it's supposed to be the breakout film for an actress named Savannah Crane. I've never heard of her, but I plan to get her autograph. It sounds as if she's going to be the next big star!"

"So you'll get to meet her?" Grams asked. "They'll allow you to be here in the shop while they're filming?"

"You bet," Emma said. "Kate made sure of it."

"This all sounds like great fun," George commented. "But won't you lose business if your shop is closed during the filming?"

"They're paying me a small fortune to use Lickety Splits as a movie set," I told him. "And it's just for one day. Tonight, the crew is coming in after I close a little early, at nine instead of eleven. They'll stay as late as necessary to get everything set up for the shoot. Then, first thing in the morning, the actors and the director and the camera people and everyone else will show up and start filming."

"And we get to watch!" Emma cried. "As long as we're quiet and stay out of the way."

"Are they using your ice cream?" George asked. Gesturing at the display case, he added, "It sure looks as if you have enough of it!"

I nodded. "My ice cream, my dishes, even my spoons. They seem really grateful that I'm being so helpful. It seems that Savannah Crane will be eating a dish of my ice cream when the scene opens. Then her boyfriend walks in, and they have an argument." Grinning, I said, "Maybe I won't get my fifteen minutes of fame this time around, but my ice cream will. It might even get a close-up!"

"It sounds thrilling," Grams said sincerely. "So, it looks as if we all have something to be excited about. You and Emma have your glamorous connection to Hollywood, I have my Halloween project—"

"And I get to build a giant foam pit," George added. "Which sounds a heck of a lot more rewarding than playing golf."

"Speaking of which," Grams said, standing up, "you and I

should be heading over to the high school gym. We need to take a few more measurements, and I want to find out if there's a place we can store supplies . . . I've got about a hundred other things to do today, too."

As soon as they had left, I turned to Emma.

Smiling, I said, "My goodness, George is certainly a cutie."

"He sure is," she agreed. "Was it my imagination or was Grams practically glowing?"

"I was thinking the exact same thing!" I exclaimed.

"I'm so happy for her," Emma said, pulling out her phone. "She could really use—oh my goodness, look what time it is! I've got to get to my Life Drawing class!" Hastily, she added, "But I'll be back as soon as it's over. You know, in case the movie people need help with anything."

"Such a dedicated employee," I teased.

"Hey, it's not every day that Hollywood comes to Wolfert's Roost!" she countered. "And if anything else happens, I don't want to miss it!"

The truth was that I was as excited as my niece. In fact, I didn't know how I was going to get through the rest of the day.

Chapter 2

The top six ice-cream-consuming countries in the world (per capita, gallons per year) are (1) New Zealand, (2) the United States, (3) Australia, (4) Finland, (5) Sweden, and (6) China.

—https://www.frozendessertsupplies.com/p-943-which-countries-eat-the-most-ice-cream-ice-cream-consumption-by-countries.aspx

Just as I'd expected, it wasn't easy focusing on ice cream for the next few hours.

For example, a customer requested a Melty Chocolate Malt waffle cone, and I was so distracted that I accidentally scooped out Chocolate Almond Fudge. (Not that the customer minded. At least not when I gave him both cones for the price of one.)

Serving up ice cream suddenly seemed terribly mundane, even if the flavors that surrounded me were as fantastically creative and irresistibly delicious as Honey Lavender and Banana Walnut Bread Pudding and Toasted Coconut with Maui Macadamia.

Not all the flavors in my display case were that exotic. My philosophy at Lickety Splits was to offer three kinds of ice cream. The first category was the classics—like chocolate, vanilla, and strawberry, but each one made with such delectable ingredients that all my customers would walk away feeling that the chocolate cone or scoop of vanilla I'd just served them was the absolute best they had ever tasted.

The ice creams in the second category were slightly more adventurous. These were more along the lines of the flavors that innovative ice cream shops all over the country have begun offering. With my own special touches, of course. The best example was Peanut Butter on the Playground, which is peanut butter ice cream made with freshly ground peanuts, then infused with generous blobs of luscious grape jelly.

The third type involved thinking totally outside the ice cream freezer. I'm talking about flavors that incorporate such unusual ingredients as cheese—any variety, from blue cheese to goat cheese. Chunks of biscotti. Pie crust. Bacon. Sweet potatoes. Potato chips. In short, all the foods people love but have probably never thought of in an ice cream context before.

But today I couldn't get excited about any of them. Not with visions of bright lights and stunningly glamorous actors and stern directors barking out commands dancing in my head.

Ice cream aside, I kept looking at the interior of my shop through the eyes of someone else. Someone like a movie director. Or a camera person. Or even a star who was about to burst onto the Hollywood scene—and onto the cover of a magazine like *People*.

I had to admit that I was certain that everyone involved in the film shoot would be bowled over by Lickety Splits.

When I'd decided to live out a lifelong fantasy by opening my own ice cream shop a mere four months earlier, I knew exactly how I wanted it to look. And the space that happened to be available for rent just as I was gearing up was perfect. Not only was the location fabulous and the size just right; the shop on Hudson Street had that gorgeous exposed brick wall that gave it a wonderful feeling of warmth as well as a sense of history. Then there was the shiny tin ceiling and the black-and-white tiled floor, two more remnants of Wolfert's Roost's past.

I'd painted the other walls bright pink, hung Willow's whimsical paintings of oversized ice cream treats, and outfitted the sitting area with six small marble tables and black wrought-iron chairs with pink-vinyl seats. What could be cuter?

I was tickled that Chelsea Atkins, the assistant director, had immediately seen its charm. And thrilled that Lickety Splits was going to be in a real live Hollywood movie.

As long as Jake approved the contract, of course.

I was in agony during the hours that passed before he showed up.

"I'm so sorry I couldn't get here sooner," he greeted me breathlessly as he scurried through the door. He was wearing his usual jeans and snug-fitting T-shirt. Even though he probably hadn't played much baseball since high school, when he was our team's star, he'd retained his lean, muscular physique. "This has been a crazy morning. For some reason, everybody in the universe suddenly seems to want organic dairy products."

"It's fine," I assured him. Jake runs an organic dairy nearby called Juniper Hill. Local interest in healthy eating had helped what was once a sleepy family business boom. "The movie people aren't coming until nine o'clock tonight. Once you look at the contract and tell me it's okay to sign, I'll text Chelsea—she's the one who came in this morning—and tell her we're all set."

Jake sat down at one of the tables, running his hands through his light brown hair as he read the contract. It didn't take him very long, given the fact that the legal document was pretty concise.

"It looks okay to me," he finally said. And then, in a very

un-Jake-like movement, he flashed his fingers and palms in that theatrical gesture that's known as jazz hands and cried, "It's showtime!"

"That's great!" I told him. "I'll let Chelsea know right away. Where do I sign?"

"I only have one question," he said earnestly.

My stomach tightened. "What's that?"

Widening his blue eyes wistfully, he asked, "Are you going to remember the little people once you're part of the Hollywood scene? Or will you forget all about the folks who knew you way back when?"

I laughed. But it was a loaded question, so much so that I immediately felt a low-grade tension between us.

The "way back when" Jake was referring to, after all, had been the years we were growing up together. Specifically, back in high school. He and I were the Romeo and Juliet of what was then called Modderplaatz High. That was long before the powers that be decided that our scenic riverside town deserved a better moniker than its colonial name, which is Dutch for "muddy place."

Unfortunately, our story ended tragically, just like Romeo and Juliet's. Not quite as tragically, of course, since we were both still up and running. But Jake had left me stranded on prom night, and I'd never completely forgiven him. Not only for what happened that June evening fifteen years before, but perhaps even more for the fact that he'd never even tried to get in touch with me since. Not to explain, not to say hello, not even to post a LIKE on a video of a kitten eating an ice cream cone that I once posted on Facebook.

Now that I was back in town, he and I had started hanging out together. Occasionally. And with major reservations on my part.

So I was happy that his reference to our shared past, however humorous it was meant to be, was cut short by Emma, who'd hurried back to Lickety Splits as soon as her morning class ended.

"Kate," she called from behind the counter, "I'm sorry to interrupt, but I think we need to open a new tub of Cashew Brittle with Sea Salt. There's a little bit left, but it's looking kind of . . . swampy."

"And I'd better get going," Jake said. "Hey, good luck with the movie thing! And let me know if the male lead gets sick and they need a last-minute replacement."

"Everybody wants to be a star," I replied, laughing. "But I promise that you'll be the first person I call. Assuming they give me that much power."

"Hey, they picked your ice cream shop to be in the movie, didn't they?" he asked. "Why not choose your local organic dairy guy and part-time semi-retired lawyer to get a star on his dressing-room door?"

Finally, the infuriatingly sluggish hands of the clock positioned themselves at the right angle that meant it was nine o'clock. Or, to be more accurate, my cell phone said "9:00" when I checked it for the eighteen thousandth time that day.

By that point, Emma had already gone over to the window at least twenty times to see if there were any signs of the film crew. But it wasn't until a few minutes after the hour that the door opened and Chelsea Atkins popped her head in.

Tonight, she was carrying a clipboard, which gave her an official look. Then I noticed the T-shirt she was wearing under a light jacket. It was bright red with the words PALM FROND PRODUCTIONS printed on it in white.

"Hey, Kate," she greeted me, sounding as if we were old friends. "Are you ready for us?"

We've been ready for almost twelve hours, I felt like telling her. Instead, I simply said, "Yup."

"Great." She turned away and addressed the cluster of people I now saw standing behind her. "Okay, let's do this."

Suddenly a dozen people swarmed in, most of them carrying things. A couple of big husky guys were dragging in cables and heavy-looking black cases that no doubt contained some sort of equipment. A third guy was lugging huge lights. Someone started snapping photos of my shop, just as Chelsea had promised, no doubt so they could put everything back the way it was once they were done. Someone else had whipped out an electronic measuring device and was checking out the room's dimensions. Through it all, Chelsea was shouting directions.

And then, amid all the unfamiliar faces around me, I saw one that I recognized. Ethan, Emma's boyfriend, had just come through the door.

As usual, his eyes were barely visible, since a curtain of straight black hair covered much of the upper half of his face. Thanks to his scrawny build and choice of hairstyle, he looks about fifteen. But he's actually eighteen, just like Emma. He was wearing grungy jeans, the kind I suspected weren't designed to be stylishly grungy but had gotten that way through his own blood, sweat, and tears. But he was also wearing the bubble-gum-pink Lickety Splits polo shirt I'd given him. He sometimes helps out with catered events, so it makes sense for him to have one at home, ready to go. And hopefully clean. As had become his habit of late, he was carrying a thick, well-worn paperback, no doubt one of the novels that's routinely on the "100 Most Important Books of Our Time" list. Dostoevsky was one of his favorites. Jack Kerouac, too.

Yet Ethan didn't belong here any more than Fyodor or Jack did. Trying to keep my irritation in check, I turned to Emma.

"How did Ethan know about this?" I demanded.

"I called him!" Emma replied. "And I told him to wear his

pink Lickety Splits shirt, since I figured that was the only way they'd let him in."

"Emma, you shouldn't have—"

I stopped mid-sentence since I'd suddenly caught sight of another familiar face. Willow, my best friend since my very first day of middle school and currently Wolfert's Roost's resident yoga instructor, was also slipping through the crowd. She, too, was wearing her pink Lickety Splits shirt, paired with turquoise yoga pants.

"How did Willow know about this?" Emma asked, her tone neutral. "And how come she thought to wear her Lickety Splits shirt?"

She had me there.

"Okay, so it's not so terrible that we each invited one friend," I said. "Just as long as everyone keeps out of the way."

"Thanks for telling me about this!" Willow gushed as she hurried over to Emma and me. Her eyes were bright, and strands of her pale blond hair, worn in a pixie cut, were sticking up at odd angles. "This is so exciting! I wouldn't have missed it for the world!"

"It's totally chill," Ethan said, nodding enthusiastically so that his bangs swung like a surrey with a fringe on top. "Probably the most clutch thing that's ever happened in this town!"

I took that to mean he was happy.

The four of us stood huddled together in the corner, content to stay out of the way and watch. Emma and Ethan kept whispering to each other excitedly, pointing out various crew members and analyzing the tasks they were performing. Willow just stood very still, her eyes wide with wonder.

It was all terribly glamorous. All that activity, all those people who were so good at what they did, matter-of-factly dealing with lights and cameras and other equipment and carrying out every single step required to turn my little shop into a movie set. It was even interesting watching them gently pack up Count Dracula and the witch, wrapping them in Bubble Wrap and hauling them to the back of the store.

Suddenly, I noticed Chelsea Atkins making a beeline in my direction.

"I need your help with something important," she said.

I stood up a little straighter. "Of course," I told her. "Any-thing."

"Can you pick out the dish and spoon that you think we should use in this scene?" she asked. "The ones Savannah Crane will use to eat ice cream?" Scrunching up her face, she added, "I'd feel kind of weird scrounging around in your cabinets. Besides, you're the ice cream expert."

"I'd be happy to," I replied, feeling very important. I smoothed the front of my pink Lickety Splits polo shirt, ran my fingers through my hair, and headed behind the counter.

Without hesitation, I picked out a classic, clear-glass tulip dish. Then I chose a stainless-steel spoon with an extra-long handle. Somehow, a metal spoon seemed just a little more el-egant than the brightly colored plastic ones that most of my customers opted for. I handed both to Chelsea, then watched with pride as she set them on the table that was closest to the display counter. I couldn't help feeling that I'd just played an instrumental role in this production.

"Thanks!" Chelsea called, then moved on to some other task.

"You're a set designer!" Emma whispered when I joined her and the others in the corner we'd staked out. "That's something you can put on your résumé!"

Or at least tell my grandchildren about, I thought.

Being part of this production, even in such a small way, was exhilarating. So I was surprised that, before long, the thrill began to wear off. After a couple of hours, I found myself growing bored with watching electricians plug things in and camera people position cameras and lighting people stand on step stools. It was after eleven by then, and I was starting to yawn.

I glanced at the little group I'd come to think of as my Ice Cream Team. Willow was texting someone, while Emma and Ethan were slumped against the wall. They were both still watching, but their eyes were drooping, and their shoulders were sagging.

"I think it's time for us to go home," I announced.

I half-expected protests. Instead, all three 'Cream Team members nodded in agreement.

I went over to Chelsea, who was scribbling furiously on her clipboard. "If you don't need me here," I told her, "I'm going to call it a night. Let me give you the keys to the shop . . ."

"That's fine," she replied, barely glancing at me as I put the keys into her hand. "I've got your cell phone number right here, so I'll get in touch if anything comes up."

So much for my first taste of Hollywood. I'd been expecting some sort of drama. Instead, I was sorely disappointed.

Maybe there will be more excitement tomorrow, I told myself as the four of us shuffled out of the shop. But frankly, I wasn't feeling very optimistic.

Early the next morning, Emma and I walked to Lickety Splits, rather than driving. It was a lovely autumn day, perfect for taking a walk. The bright October sun gently warmed the crisp, cool air, and all around us the trees were tinged with vibrant reds, oranges, and yellows. Emma chattered away nonstop, still scarcely able to believe that a scene in a real Hollywood movie was about to be filmed at her aunt's ice cream shop.

As we turned the corner of Wolfert's Roost's main intersection, I wondered if I'd even be able to tell that a film shoot was about to take place at Lickety Splits. I pictured a small van parked outside, perhaps with a half dozen cables running from the vehicle to the shop, a camera or two, and some of the people I'd seen the night before standing around with clipboards or cameras or lights.

So I froze when I saw the chaos outside my store.

A moving-van-size truck that took up several parking spaces stood in front of Lickety Splits. The sidewalk in front of the shop was cordoned off, preventing anyone from walking by.

And there was a huge crowd. People were standing out on the sidewalk or going in and out of Lickety Splits, all of them looking busy. Not only the men and women who'd shown up the night before to set up, but at least ten or fifteen others. Some were hauling equipment around, some were fiddling with the thick black cables that snaked across the pavement, and some were talking animatedly on cell phones.

"Wow!" Emma said breathlessly. "This really is a big deal, Kate. Look at all these people! I wish Ethan could be here!"

"Yes, jobs do tend to get in the way a lot of the time," I commented. But I had just been thinking that it was too bad that Willow had to teach three classes in a row that morning at her yoga studio, Heart, Mind & Soul.

I quickly spotted Chelsea. She was standing near Lickety Splits' front door, clutching her clipboard. I wondered if she'd slept with it.

"Good morning, Chelsea," I greeted her. "It looks like you're already in full swing."

"Time is money," she replied with her usual brusqueness. "Especially in the movie business."

"Are you allowed to close off the sidewalk like this?" I asked nervously, wondering how my neighboring shopkeepers would feel about all this disruption.

"Don't worry, I got all the necessary permits," she assured

me. With a shrug, she added, "I've done it a million times before. We cordon off the area in order to—hey, Carlos? Could you please move that boom pole? It's kind of in the way. Thanks."

"Who are all these people?" I asked.

"That guy over there is Skip DiFalco, the director," she said. She pointed at a man in a backward baseball cap who was standing inside the shop, earnestly addressing three people. "And those people he's talking to right now are the gaffer—the chief lighting technician—and two of the cameramen. Those women in the corner are the hair stylist and the makeup artist. The woman behind them is the prop master."

"Wow, I had no idea they needed so many people to shoot a simple scene like this," I said breathlessly.

Emma, I noticed, didn't say a word. But the expression on her face was that of someone who had been hypnotized. Her brown eyes were the size of ice cream scoops. And they were as glazed as if they were made of the same type of metal.

"That woman over there is the script supervisor," Chelsea went on. "She takes notes constantly, keeping track of what's been filmed, checking for continuity, noting any changes the actors have made to their lines, things like that. Carlos over there is the boom operator, who positions the microphone during filming. And that tall man over there is the best boy, the head electrician. Let's see, who else is here . . . ?"

I remembered seeing some of those terms in the screen credits at the end of movies. I'd always wondered what they meant. Now I knew.

Suddenly the door of the white truck opened. A tall, slender woman stepped out, blinking in the bright sunlight of the crisp October morning. Her long blond curls looked as if they'd been arranged strand by strand to fall in perfect symmetry across her shoulders. Her features were delicate: pale blue eyes, a patrician nose, high cheekbones. She wasn't conventionally beautiful, but she was definitely one of those people who gave off an inner light that somehow let everyone around her know that she was special.

She was wearing a flowing dress made from a fabric that reminded me of cotton candy. It looked as if it would dissolve in your hand if you touched it. The dress was a color that looked great on her: the same shade of peach as my Peaches and Cream ice cream.

She drifted past us, flashing Chelsea a dazzling smile.

"Who's that?" I asked, even though I already knew.

"That's Savannah Crane," Chelsea said. "She's the star."

Emma uttered a little throaty sound. I had a feeling she was picturing her on an upcoming issue of *People*.

I followed Savannah Crane with my eyes as she floated into my shop. As she neared the display case, the hair stylist stopped her. She began fussing with the long, blond strands that as far as I could tell were already flawless. The makeup artist leaped into action as well, frowning pensively as she brushed blush over the actress's cheekbones.

The door of the truck opened once again. This time, a young man who also had an air of specialness around him stepped out. He, too, was lean. On the short side, too. I remembered reading that short men came across especially well in movies because of the way the camera caught their proportions.

He was startlingly handsome, his rugged features an interesting contrast to his leading lady's delicate look. His dark hair and dark eyes would be a pleasing complement to her fair coloring, too.

Before I had a chance to ask the obvious question with the obvious answer, Chelsea said, "And that's Damian Reese. He's got the other lead role."

"I'm impressed that all these people are managing to fit inside my store," I commented. "This isn't exactly a large space."

"We're used to working in all kinds of situations," Chelsea

told me. "Besides, some of these people will be moving out shortly. We're about to begin filming."

By this point, Savannah had taken a seat at one of the round tables. In front of her was the glass tulip dish I'd picked out the night before, along with the long-handled spoon. She sat facing the front of the store, with her back to the display case. Frankly, I didn't consider that the best way to shoot the scene. I thought she should have her back to the display window, since it would provide a much better view of my shop. But no one had asked me.

"We're ready for the ice cream," someone suddenly called.

Chelsea turned to me. "That's your cue, Kate. Could you please put a nice big scoop of something chocolate in front of Savannah? Just use the dish that's already in place."

"Chocolate?" I repeated, wanting be sure I got it right.

"That's right," Chelsea replied. "The dark brown will be a nice contrast to the color of her dress."

"I'm on it," I said.

My heart was pounding as I strode through the shop, picked up the dish, and took my place behind the counter. My hands were actually shaking as I scooped out a big ball of Chocolate Almond Fudge. It was a lovely shade of brown, and I figured the darker-colored fudge running through it would add visual interest. Nice texture, too. I pressed it into the dish, then rounded off the top so it would have a pleasing shape.

I sashayed over to Savannah's table and set it down in front of her.

"Here you go," I said.

She looked up and flashed me the same dazzling smile I'd seen before. "Thanks," she said, sounding a little breathless. "I don't usually eat ice cream at this hour."

"I think you'll find this is the best ice cream you've ever had," I couldn't help saying.

She laughed. "I just hope we do this scene in one or two

takes. If I keep eating ice cream all morning, I won't fit in my costume for the scene we're shooting tomorrow!"

I laughed too. *Friends.* Savannah Crane and I were now friends. I was friends with a movie star. Or at least a soon-to-be movie star.

I glanced over at Emma, who was standing in the corner closest to the front door. She was so green with envy that she looked like a scoop of Mint Chocolate Chip.

I wove through the crowd and joined her in the corner. It was an excellent spot, one that enabled us both to see perfectly.

"Quiet on the set!" Chelsea called out.

Emma and I looked at each other and grinned.

Just as Chelsea had explained, the scene opened with Savannah, playing the role of Suzi Hamilton, sitting at the table eating ice cream. I was pleased to see that the two shades of brown in my Chocolate Almond Fudge did indeed provide a nice contrast to the peach color of her dress. Vanilla would have looked too washed out. Strawberry, forget it. Mint Chocolate Chip and Pistachio Almond would have worked well, too, but again, no one had asked me.

And then the director called, "Action!" Just like I'd seen in the movies.

The actor Damian Reese strode in, his fingers clenched into fists and his expression angry. As he passed by Emma and me, I got a whiff of his cologne. He headed over to the table, sat down opposite Savannah, and stuck his hands in his pockets.

"What are you doing here?" Savannah asked, her eyes growing wide. Her voice was much more even, and considerably more controlled, than it had been when she and I had spoken.

"I just talked to Steve," Damian replied. "He told me you're leaving tomorrow."

Savannah had the next line.

"Honestly, Shane," she said, casually reaching for the spoon lying on the table, "I don't see what you're so upset about."

"Cut!" Skip DiFalco yelled. Everything immediately came to a halt.

With great patience, Skip said, "Savannah, you're supposed to be infuriating. This scene should be fraught with tension. But you're sounding just a bit too nice. Can you put a little more coldness into what you're saying? Can you be meaner?"

Savannah nodded. I got the feeling she was someone who didn't find it easy to be mean. Then again, she was an actress.

She closed her eyes, relaxed her shoulders, and took a deep breath. A few seconds later, she straightened up again and said, "Okay, I'm ready."

"Action!" the director called.

For the second time, Damian Reese strode over to the table and sat down opposite Savannah, then stuck his hands in his pockets.

"What are you doing here?" Savannah asked. She widened her eyes in the exact same way she had before.

"I just talked to Steve," Damian said. "He told me you're leaving tomorrow."

"Honestly, Shane," she said, once again reaching for the spoon, "I don't see what you're so upset about."

I guess she sounded mean enough, because this time Damian got to say his next line. As Savannah scooped up one spoonful of ice cream, then another, then one more, he stared at her angrily.

"You don't?" he yelled. "You seriously mean you don't understand how much you mean to me?"

"I'm tired of hearing you say that," she replied, eating more ice cream. I was starting to get alarmed. At the rate she was downing the stuff, I was afraid she'd run out before the scene was finished. I wished someone had told me how many lines of dialogue there were so I'd have known how much to dish out.

"You know you're the most important person in my life," Damian-as-Shane insisted. "That's been true since the first time we met. Have you forgotten Paris? Didn't all those evenings at that piano bar mean anything? You said yourself that those were the best ten days of your life!"

By that point, Savannah Crane had eaten almost the entire dish of Chocolate Almond Fudge. I glanced at the director, but he seemed so intent on his two actors' performances that he didn't seem to notice.

Finally, she scraped up what remained of the ice cream, sucked it off her spoon, and looked at Damian defiantly. She was silent for a few seconds, just staring at him.

I had to admit, it was a pretty dramatic moment. This Savannah Crane was a good actress. Even I could see that.

I glanced at Skip DiFalco. He was positively glowing with satisfaction.

"Shane," Savannah finally said, speaking with the same cold indifference with which she'd delivered her earlier lines, "I've told you all along that I have to—I have to—"

A sense of stillness gripped the entire room as she stopped mid-sentence. I could feel the tension in the air even before I glanced at the director and saw the shock on his face.

Was it really possible that Savannah had forgotten her next line and was about to flub what had clearly been exactly the performance that Skip DiFalco had hoped for?

But I quickly saw that something entirely different was going on. Savannah hadn't simply forgotten her lines.

Her entire demeanor had changed, her expression becoming stricken and her body hunching up in a peculiar way.

"Savannah?" Chelsea called from across the room. "Is everything okay?"

Savannah didn't reply. Instead, her eyebrows shot up, and her eyes widened as she clasped both hands to her heart.

A buzz rose up in the room.

"Savannah?" Chelsea cried again. "What's going on?"

"I—there's—" Savannah whispered hoarsely.

"Cut!" the director finally remembered to yell.

Savannah was shaking her head hard. Her eyes fluttered for a few seconds, then her shoulders slumped, and her entire body seemed to go limp.

As she slid off her chair and onto the floor, somebody let out a scream.

Chapter 3

George Washington had an absolute sweet tooth,
and his real love was for ice cream. He was
introduced to it around 1768 or 1770, and then
he became an addict. He started serving it at
Mount Vernon all the way back in 1784. And
when they did a catalog of his possessions,
he had a 306-piece ice cream serving set.

—*Amy Ettinger, author of* Sweet Spot: An Ice Cream Binge
Across America, *in an interview on NPR's* All Things
Considered

Total chaos immediately descended upon my shop.
"Somebody call nine-one-one!" someone shrieked.

"I'm doing that right now!" another voice yelled back.

"I already called!" a third person chimed in. "They're on
their way!"

Meanwhile, several people crowded around Savannah as
she lay sprawled on the floor. A man hunched over her, doing
CPR. A young woman with tears streaming down her cheeks
was clutching her hand, crying, "Savannah, can you hear
me? Savannah, talk to me!"

Damian Reese sat frozen in his chair, looking as if he were
in shock.

"Stay calm, everybody," the director, Skip DiFalco, called.
"And please clear the room. Hopefully the EMTs will be here

any minute, and they'll need to get in. Wayne, keep administering CPR. You look like you know what you're doing."

Most of the crew members dutifully moved out to the street, their expressions distraught and their voices hushed. The few people who remained included Skip DiFalco, Chelsea Atkins, and the man named Wayne, who continued doing CPR. I noticed that Damian Reese had shot out of there, practically pushing his way through the crowd.

Emma and I were among the last ones out. I was feeling completely dazed by what had just happened, and I sensed that my niece felt the exact same way.

"How could this be happening, Aunt Kate?" she asked in a high-pitched, little-girl voice once we were standing outside on the sidewalk. "Do you think Savannah Crane is just sick, or do you think something worse happened? What should we do? Should we call Grams?"

"None of us know what's going on yet," I told her, putting my arm around her and doing my best to sound reassuring. "I hope she's just fallen a bit ill and that it's nothing serious. I think we should stand by until we find out more about what's going on. And to answer your other question, I don't think there's any reason to call Grams. Not at this point."

It took only a few minutes for the ambulance to arrive. Two EMTs hurried into Lickety Splits as everyone stood around watching them. The air was so thick with tension that it seemed as if the people who were gathered there were barely breathing.

The last thing I wanted was for my niece to see something she wouldn't be able to get out of her head. So I pulled her away and said, "Let's take a walk around the block. It's so crowded that the best thing we can do is give the EMTs some space."

She nodded, then silently followed me as I led her down the street.

It wasn't until I saw the ambulance driving back down

Hudson Street, its sirens blaring, that I veered back to my shop. The same crowd was still standing on the sidewalk. But there was a new addition: a black-and-white police car had pulled up in front of Lickety Splits. As we got close, the driver's door opened, and Pete Bonano got out, pulling his navy-blue hat over his head of curly, dark brown hair.

Officer Pete Bonano, I had to remind myself. It was still difficult to comprehend the fact that my high school's good-natured star football player, with his chubby cheeks and his big grin, had grown up to become a police officer.

"Can I have everybody's attention, please?" he said authoritatively, addressing the crew members as well as a small group of passersby who lingered on the sidewalk, eager to see what all the commotion was about. "I'm going to ask any of you who were inside the store this morning for the film shoot to remain right where you are. I'd like to speak with each one of you briefly, primarily to take down your name and contact information. Everyone else, please clear the scene."

As a few members of the crowd shuffled away, I turned to my niece.

"Emma, I think you should go home," I said.

"But, Kate! You shouldn't be alone right now!" Emma protested. "Besides, the police officer just said that everyone who was there when this happened should stay."

"I insist," I told her firmly. "I'll tell Pete you were there and answer any of his questions for both of us."

"Besides," I added, as I noticed someone crossing the street and heading in our direction, "I'm not going to be alone."

Jake rushed over to the spot where we were standing, his expression grim.

"Is the rumor true?" he immediately asked. "Was the actress in this movie poisoned?"

Emma let out a cry. "Savannah Crane was *poisoned*?" she wailed.

"That's the rumor that's going around," Jake replied somberly. "I just got a call from a friend of mine who knew they were filming here this morning, and he said that's what he heard. So, of course, I came right over."

"I wish Ethan was here," Emma said, her voice thin. "Is he coming, too, Jake?"

"He's still at the dairy," Jake said. "I had to leave somebody there to keep things running. But you should call him. I'm sure he's anxious to hear how you're doing."

Just then, another vehicle pulled up in front of my store. This one was a van bearing the logo of our local cable TV news station.

Jake gently took my arm. "Let's go inside."

I turned to my niece. "Go home, Emma," I instructed her. "In fact, you can do me a big favor by telling Grams what happened. If Savannah Crane really was poisoned, I don't want her hearing about this from someone else. And please convince her that I'm totally fine!"

Emma scooted off with her phone in hand, no doubt calling Ethan.

But as Jake and I started to go inside Lickety Splits, I saw that Pete Bonano was blocking the way. He was standing in the doorway with his back to us, leaning forward awkwardly. I couldn't imagine what he was doing.

And then he turned around and I found out. He had fastened yellow tape printed with the words CRIME SCENE DO NOT CROSS across the doorway.

"Pete!" I cried. "What are you doing?"

Pete's full cheeks reddened. "Sorry, Katy," he said. "I had no choice."

"But—but—!" I protested.

A hundred *buts* were running through my mind, the predominant one something along the lines of "But Lickety Splits is mine! You can't close it off to me! It's autumn, one of Wolfert's Roost's prime tourist seasons! The Hudson Valley is crawling with leaf peepers, tourists who came to the area to look at the beautiful autumn leaves—and hopefully eat ice cream while doing so!"

Following that one were some more practical *buts*: "But how will I make a living if I can't run my shop? But what about all the ice cream I've got stashed in the freezer? But what about the milk and cream and all the other ingredients in the refrigerator?"

Before I had a chance to ask any of those questions, Pete said, "I know it's tough to be shut out of your own store." His tone was sympathetic. "But I just got word that Savannah Crane died on the way to the hospital. We'll have to wait for the toxicology report, of course, but at this point it looks like she was poisoned. And that makes Lickety Splits the scene of a homicide investigation."

I suddenly felt like a blob of melting ice cream lying on a hot sidewalk.

Jake must have guessed that my knees had suddenly turned into something resembling soft serve because he grabbed hold of me.

"It's okay, Kate," he said. "This whole mess won't last long. They'll take that tape down in a day or two, as soon as the forensics people are done."

I nodded, trying to believe him.

"What now?" I asked him. "Should I just go home?"

"It looks as if that may not be an option," Jake replied warily. "At least, not yet."

Confused, I glanced over at him and saw that his gaze was fixed on something up the street. I followed his eyes and saw a gray car heading in our direction. The driver was tall with dark blond hair cut short. Just like Jake, I knew who he was immediately.

So I wasn't at all surprised when the car pulled up right in front of us and the driver rolled down his window.

"Ms. McKay?" Detective Stoltz said. "Would you mind coming down to the police station so I could ask you a few questions?"

I was grateful to have Jake with me in the small, dreary, windowless room in the Wolfert's Roost police station, a place I'd unfortunately been before. I found myself wondering if the Palm Frond Productions people knew about it. It would have been perfect for one of those tense, hard-to-watch scenes in a movie in which someone is being given the third degree.

Fake wood paneling, a scuffed linoleum floor, an ugly metal table, and impressively uncomfortable metal chairs . . . the room truly captured the demoralizing feeling that invariably accompanied being questioned by the police. A feeling that was impossible to shake even if you knew you hadn't done anything wrong.

Finally, after what seemed like a very long time, Detective Stoltz strode in. As usual, his posture was as upright and wooden as a four-star general's. His suit, meanwhile, was as far from a military uniform as it could be. In fact, it looked as if he had grabbed it off the clearance rack in a store that had particularly bad lighting and hadn't cared in the least that it wasn't actually his size.

"Ms. McKay," he said dryly as he sat down. "Here we are again." As usual, he was the picture of politeness. But there was a hard look in his eyes. They were a pale, nondescript shade of gray, something I didn't remember noticing before. Somehow, that seemed to suit his personality perfectly.

Turning to Jake, he curtly asked, "And you're here as her attorney?"

"That's right, I am," he replied, returning Stoltz's steely stare.

While Jake had taken over his family's dairy several years earlier, prior to that he had been a criminal defense lawyer, working for a big law firm in New York City. Since I'd come back to Wolfert's Roost, his background had come in handy. Repeatedly.

Detective Stoltz took out a spiral pad of paper and opened it to a blank page. I was glad that he still used a paper and pen, like in the old days. Somehow, it seemed less intimidating than having him type every word I said into a computer.

"I'd like you to tell me your version of what happened," he began, his voice showing not even a trace of emotion.

I didn't like the phrase "your version." Somehow it seemed to imply that my version wasn't the most valid version. Or even truthful.

But I glanced at Jake, and he nodded.

"I suppose I should start with what happened yesterday," I began, trying to sound as matter-of-fact about all of this as I could. "A woman named Chelsea Atkins came into my shop at around ten in the morning, before it had even opened. She said she was the assistant director on a movie that was being made in the Hudson Valley and she needed a place to film a scene in a hurry. The spot they'd planned to use had become unavailable at the last minute, and the director and the actors and the rest of the crew were all ready to go. She offered me a ton of money. And I have to admit that it sounded like fun. So I said yes.

"Later that evening," I went on, "at a time we'd agreed upon, nine o'clock, a bunch of people who were involved in making the movie showed up and began setting up—"

"Let me stop you there," Detective Stoltz interrupted. "Who, exactly, came into your shop last night?"

I squirmed in my seat, just a little, then forced myself to stop as soon as I realized what I was doing. "I don't really know. There were probably about a dozen people there, and

I didn't know any of them. To me they looked like camera people, lighting people . . ."

I shrugged. "I'm afraid I can't be very helpful about specifics. I suggest that you talk to Chelsea Atkins, the assistant director I mentioned, since she'll know exactly who was there. She was in charge of the setup last night."

Detective Stoltz nodded. "Who was there that you did know?"

"My niece was there," I replied. "Emma Pritchard is my sister Julie's daughter. She lives in Washington, D.C., but she's staying with my grandmother and me here in Wolfert's Roost right now. She's taking classes at the community college and working part-time at Lickety Splits. You've met her."

"Anyone else?"

"Willow Baines," I said. "She runs the Heart, Mind, and Soul yoga studio in town. And then there's Ethan—" I realized I didn't know his last name.

"Love," Jake said. "He works for me at the dairy."

"Really?" I couldn't help asking. "Ethan's last name is *Love*?"

Jake just shrugged.

"And that's it?" Detective Stoltz asked.

"Yes," I said. "Just the four of us."

"How long were you there?" he asked.

"Until a few minutes past eleven," I replied. Speaking more to myself than to him, I added, "We'd all had enough by then. I thought the setup would be exciting, but it was actually kind of boring."

"And this morning?" Detective Stoltz asked.

"Emma and I were the only ones who went to the shop," I said. "Willow had classes to teach, and Ethan had to work at the dairy. The two of us showed up at around nine. There was already a whole crowd of people there." I gave him an overview of who and what I'd seen.

"And while you were there," Detective Stoltz said when I'd finished, "either last night or this morning, did you notice anything out of the ordinary? Anything at all? Anyone who looked as if they shouldn't have been there? Anyone who seemed angry? Or was acting strangely?"

I shook my head.

"Did you see anyone who seemed to have a particular interest in watching what was going on?" he asked.

I shook my head again. "Everything seemed to be going along just fine. Of course, it's hard to say, since I've never been at a film shoot before," I noted. "At least not for a big Hollywood movie. I went to plenty when I worked in public relations. The firm I worked for was involved with corporate films. But this Hollywood thing is new to me."

"But you have had some exposure to film sets," Detective Stoltz prompted. "Did anything strike you as unusual?"

I thought for a few seconds. "Only how thorough everyone was," I finally replied. "They were meticulous about setting up everything that would be needed for the next morning. The idea was to make it possible for the actors and the director and everyone else to just show up and immediately get right to work."

"And that included putting the dishes and silverware on the table?" Detective Stoltz asked.

I stiffened. "Yes, that's right."

"Where did the dish and spoon that Savannah Crane was using to eat the ice cream come from?" he asked.

The fake wood paneling began swirling around me like a set in a horror movie.

"They were both mine," I finally managed to reply. "I mean, the dish and the spoon belong to my shop."

"I'm a little confused," Jake interjected. "Why do the dish and spoon matter so much?"

Detective Stoltz glanced at him coolly. "One theory I'm

considering is that the person who murdered Savannah Crane did so by putting poison into the dish, rather than into the ice cream. That way, it would have been in place no matter what flavor was used. The spoon could also have been dipped in poison, but that's not as likely because it's smaller and flatter and would therefore hold less."

"That sounds right," I said thoughtfully. "Especially since no one knew in advance which flavor of ice cream would be used."

I repeated what Chelsea Atkins had said on the morning of the shoot, which was, "Could you please put a nice big scoop of something chocolate in front of Savannah?" I also told him that she had then added, "Just use the dish that's already in place."

"So the poison *has* to have been in the dish," I concluded.

"The dish you told me *you* picked out and put on the table," Detective Stoltz said.

The faux-wood panels were doing the boogie-woogie once again.

"Look, Detective, I didn't even know Savannah," I said firmly. "I'd never *heard* of her until Chelsea Atkins told me her name yesterday. I had absolutely no reason to wish her any harm. But there were plenty of people in that room who *did* know her. Which means Savannah Crane's killer must have been a member of the crew."

My mind continued to race as I tried to reconstruct what had happen. "They were the only ones who had access to the dish and the spoon. There was nobody else there last night or this morning, at least not besides the three people I told you about and me. And I know for certain that none of us had anything to do with what happened."

"I can assure you that we'll look at all the crew members carefully," he said. With a meaningful look, he added, "But when it comes to murder, sometimes what seems like the most obvious explanation doesn't turn out to be the correct one."

Jake leaned forward. "Surely you don't consider my client a suspect in this actress's murder," he said. "As she just told you, she had never even heard of her before yesterday, much less met her and had something transpire that gave her a reason to want her dead."

Detective Stoltz was silent for what seemed like a very long time before he said, "But we don't actually know that, do we?"

I opened my mouth to protest, then immediately snapped it shut. I'd just gotten the answer to Jake's question about whether or not I was a suspect.

Clearly, I was.

I was still trying to digest that ugly fact when Detective Stoltz said, "You can be sure that we'll be looking into every possible option. In the meantime, Ms. McKay, there's something you can do for me. Once your store is open again, I'd like you to pay extra attention to everyone who comes in."

I blinked. "What do you mean?"

"Often, a murderer can't resist the urge to return to the scene of the crime," he said. "If someone shows up who doesn't normally come into your shop, or if someone appears to be acting a little strange, take note."

There was something chilling about the idea of Savannah Crane's murderer sailing into Lickety Splits, pretending to crave ice cream but, in reality, wanting to be there for an entirely different reason. An unimaginably sinister reason.

"I will," I assured him.

The detective asked me a few more questions, mostly about logistics. He wanted to know about all the ways of gaining entrance into Lickety Splits, other people who may have had keys, and spots in the downtown area where someone might stand in order to get a good view of the shop. He also asked if I'd noticed anyone watching my store or asking unusual questions, not only the day before but at any time. I did my best to give helpful answers.

Finally, he shifted in his seat, his body language telling me that our interview was over.

"Thank you for your time, Ms. McKay," he said. Glancing at his notes, he added, "I'll also be talking to your niece, Emma Pritchard, as well as your other two associates."

"When can I go back to business as usual?" I asked.

"I'm afraid I can't answer that," Detective Stoltz replied seriously. "Your ice cream shop is now a crime scene. No one can go inside until the investigation has been completed. Or even touch anything on the exterior, for that matter, since that's been taped off, too."

"But—but—"

The same *buts* that had run through my head before were making a comeback. Big-time.

I never did have a chance to voice any of them since the detective was already on his feet. It was clear that, as far as he was concerned, we were done.

Lickety Splits was also done. At least for now.

"I don't think you should be alone right now," Jake said as the two of us stood outside the Wolfert's Roost police station. "It's still a little early, but let's go get lunch."

"Sounds good," I said. Especially since I didn't know where else to go.

Jake drove back into town, using a circuitous route that kept us from driving past Lickety Splits. But as soon as I realized what he was doing, I asked him to take me there.

"I just want to see it," I explained.

Hearing Detective Stoltz say that I had to keep Lickety Splits closed indefinitely had been bad enough. The actual experience of parking outside it and seeing the yellow crime-scene tape crisscrossed along the front was an experience that was on another level entirely.

My beautiful shop looked so forlorn. So miserable. So hopeless.

Which was exactly the way I felt.

Jake put his arm around me protectively. "Come on, Katy," he said softly. "Let's get out of here. And I know just the place to go."

Toastie's was the obvious place to recover from the morning's events. The small eatery was right in town, but not close enough to Lickety Splits that I'd have a view of my poor, pathetic shop. It was also the embodiment of homeyness. Familiarity, too, since it was a place I'd been coming to for so long that I used to have to climb up onto the seats.

Toastie's was a genuine, old-fashioned diner, rather than merely being a more modern place that was simply designed to look like one. That was a nice way of saying it was kind of a dump. The Formica on the tables was the real thing, probably there since the 1970s. The same went for the cigarette burns and mysterious stains that dotted it.

It was pretty empty, so Jake and I slid into one of the booths in front, next to the line of windows overlooking Hudson Street. My pants snagged a bit on the strip of duct tape that held the seat together.

Toasties's proprietor, Big Moe, immediately lumbered over to our table with two white mugs of steaming coffee. I swear, the man must be psychic. Tucked under his arm were two laminated menus, multipage tomes that listed everything from basic egg sandwiches to heavenly waffles with Nutella to turkey dinners complete with stuffing, gravy, and cranberry sauce. I knew from past experience that the menus would add to the diner's feeling of authenticity by being sticky.

Jake drank his coffee black, no sugar. I, meanwhile, always loaded mine up with enough cream and sugar that it practically became a melted version of Cappuccino Crunch ice cream.

He took a sip, then with mock serious said, "This seems to be becoming a tradition."

"What does?" I asked, tearing open a packet of sugar.

"You and me coming to Toastie's after you've been implicated in a murder," he replied.

"Ha ha," I said sullenly.

"Too soon, I guess," Jake said, shrugging. "Come on, Kate. I wouldn't be teasing you if I thought you had anything to worry about."

"No? What about the fact that someone was murdered—and it happened in my shop?" I shot back. "That doesn't exactly do much for my reputation. You know that saying about how there's no such thing as bad publicity? I, for one, have never believed that. And this is from someone who used to work as a publicist!"

My eyes were burning as I muttered, "I can't believe I'm in the middle of a murder investigation again."

I waited for Jake to say something comforting. Something like, "Yeah, but it's pretty clear that Detective Stoltz doesn't really believe you had anything to do with it." Or at least, "I'm sure Stoltz will get this case cleared up fast."

Instead, he said, "It's not good, is it?"

"Well, I guess the upside is that Lickety Splits being closed for a while because it's now considered a crime scene will give me plenty of free time," I quipped. I was trying to sound lighthearted, but I wasn't doing that great a job.

Jake eyed me warily. "Yeah, it will. And what exactly are you planning on doing with that free time?"

I kept my eyes on my coffee mug. "What do you *think* I'm planning on doing?" I asked.

"Kate, I hope you're not thinking of conducting your own investigation," Jake said earnestly.

I just shrugged, then took a big gulp of coffee. "I haven't actually thought about it," I replied.

He leaned forward so he was only a few inches away from me, studying my face.

"Is there something wrong?" I asked, frowning.

"I'm just checking to see if your nose is growing," he said, trying not to smile.

Personally, I wasn't in the mood to smile. "I haven't decided anything, Jake. But if I did decide to be a little—shall we say, *proactive*—in absolving myself of guilt, since I'm clearly a suspect in Detective Stoltz's mind, I don't see the problem with that."

"*I* see a problem," Jake said. "In fact, I see a serious problem. First, there's a killer out there. Someone dangerous. Second, you don't know anything about the movie business or the people in it. Third, you have no training, aside from the fact that you've gotten involved in murder investigations a couple of times before. Both times with nearly disastrous consequences, I might add—"

"Point taken," I said.

I hoped I was making it clear that I didn't want to have this discussion. Not now, possibly not ever. What I wanted was to drink my coffee, stuff my face with some comfort food, and find something else to talk about.

Besides, I got the feeling I wasn't going to change Jake's mind anyway.

So it was a great relief that Big Moe chose that moment to reappear. Jake and I ordered. We were both familiar enough with the menu that we already knew exactly what we wanted. A burger for him, emotional support in the form of strawberry-banana waffles smothered in whipped cream for me.

When Big Moe went off to make all our dreams come true, I immediately told Jake, "I can't think about this anymore. Let's talk about something else. Anything new with you?"

Jake leaned back in his seat and casually draped his arm across the back. "Funny you should ask," he said, his tone a bit strained. "Actually, there is. And, well, it has something to do with you."

"With me?" I repeated, blinking.

"It *might* have something to do with you," he corrected himself. Grinning, he added, "That is, if I can talk you into it."

"Okay, now you've got my attention," I told him.

"So, here's the thing," Jake said. He pushed aside his mug, folded his arms across his chest, and leaned forward so his elbows were on the table. "I've been thinking about expanding Juniper Hill's scope. Up until now, the dairy has been focusing on wholesale, but the Hudson Valley is going through a major shift—"

"Cut to the punch line," I interrupted.

He took a deep breath. "I want to open a store."

I was still trying to absorb what he'd just said when he went on. "I found the perfect place. It's this old roadside stand, right on Route 9 a few miles south of Wolfert's Roost. It's bigger than the usual roadside stand, though. I think it was a mom-and-pop operation a million years ago that mainly catered to tourists. They may even have had a gas pump there at one point, if the big concrete slab in front is any indication.

"Anyway," he went on, "a few other businesses have been in that building over the decades, but it's been sitting there empty for at least two years. I think I can get it cheap."

"And turn it into what?" I asked.

"A modern-day version of a roadside stand, with enough old-fashioned touches that it feels like an original," he replied proudly. "It would sell all the things that tourists like to shop for. Locally grown fruit and vegetables, when they're in season. Flowers, too. I can picture huge, colorful bouquets out front that would catch the eye of people driving by. And food, especially things made by local people. Jams and jellies, baked goods, cheeses, whatever I can find. Basics, too, so people who live around here would have a reason to stop in. Milk and other dairy products from Juniper Hill, for one thing.

"But it would have other things, too," he went on, growing more and more excited the longer he talked. "Local crafts, souvenirs . . ."

"You could call it something cute like the Broken Bucket," I said, thinking out loud. "Or something memorable, like, I don't know, the Flying Frog or the Happy Cow."

"One idea I came up with is simply calling it Pratt's," Jake added. "Or there's always the Juniper Hill Farm Stand."

"Tell you what: I'll put Emma on it," I told him. "She's great at this kind of thing."

"So it sounds as if you think this is a good idea," Jake said lightly.

"I absolutely do," I said. "I think that between the steady stream of day-trippers and all the city people with weekend houses around here, not to mention all the new people who are relocating to this area, you can't go wrong."

Suddenly I remembered that Jake had said something about me being part of this.

"But where do I fit in?" I asked, even though I already had an idea.

"Ice cream, of course," he replied. "I was hoping you'd be willing to let me sell Lickety Splits ice cream at my shop. It *is* made with Juniper Hill products, after all."

"Do you mean packed ice cream, like pint containers, or cups and cones that are scooped out on-site?" I asked.

"Up to you," he said. "But selling gourmet ice cream like yours would be a real plus for my shop. Especially since you've already built yourself a nice reputation."

"Have I?" I asked, genuinely surprised by his comment.

He laughed. "You obviously haven't Googled 'Lickety Splits' lately, have you? Check out the reviews on Yelp and TripAdvisor. You're pretty much getting five stars everywhere. Although there is this one guy who blasted Prune 'n' Raisin," he noted, chuckling.

"Not my finest hour," I admitted. "But at least I'm willing to experiment."

"Lickety Splits has even been mentioned on some special web sites that are geared toward ice cream lovers," Jake added. "This one web site, IceCreamFanatics.com, actually named you the number-three gourmet ice cream purveyor in the country."

I was dying to know who'd captured the top two spots on that list.

"In fact," Jake went on, suddenly breaking eye contact and instead acting as if the answer to the secret of life was written on Big Moe's sticky, cigarette-stained table, "I thought you might even consider becoming my business partner."

That comment sent my eyebrows jumping up to the stratosphere. "But—I'm not looking to—we don't—if it's start-up money you need, I could certainly—"

"It's nothing like that," Jake insisted. When he finally looked at me, his eyes positively bored into mine. "I thought it would be fun."

I had nothing to say to that.

Jake wanted the two of us to become partners. A pair. A unit.

I wasn't quite sure what he meant by that. Was he saying he wanted to be *business* partners or *partner* partners?

Either way, the complications could be monumental.

"Just think about it," Jake said. "I know it's a major decision. You've already got so much going on, what with running the shop and catering and all the other things you're doing—"

Jake was right. I did have a lot going on. And not all of it was related to ice cream.

Still, I had a feeling that no matter how distracted I was about Savannah Crane's murder, it would be difficult not to think about his proposition.

Chapter 4

Jacob Fussell of Baltimore, Maryland, was the
first to manufacture ice cream on a large scale.
Fussell bought fresh dairy products from farmers
in York County, Pennsylvania, and sold them in
Baltimore. An unstable demand for his dairy
products often left him with a surplus of cream,
which he made into ice cream. He built his first
ice cream factory in Seven Valleys, Pennsylvania,
in 1851.

—*https://en.wikipedia.org/wiki/Ice_cream*

Now that Lickety Splits was a crime scene, I had nowhere to go but home. Fortunately, that was exactly where I wanted to be.

As I drove up to 59 Sugar Maple Way, I could practically feel the dilapidated old house reaching its arms out to me and pulling me into a soothing bear hug. I had spent most of my childhood there, ever since I was five years old. That was when my father passed away and my mother brought my two sisters and me to Wolfert's Roost to live with Grams. Julie, the oldest of us three, was twelve, and Nina was ten.

I would have loved any house I lived in with the four of them. But this particular house happened to be the very image of—well, comfort.

Back in the 1880s, when the three-story Victorian was built, it had undoubtedly been majestic. It has a turret jutting out of the center, an elegant white porch that runs along the entire front, and curved bay windows on both sides of the front door, one in the living room and one in the dining room. Due to a misunderstanding between my great-great-great-grandfather and the builder, the shingles had been painted yellow—rather than "mellow," as my ancestor had intended.

The house was still dignified, but the past century and a half had taken a bit of a toll. These days the porch sagged, the paint on the shingles and window frames was chipped, and the front yard looked so bedraggled that I was actually grateful when it snowed.

Yet the house still epitomized hominess, at least in my eyes. Grams kept three rocking chairs on the front porch, one wicker, one wood, and one painted with peeling blue paint. There was a colorful needlepoint pillow featuring a different flower on each one. My grandmother's handiwork, of course. A line of flowerpots stood along the banister, and Grams had hung one of her dried-flower wreaths on the front door. Late that summer, she had even painted huge pink and purple flowers on the wooden ramp we'd had built to make it easier for her to get in and out of the house.

The inside of the house was filled with her creations, too. The sunny living room was dominated by large, well-worn furniture: a dark red velvet couch with gold carved legs, over-stuffed upholstered chairs, and three heavy wooden curio cabinets displaying souvenirs of Grams's countless trips all around the world. And superimposed over them were more items she had made. Spread along the back of the couch was an orange, gold, and lime-green afghan, the startling colors a throwback to the seventies, when she'd crocheted it. She had needlepointed the pillows crowding the back and hooked the footstool in front of the green upholstered chair that was her favorite. Her meticulously made patchwork quilts hung on the walls, all made with wonderfully bright fabrics.

As I opened the front door, I was immediately greeted by the two individuals charged with keeping the place cute. Digger is our resident cheerleader, always happy and full of energy—so much so that just being in his presence can often be exhausting. Then again, the scruffy little guy is a terrier mix, so he can't help having the personality of someone who's hit the espresso pot a little too hard.

Our feline, Chloe, is a grand dame who may be aging but still considers it her job to keep Digger under control. He's been a big influence on her as well, since she's almost as sociable as he is. If there's a human in the room, she has to be there, too.

Grams was in the living room, no doubt waiting for me. She was dressed comfortably in sweat pants and an apple-green, long-sleeved knit shirt, along with a hand-knit, dark green vest. Draped across her lap was her latest craft project, a small gold and brown patchwork quilt with appliquéd pumpkins. She jumped up as soon as I came in.

"Katydid!" she cried, still holding her needle and thread as she came into the foyer. "Are you all right?"

"I'm fine," I assured her, crouching down to give Digger and Chloe the welcoming tummy scratching they had both come to expect. "I take it Emma told you what happened?"

She nodded. "You must be devastated. What a horrible thing to witness!"

"It was pretty bad," I agreed. "And there's been a new development: Lickety Splits is closed. It's now a crime scene."

"Oh, my goodness," Grams said breathlessly. "Do you know how long it will be before you can reopen?"

"Probably not too long," I replied. "At least that's what Jake said."

"You've talked to Jake?" she said.

"He came to the police station with me," I told her. "Detective Stoltz wanted to question me. But that was mainly because Savannah Crane was killed inside my shop." I didn't see any reason to worry her about me being a suspect.

"You poor thing," she said. "What a morning!" And she gave me exactly what I needed: a long, hard hug.

I was still feeling pretty shaken up, but not so much that I didn't know exactly what to do next. I went into my bedroom and fired up my laptop, determined to find out everything I could about Savannah Crane.

Maybe the young actress was about to become a star, but she wasn't there yet. So even though she was on the verge of fame and fortune, the irony was that, at this point, there simply wasn't that much about her online aside from several articles about her murder that didn't tell me anything I didn't already know.

But plenty of photos came up. A string of pictures of the blond actress with the not-quite-perfect yet infinitely intriguing face stared back at me. In some of them, she looked as glamorous as an old-time movie star. In others, she looked much more down-to-earth, like someone you could talk to. Someone you could even joke around with. About eating too much ice cream, for example, and not fitting into her costume. Those were the photos that made me feel as if someone was squeezing my heart in their fist.

There were also listings for her on Wikipedia and the TV and film web site IMBD.com.

I learned that Savannah had been born in Columbus, Ohio, then majored in theater at Ohio State before moving to New York. She continued studying acting at the New York Acting Workshop, meanwhile doing television commercials and picking up small parts with small theater companies. Then came some tiny roles in movies, none of which I'd ever heard of.

I found it sad that *The Best Ten Days of My Life* was listed as one of her credits, with a release date one year in the future. Now, of course, that wasn't going to happen.

As for her personal life, the Internet was willing to tell me plenty. Her father was a high school math teacher, her mother was a real estate agent, and she had a brother who was in the military and stationed abroad.

She also had a serious boyfriend.

Timothy Scott, born Timothy Randall Scott, was an actor as well. The web pages about Savannah just mentioned him in passing, so I moved on to Googling him.

Once again, a line of photos came up. Timothy Scott was nice-looking, but not over-the-top handsome. More like the boy next door. Light brown hair, light brown eyes, an engaging smile. Late twenties or early thirties, I surmised. Nice build, but not exactly a muscleman.

Below the photos I found the same thing I'd found when I'd Googled Savannah: Wikipedia and IMBD.com listings. Timothy was born and raised in the New York area, then studied theater at New York University and a few different acting schools in the city. Since then he had landed small parts in a variety of television shows, including playing Thug with Knife in an episode of the popular crime drama *Mean City Streets* and Jogger in the comedy series *Miami Minutes*. He had also done some commercials, including one for Verizon that I figured must have paid the rent for quite some time.

I wondered if I'd ever seen him on television. I scrolled back to the photos and began studying them, one by one.

I didn't recognize him. But I suddenly froze as I realized I did recognize something.

In one photograph, Timothy and Savannah were standing with their arms around each other, grinning at the camera, in front of a house. It was a cute bungalow, nothing too fancy, with stone steps in front and window boxes dripping with flowers. The front door was painted a startling shade of lime green.

A weekend place, I figured. Interesting that two aspiring actors could afford something like that.

But I was much more interested in the truck parked in the driveway. Printed on the side were the words NEW PALTZ PLUMBING.

New Paltz was right across the Hudson River from Wolfert's Roost. Which meant that Savannah Crane's weekend getaway was close by.

Excitedly, I clicked on photo after photo, looking for more clues. And then I spotted something else that was familiar. I came across a photo of Timothy—alone, this time—sitting at a café, sipping a cold drink through a straw. Behind him was a sign identifying the restaurant as the Coffee Break Café.

I knew the Coffee Break Café. It was located on Main Street in Cold Spring, a charming village that overlooked the Hudson River and was located just a few miles south of Wolfert's Roost.

I did some more Googling. I put in Timothy's name again, this time adding "Cold Spring." Nothing.

I tried again, this time using Savannah Crane's name.

Bingo. An address in Cold Spring came up.

The house belongs to *Savannah*? I thought. An aspiring actress like her had had the money to buy a house? In a desirable place like Cold Spring, no less?

There were some perfectly good explanations for that, of course. They ranged from family money to a large inheritance to working hard from an early age and investing well.

But while the question of how Savannah had managed to buy a house was intriguing, what mattered to me even more was the fact that I'd just found my first good lead.

*   *   *

Once I had the address of Savannah's house in Cold Spring, finding it was easy. Thank you, Google Maps. And because of all the information available on real estate web sites like Trulia and Redfin, I was able to learn that the one-story ranch had three bedrooms and two bathrooms, occupied 1,296 square feet on a 1.1-acre lot, and was worth almost $400,000.

Quite a price tag for a struggling actress.

As I drove down her street, I spotted the house from a block away. The lime-green door was hard to miss. It was a charming little place, with white shingles, black shutters that looked as if they'd been painted recently, and an expansive front lawn.

I was nervous as I strode up the walkway, my heart pounding and my mouth dry. My anxiety was alleviated only slightly by the sight of a cute, foot-high ceramic garden gnome with a tall red hat, perched on the corner of the stone steps.

I was poised outside the door, rehearsing my opening lines one more time, when the sound of someone yelling made me freeze. It was a man's voice, coming from inside the house.

While my instincts told me to run, my determination to do what I'd come here to do propelled me a few steps forward.

And then: "What the hell do you think you're doing! I'm gonna kill you, you animal!"

I froze.

Maybe this isn't such a good time, I thought, glancing longingly at my truck.

"I'm gonna kill you, you animal!" I heard once again. And then, in a softer voice, "I'm gonna kill you, you animal!"

Something sounded wrong.

And then, in a low, gruff voice, I heard, "What the hell do you think you're doing? I'm gonna kill you, you animal! I'm gonna kill you, you—no, wait."

And then, a loud groan. One of frustration, not fury.

"I can't do this!" the voice from inside the house wailed.

Peering through the front window, I saw a man standing in the living room, alone. In one hand he held a stack of paper that I immediately surmised was a script.

But while the lines I'd just heard him screaming may have been nothing more than words he was reading off a page, the desperation that was now in his voice sounded real.

I watched him sink onto the couch, drop the script, and bury his face in his hands.

I realized that I'd come at a very bad time.

I turned away to retreat to my truck, thinking that I'd come back another day. But in my rush to get away, I accidentally kicked the garden gnome. It tumbled down the stone steps, landing on the walkway with a loud crash. At least it wasn't completely destroyed. Only the top of its red hat had broken off, like an ice cream cone that someone had snapped in two.

A few seconds later I heard the front door open behind me. I turned, certain that the guilt I was feeling was written all over my face. Not only guilt over breaking the garden ornament, either. I also felt bad that I'd come here so soon after the tragedy that Timothy had just suffered.

And the man standing in front of me was undoubtedly Timothy. I recognized him from the Internet immediately. He was wearing jeans and a rumpled navy-blue T-shirt. His shoulders were slumped, giving him a defeated look. His thick, light brown hair was shaggy, not in a cool way but in a way that said he needed a haircut. His eyes were rimmed in red, and his expression was distraught.

"Can I help you?" he asked, running one hand through his hair distractedly.

"I'm afraid I broke your gnome," I said apologetically, pointing to the ceramic figure lying on the ground.

"No big deal," he said. "Just give it to me, will you? I don't want anyone to trip on it."

I retrieved the gnome and its broken-off hat and handed them to Timothy.

"Is there a reason you're here?" he asked, sounding confused. "Aside from coming onto my property to break my stuff?"

"You're Timothy Scott, right?" I said. "I wondered if I could talk to you."

"Who are you?" he asked. He was cradling the gnome in his arms as his eyes traveled past me, toward the street. I suspected that he was looking for a van from a television station. Or maybe some other indication that I was a reporter or an overzealous fan or someone else who was anything but welcome.

"My name is Kate McKay," I said. "I hope I'm not interrupting . . ."

"What do you want?" he demanded.

I took a deep breath. "I'm really sorry to bother you," I said. "But I'm the owner of Lickety Splits, the ice cream parlor in Wolfert's Roost where—"

"Now I understand." Still looking puzzled, he added, "Sort of. Why are you here?"

"A few reasons, actually," I said. "One is to extend my condolences. I didn't know Savannah—in fact, I just met her briefly the day of the shoot, but—"

"Thanks," he said brusquely, "but there's got to be another reason."

I took a deep breath, then said, "I'm here because I'm involved. This terrible thing happened in my shop. I was standing just feet away from Savannah when she ate *my* ice cream out of one of *my* dishes with *my* spoon . . ."

Through some quirk of fate, a van emblazoned with the initials of a national cable television news station chose that exact moment to pull up in front of the house.

Timothy's expression immediately hardened. "Come inside," he instructed, waving me in.

As soon as we were in the foyer, he slammed the front door shut.

"Those idiots have been bothering me nonstop," he said. "As if I don't have enough to deal with right now."

"It's the kind of story that makes headlines," I said gently. "Unfortunately."

"Yes, I guess it is," Timothy said. He put the damaged gnome on the windowsill, gently placing the chunk that had broken off its hat beside it. Then he collapsed onto the couch and stared off into space for what seemed a very long time. I wondered if he'd forgotten I was there.

But then he turned to me. "Do the cops consider you a suspect?" he asked. The tension in his face told me he wasn't sure whether or not he should, too.

"Yes and no," I replied. "They brought me in for questioning simply because it happened in my store. As I said, I'd never met Savannah until two days ago. I'd never even heard her name. There's absolutely no reason why I would have wanted anything bad to happen to her."

Timothy's eyes narrowed. "I still don't understand why you're here."

I decided to be honest. "I'm trying to clear my name. And to solve this mess so my shop's reputation isn't tarnished— the faster, the better."

"Isn't that why we have homicide detectives?" he asked, sounding a bit skeptical.

"Of course," I said. "It's just that it's hard *not* to get involved in something like this when you're one of the people those homicide detectives are looking at. The sooner the case is solved, the faster I can get back to my normal life." I couldn't resist adding, "At the moment, my shop is closed for business. It's now a crime scene."

"I get it," he said.

"In that case," I said, "I wonder if there's anything you

can tell me about Savannah's life. Anything out of the ordinary that might have been going on. There was obviously someone who was very angry with her. Or who wanted her out of the way for some reason. Do you have any idea who that might be?"

He thought for a few seconds. "Believe me, I've been thinking about very little else for the past two days. But there are no obvious answers. Everybody loved Savannah. She was the sweetest, kindest, gentlest person—"

His face crumpled. "You know, I spent the morning arranging a memorial service for her. It'll be here in the Hudson Valley. Even though she lived in the city, this weekend place of hers was where she really felt at home, so it seemed like the right thing to do."

I blinked. So not only had Savannah bought this house; she had done so in order to have a second home—rather than, say, for rental income. It was her weekend place. I was more puzzled than ever about how she had managed to pull that off.

"I can't describe how horrible all this is," Timothy went on, his eyes moist. "She was twenty-six years old, for heaven's sake! And—and I loved her."

He dissolved into tears, his anguish erupting in deep choking sounds that made my eyes fill with tears, too.

Seeing how distraught this man was made it pretty much impossible to believe that he could have had anything to do with her death.

I left soon afterward, not wanting to intrude on his grief. It wasn't until I was driving away that I was able to put our meeting into perspective.

Timothy had seemed sincerely devastated. Then again, I reminded myself, he was an actor. And pretending was what actors did best.

Then there was his claim that Savannah Crane hadn't had

a single enemy. I found that difficult to believe about anyone, no matter how sweet she was. Someone had wanted her dead, and it was undoubtedly someone she knew. And Timothy, of all people, should have known that there were many possibilities. Actors became jealous of other actors' success, current and former lovers became possessive, people from one's past dug up old conflicts and became vengeful.

Timothy's insistence that everyone in the world was as crazy about Savannah as he was made me wonder if he was protecting someone.

Or even himself.

There was one—and only one—advantage to Lickety Splits being closed. And that was that I now had more time to spend with Grams.

That evening was one of those rare occasions when the three of us were able to sit down and enjoy a meal together. Grams had set the dining room table with her "good" china. She had also used her favorite tablecloth and matching napkins, a blue and green block-print design with elephants she'd bought on a trip to India.

Emma, meanwhile, had insisted on doing all the cooking. She had declared that the meal she was preparing had a theme: comfort food. She spent hours in the kitchen whipping up herbed meatloaf, made-from-scratch macaroni and cheese, carrots dripping with honey, and fluffy biscuits the size of baseballs. If a person couldn't find comfort in a menu like that, the poor sad sack was beyond being consoled.

As usual, I was in charge of dessert. For tonight, I'd made something I was thinking of selling at the shop: an Italian dessert called *affogato*, which means "drowned." It's simple enough to make, since it's basically vanilla ice cream that's been drowned in hot espresso.

But one of the fun things about *affogato* is that you don't have to use vanilla ice cream. The sky's the limit there, as long as you choose a flavor that's compatible with the flavor of the coffee. And you can add other things, such as shaved chocolate or nuts or coconut. You can even top it off with amaretto or hazelnut-flavored liquor. I was still experimenting with different combinations. But one thing I was certain of was that I would use decaf espresso in case the person who was eating it liked the flavor of coffee but didn't want a caffeine jolt.

Yet while all the trappings of our family dinner were festive, the bottom line was that even colorful cloth napkins and drippy melted cheese couldn't keep us from ruminating about the matters at hand.

"Did Detective Stoltz say anything about how long Lickety Splits will be closed?" Emma asked as she slathered butter on the cloud-like biscuit she'd just broken in half.

"You know how he is," I said, stabbing a piece of meatloaf with my fork. "He says as little as possible. Getting information out of that man is impossible."

"What about Jake?" Emma asked. "He was a criminal lawyer. Does he have any idea how long it usually takes the police to collect the evidence they need in a situation like this?"

"He said it shouldn't take too long," I replied. "But every day that goes by is costing me money." Not to mention what it's doing to my shop's good name, I thought. *And* mine.

As Emma and I talked, I gradually became aware of a strange sound in the background. It wasn't until Emma and I stopped talking long enough to pass the butter from her side of the table to mine that I realized what it was.

"Are you humming?" I asked, turning to Grams.

"Was I?" she replied, looking surprised. And, I thought, a little guilty. "I'm sorry. There's a song playing in my head, but I didn't realize I was humming it."

Emma and I exchanged puzzled looks.

"What's going on, Grams?" Emma demanded. Even though Caroline Whitman, my grandmother, is actually Emma's great-grandmother, she calls her Grams, the same way my two sisters and I do. Their husbands call her Grams, too. Somehow, coming up with another name for Emma to call her by would be, well, just too complicated.

Grams glanced up from her plate. "Nothing is going on!"

"Come on, Grams," I said. "I've never heard you hum while you were eating dinner before. Emma's spread of comfort food is truly spectacular, but I don't know that it's something to hum about."

She sighed. "All right. Maybe I am in a particularly good mood."

"And why would that be?" Emma asked teasingly. "I don't suppose it has anything to do with Georgie-Porgie, does it?"

I braced myself for a denial. Instead, Grams's face softened into a smile. "As a matter of fact, it does. My relationship with George is—let's just say it's suddenly going beyond planning the Halloween event for the kids."

"Do you mean he asked you out on a date?" Emma asked, widening her big brown eyes.

"As a matter of fact, he did," Grams replied. "He invited me to have dinner with him at Greenleaf this Sunday evening."

"Greenleaf!" I cried. "This guy is serious!"

Greenleaf is easily the best restaurant in Wolfert's Roost, if not the entire Hudson Valley. A few months earlier, the *New York Times'* restaurant critic had trekked up to our little town to check it out. After tasting the farm-to-table cuisine, brought to thrilling new levels with the addition of ingredients that most people didn't even know how to pronounce, he had awarded it the maximum number of stars.

Since then, foodies from all over the metropolitan area had been descending upon Wolfert's Roost to enjoy Greenleaf's exceptional cuisine. While the restaurant's founder and executive chef no longer lived in town, he apparently oversaw its menu from afar. I hadn't gotten around to eating there myself yet, but from what I heard, it was as fabulous as ever.

"George and Caroline, sitting in a tree," Emma began chanting, "K-I-S-S—"

"Oh, stop," Grams insisted, waving her hand in the air dismissively. "For all I know, it's not even an actual date. I may simply be leaping to conclusions. Maybe he just means it as a friendly gesture."

"Ri-i-ight," Emma said dryly. "A man takes you out for an expensive dinner because he wants to be friends."

"It's not impossible, is it?" Grams countered.

"Not impossible," I replied. "But I agree with Emma. It's highly unlikely."

"The important question," Emma said, waving her fork in the air, "is what are you going to wear?"

For the rest of the meal, the three of us had fun speculating about hilarious outfits, everything from an evening gown to a chef's hat and apron to show how much she appreciated fine cuisine. It was a welcome distraction, much better than talking about Savannah Crane's murder and the toll it was taking on me, my business, and every other aspect of my life.

"Maybe you and George could double-date with Ethan and me some time," Emma teased as we all cleared the table. "He keeps talking about this club he heard about that specializes in grunge music from the nineties. That's ancient history to me, but maybe that's your thing, Grams."

"Of course it's her thing," I joked. "Haven't you noticed the Nirvana T-shirt hanging in her closet?"

"Don't get ahead of yourself, Emma," Grams warned. "We're not at the double-date stage yet, and we might never be. I still think George may just be interested in an occasional dinner companion."

But I noticed that her eyes definitely had that same twinkle I'd seen in them before.

Later that evening, as Grams was beating me at Rummy 500, Emma came rushing into the living room, her cloud of dark, blue-streaked curls flying behind her. Her laptop computer was tucked under her arm.

"Kate, you're not going to believe what happened!" she cried.

"Whatever it is, I hope it's better than what's happening with this hand," I replied, grimacing at the mismatched twos, threes, and fours I was holding.

"Kate, this is serious!" Emma insisted.

That got my attention.

"What happened?" I asked.

"I was just checking some of the web sites I like to follow that have news about celebrities. And I just read that Jennifer Jordan has disappeared!" Emma exclaimed. "She was last spotted on Wednesday afternoon, picking up dry cleaning in Greenwich Village, the section of New York City where she lives. No one has seen her since then!"

Jennifer Jordan, Jennifer Jordan . . . I couldn't place the name. I certainly didn't have any idea why we should care.

"Who on earth is Jennifer Jordan?" I finally asked.

Emma rolled her eyes. "Ka-a-a-ate!" she moaned, as if I was the most clueless person in the universe. "Jennifer Jordan is the actress who lost the part of Suzi Hamilton in *The Best Ten Days* to Savannah Crane! According to this web site, she really, really wanted that role. And just a few hours after Savannah was murdered, she mysteriously vanished!"

Chapter 5

Rocky Road ice cream became the first widely available flavor other than vanilla, chocolate, and strawberry in 1929. It was invented in Oakland, California, by William Dreyer, who had an ice cream company with his partner, Joseph Edy. Dreyer used his wife's sewing scissors to cut up walnuts and marshmallows, which he added to chocolate ice cream. The walnuts were later replaced with toasted almonds. Dreyer and Edy named the flavor after the period that followed the Wall Street Crash of 1929 "to give folks something to smile about in the midst of the Great Depression."

—*https://en.wikipedia.org/wiki/Rocky_road_(ice_cream)*

"She vanished?" I repeated, confused. "Where did she go?"

"Kate, that's the whole point of vanishing!" Emma exclaimed, sounding exasperated. "It means that no one *knows* where she went!"

"But there could be all kinds of explanations, couldn't there?" Grams said.

My mind raced as I tried to come up with a few. "Like she decided she wanted to get out of the public eye for a while," I said. "Like a favorite aunt got sick and she flew off somewhere to take care of her. Like—like—"

"Here's one," Emma said breathlessly. "How about she disappeared because she just murdered her rival, Savannah Crane?"

My mind was still clicking away. "But was Jennifer Jordan even anywhere *near* the Hudson Valley?" I asked, trying to figure out a way that Emma's theory could hold water.

"That's something I hope to find out," Emma said. "But there's another possibility."

"What's that?" I asked.

"That she hired one of the crew members who was at the shoot to kill Savannah!" she said excitedly. She plopped down in the dark green upholstered chair. "Think about it. It makes perfect sense. Or maybe both Jennifer and the person she hired wanted Savannah dead, so Jennifer didn't actually have to hire him or her, since they were working together as a team. And now that she's a murderer, she's disappeared . . ."

"It's not impossible," I said thoughtfully. "Maybe it's not the most likely scenario, but it could be what happened."

Detective Stoltz's declaration about the most obvious explanation in murder cases not always being the correct one had stuck in my mind. So did the other side of it: that the correct explanation could sometimes be one that wasn't obvious at all.

"I've been doing some research on Jennifer Jordan," Emma went on animatedly. She opened her laptop and placed it on the coffee table so Grams and I could see the screen. "Apparently she and Savannah have been rivals for ages. The two of them went to the same acting school in New York together. According to this web site, CelebScoops.com, they were both the same type. You know, young, pretty, innocent-looking. What used to be called debutantes back in the old days. Anyway, every time there was a role that they were both suited for, they ended up competing."

"Who usually won?" Grams asked, craning her neck to get a better look at the computer.

Emma pointed at the screen. "Over here it makes it sound as if Savannah was the favorite most of the time. Jennifer Jordan didn't get famous until she married a big-shot movie producer." Turning her laptop so I could see the screen, she added, "He's the yucky-looking guy in this picture, Harry Steinberg."

"He looks as if he's much older than she is," I commented, peering at the photo. And that was being polite. He was also short, chubby, bald, and kind of ugly.

But Emma had made it sound as if he was very influential. Wealthy, too.

"They got divorced after only a couple of years," she went on. "But while they were married, she landed some great roles in a bunch of his movies. She even got an Oscar nomination for her performance in *Young Eleanor*. But as soon as she got famous, she ditched him."

"Marrying someone powerful is one way to get ahead in Hollywood, I suppose," I mused. "But if she's so famous, why would she give a hoot about Savannah Crane's career?"

Emma did some more clicking. "This website, StarGazer. com, says that once Jennifer Jordan divorced Harry Steinberg, no one would touch her. She couldn't get any good parts. But then the role of Suzi Hamilton in *The Best Ten Days of My Life* came up. Jennifer was sure that would be her big comeback. And apparently the studio that's making it was one of the few places where Harry Steinberg didn't have any influence. At any rate, she desperately wanted that role—"

"And instead Savannah Crane got it," I said, finishing her sentence. "Once again, Jennifer Jordan's longtime rival got something she really, really wanted."

The relationship between the two actresses reminded me of the one I'd had with my nemesis since childhood, Ashley

Winthrop. Ashley had resurfaced right after I'd opened Lickety Splits four months earlier. It turned out that she ran the bakery right across the street from my ice cream shop, and as soon as it opened, she put up a big sign announcing that the Sweet Things Pastry Palace was now selling ice cream.

That hadn't ended well. But it had certainly given me a good lesson in the bitter feelings that rivalries can cause.

"So Jennifer Jordan had a strong motive for killing Savannah Crane," I said, thinking aloud.

"She sure did," Emma agreed. "And now she's vanished! Kate, I think we may have found our murderer!"

"Not so fast," I warned. "There are a few other suspects, too, some of them right in the area."

I was mainly thinking about Savannah's boyfriend, Timothy. But there were also all the other people who were part of the film crew, people who had been at Lickety Splits at the time Savannah was poisoned. The possibility that one of them was working with the victim's rival was worth considering, but that still left us with the problem of figuring out who that person was.

And how on earth he or she had managed to put poison into Savannah's ice cream dish.

I was still lost in thought as Emma asked, "So you're going to do it again, right?"

I puzzled over her question, wondering if she was talking about some ice cream flavor I'd once made or an unusual catered event I'd put together . . .

But before I had a chance to figure out what she was talking about, she added, "You're going to see if you can figure out who killed Savannah Crane, aren't you?"

I was about to protest, to insist she had it all wrong. Instead, I let out a deep sigh.

"I don't think I have any choice, do you?" I said. "In fact,

I already tracked down her boyfriend. I wanted to ask him if he had any ideas about who might have been behind this."

I glanced over at Grams, nervous about her reaction.

So I was greatly relieved when she said, "Just be careful, Kate. I understand that this terrible thing really hit you close to home. After all, it happened right in your shop, with *your* ice cream in *your* dish . . . But please promise me that you won't put yourself in any danger."

"I promise," I told her earnestly.

"You know that I'll do everything I can to help you, right?" Emma said. "Computer stuff, research stuff, even going undercover."

I couldn't resist leaning over and giving my niece a big hug. "You're the absolute best, Emma," I told her. "Thank you."

"You're welcome," she replied. Snapping her computer shut, she added, "But so far, I'm betting on Jennifer Jordan. She played a killer in *Dark Days in Denmark*, and I always thought she was just a little too convincing. She was much better in that movie than any of the others I'd seen her in."

I doubted that that argument would hold up in a murder trial. But the two actresses' long-term rivalry, along with the fact that Jennifer Jordan had really wanted the role of Suzi Hamilton, were definitely worth taking into account.

Not to mention the reports that Jennifer Jordan had inexplicably disappeared.

I wondered if Detective Stoltz read CelebScoops.com or StarGazer.com. But since I was pretty sure he didn't, I decided this was a piece of information I should keep in mind.

The following morning, a Saturday, I was lingering over breakfast when my cell phone buzzed. I'd been sipping my second cup of coffee as I read and reread that day's *Daily Roost*. "MURDER STILL UNSOLVED!" the front-page headline screamed. It was a harsh reminder that I had work to do. Even with Detective Stoltz on the case.

Then came the call from the very same individual I'd been thinking about only moments earlier.

"The crime-scene tape has been taken down from your shop, Ms. McKay," Detective Stoltz informed me as soon as he'd identified himself. "You can open for business again."

At first, I was so thrilled that I let out a whoop that caused Digger's ears to jump up to the ceiling. The scruffy terrier gave me a look that said, "Hey, I thought *I* was the one who was supposed to do the barking around here!"

But two seconds later, I was in panic mode. It was already nine AM. That meant I had exactly two hours to get ready to reopen.

I gulped down the remains of my coffee, then shrieked, "Emma!"

Half an hour later, the two of us were bustling around the shop, getting ready for what would hopefully end up being a day that could be described as business as usual.

That turned out to be more demanding than I'd anticipated. Not the ice cream part, which by that point I'd pretty much mastered. It was the fact that my shop no longer looked like Halloween Central.

Despite Chelsea Atkins's promise about restoring Lickety Splits to its original state, Halloween decorations and all, that hadn't happened. Not when immediately after the movie shoot—right in the middle of it, in fact—my beloved little store had become a crime scene.

The cobwebs, the pumpkin lights, the lovable life size monsters . . . none of it was on display. Fortunately, we found all of it stashed in back, in the kitchen area where I whip up my fresh, homemade ice cream and all the other related concoctions.

"The bat fell off Dracula's shoulder!" Emma wailed as she pulled off the Bubble Wrap he'd been cocooned in.

"We can prop him up at the table anyway," I assured her. "And next time you come, bring a needle and thread, and you can perform emergency surgery."

Thanks to being highly motivated, not to mention downing that second cup of coffee, my niece and I quickly restored Lickety Splits to its original state. By five minutes to eleven, the Count was seated at a table, the witch was at the door, and Frankenstein was sitting outside, drooling over his towering ice cream cone. The cobwebs, the spiders, the lights . . . everything was back in place.

"It looks great," I told Emma. "Now all we need is customers."

I held my breath as I turned around my CLOSED sign so that it read OPEN.

It's showtime! I thought. But this time, the phrase had an entirely different meaning.

I usually love opening my shop in the morning, but today I was filled more with apprehension than optimism. I was truly worried about business being slow. A couple of months earlier, back in August, a similar incident had all but closed down Wolfert's Roost. The tourists and day-trippers were scared away.

And here we were, dealing with another murder.

So I was relieved that it didn't take long for customers to start drifting in.

Even though it was a Saturday, the most popular day for tourism in the Hudson Valley, foot traffic did seem lighter than usual. But Halloween being less than two weeks away seemed to have put the local residents in a holiday mood.

The first customer of the day was a young mother who ordered a dozen of Emma's ice cream characters for her seven-year-old son's Halloween party. She decided on an assortment of pirates, clowns, and monsters. Quite a few of the customers who followed were also up for seasonal treats, including the makeshift version of Monster Mash that Emma quickly put together by topping green mint ice cream with chocolate chips, two kinds of nuts, and crushed chocolate cookies. All that was missing from the original concept were the tiny eyeballs, but the new flavor proved to be pretty popular even without them.

Not everyone was in a Halloween mood. The two earnest teenage girls who came in, lugging heavy backpacks, for example. I suspected that they were gearing up for an intense studying session. After spending nearly ten minutes agonizing over what to get, they ended up sharing a Bananafana Split. Their choice of flavors: Dark Chocolate Hazelnut, Classic Tahitian Vanilla, and Berry Blizzard—an updated, very Lickety Splits version of the classic chocolate, vanilla, and strawberry. Then three businessmen came in and loudly ordered cones stuffed with all the ice cream that would fit. From the giddy way they were high-fiving each other, I got the feeling they'd just closed a deal.

But the customer who really made my day was the young man who wandered in. He was about Emma and Ethan's age, with a wild mane of jet-black hair. At least it managed to stay out of his eyes.

"I was totally into the thing you did the other day," he remarked after he ordered a Hudson's Hottest Hot Fudge Sundae made with English Toffee Caramel and Black Raspberry with Dark Chocolate Chunks.

"Thanks," I said automatically. Then I added, "What exactly are you talking about?"

"The crime-scene tape," he replied with a grin. "It took the concept of Halloween decorations to an awesome new level. It was totally chill! But I can see why you couldn't leave it up. It was kind of blocking the door."

I was smiling as I opened the cabinet to take out a glass tulip dish for the man's sundae. I hoped most other people had made the same assumption he had, that the crime-scene tape was just another clever Halloween decoration.

As I was reaching for the dish, I suddenly stopped, my hand frozen in midair. I had just spotted a single strand of human hair curled up on the shelf. At first, I assumed it was mine, and I told myself that I needed to be more careful. But when I pulled it out and studied it, I noticed it had a reddish tinge.

Definitely not mine.

A shock wave passed through me. I knew someone with long red hair. Chelsea Atkins, the assistant director.

My mind was racing. Of course, she had spent hours in the shop, both the night before the shoot and early that morning. But she had specifically said that she wanted *me* to pick out the dish and spoon that would be used during the film shoot because she felt uncomfortable scrounging around in my cabinets.

Now it looked as if she had done precisely that.

There could be a hundred different reasons why Chelsea had been rummaging through my cabinets, I thought. But I still felt uneasy about the fact that she had clearly done exactly that. I decided that this was a fact worth filing away. As for the hair, I wrapped it up in paper and stuck it on a shelf.

A few more customers wandered in, and then suddenly there was a lull. Lickety Splits was empty. Emma had plans to meet with two classmates from her computer course to work on a group project, and I assured her that I could handle the shop by myself while she focused on her schoolwork. The fact that she had her own car now was what made juggling her complicated life possible. Her parents had been so thrilled that she was taking classes at the community college that they had bought her one. It was practically an antique, but it gave her the mobility she needed.

Which left me alone in my shop. As I stood behind the counter, I looked around, still trying to digest the fact that this lovely place had actually been the scene of a murder.

I stared at the seat Savannah Crane had been sitting in, wondering if I'd ever again be able to see it as just another chair. It was difficult not to keep replaying that horrible morning over and over again in my head.

But what was even worse was the idea that Detective Stoltz thought I might have had something to do with it. That continued to plague me like a low-level headache that simply wouldn't go away.

I was sinking deeper and deeper into negative thoughts, so I was relieved when the door opened and another customer came in. At least, I assumed the woman was a customer. She looked as if she was in her late twenties, small in both height and build, with wavy, shoulder-length, dark brown hair. Her large brown eyes and full lips gave her round face a doll-like appearance.

She didn't come right up to the counter. That was what most customers did, either to scan the giant tubs of ice cream in the display case or to study the menu posted on the wall behind me. Instead, she immediately slumped into a chair. Then she looked around, as if she was trying to drink in her surroundings.

A wave of panic came over me as I realized that she might be a reporter. I'd prepared myself for that possibility, deciding in advance that I would refuse to talk to anyone looking for an inside scoop or even a catchy sound bite.

But this woman didn't strike me as someone who'd come here to interview me. In fact, I immediately picked up on the heavy sense of sadness she exuded.

An awkward silence hung over the shop. Finally, I asked, "Is there something I can get you?"

She glanced up, looking surprised. It was as if she'd just noticed that she wasn't alone. But instead of responding, she stared at me blankly.

"You're welcome to sample any of our flavors before deciding," I went on cheerfully. Gesturing at the listings behind me, I said, "And in addition to cones and cups, we have Hudson's Hottest Hot Fudge Sundaes, Bananafana Splits . . . and for Halloween, we've come up with a bunch of fun seasonal creations."

"Actually, I didn't come here for ice cream," the young woman said somberly.

Now I was really confused. But before I had a chance to ask what she *had* come in for, she added, "I was Savannah Crane's best friend." Tears welled up in her eyes as she choked out the words, "I wanted to see this place for myself."

"I see," I replied. I could feel my own shoulders slumping. "You're welcome to spend as much time here as you like."

"Thanks," she said. Her eyes filled with tears.

I desperately wanted to do something more for her. But the only thing I could come up with was giving her ice cream.

So I dished out big scoops of Classic Tahitian Vanilla, Chocolate Almond Fudge, and Blueberry Pomegranate, filling the biggest dish I had. Then I covered the ice cream with rainbow sprinkles. I figured the bright colors might cheer her up. And she was clearly someone who needed cheering up.

"I don't know about you," I said as I brought the concoction over to her table, "but I find that ice cream goes a long way in making even the worst situations just a little bit better."

"Thanks," she said, casting me a woeful glance as I set it down in front of her. "I don't know if I can eat it, though. I haven't had much of an appetite since . . ."

"I understand completely," I told her. "But another good

thing about ice cream it's that it's easy to eat, even if you don't have the least interest in food."

She picked up the spoon, treating it like it was made of lead.

"Do you mind if I sit down?" I asked, nodding at the seat opposite her.

She shrugged. I took that as permission.

Maybe it was because I was sitting a few inches away from her, but she finally forced a minuscule bit of vanilla into her mouth. I was glad to see that her tense expression softened, just a little.

"Hey, this is really good," she commented. "I'm not usually a big fan of vanilla, but this is delicious."

"The vanilla is imported from Tahiti," I told her, glad we'd found something lighthearted to talk about. "I call the flavor Classic Tahitian Vanilla. My intention in creating it was to bring regular old vanilla ice cream to a brand-new level."

"You sure managed to accomplish that," she said, helping herself to more.

Neither of us spoke as she continued to eat, scooping up one tiny spoonful of ice cream after another. Finally, the silence started to make me uncomfortable.

"By the way, I'm Kate McKay," I said.

"Nice to meet you," she replied. "I'm Amanda Huffner."

"Are you an actress, too?" I asked. "Is that how you know Savannah?"

She shook her head. "No, but we did meet through her acting career. It was while she was in an off-off-Broadway play. It was called *Next Stop: Brooklyn.*" She grimaced. "Savannah was great in it, but it was a pretty terrible play."

"How did you come to be involved with it?" I asked.

"I work for a props house," Amanda said. "It's called Monarch Cinema Props. It's in Queens." She sounded proud as she added, "It's the biggest props house on the East Coast.

We handle everything: furniture, lamps, rugs, fake flowers, dishes, toys, you name it. We've got anything anyone could possibly need for movies, television, theater, commercials, fashion shoots . . . Everything is stored in a one hundred thousand square foot warehouse that's also our showroom."

"Wow, that sounds fun!" I said. I was already wondering if it would be possible to go see it. Especially with Emma. Given my niece's artistic bent, not to mention her love of anything related to the entertainment industry, I had a feeling she'd get a real kick out of touring a place like that.

"It is fun," she agreed. "I really love my job."

Suddenly another thought occurred to me. "Did Monarch handle the props for *Ten Days*?" I asked.

Amanda shook her head. "Unfortunately not. It would have been cool to work on a film that my best friend was starring in. Especially since that connection is how we met in the first place. A few years ago, I was part of the crew that was delivering props to the theater where *Next Stop: Brooklyn* was rehearsing. Savannah and I started chatting, and before we knew it, we'd exchanged phone numbers." With a little shrug, she added, "That was about two years ago, right after Savannah moved to New York from Ohio. She didn't know many people, and we started hanging out together a lot."

Her voice had become strained, as if talking about her close friendship with Savannah was difficult. Instead, she went back to eating ice cream.

But after just one more mouthful, she set down her spoon. The corners of her mouth drooping downward, she mumbled, "I knew he was a creep, but I had no idea he was this psycho."

I blinked. "Who are we talking about?"

"Ragnar, of course. Ragnar Bruin." She practically spit out the syllables.

Ragnar Bruin, Ragnar Bruin . . . it took me a few seconds to remember why that name sounded familiar.

"The director?" I finally asked, my eyebrows shooting up. "The guy who directed *The Hartford Trilogy* and *Too Much Time?*"

"That's right," she replied, her tone colder than the ice cream in her dish. "The great Ragnar Bruin. Academy-Award-winning director, artistic genius, and total nutjob."

I knew that film directors had a reputation for having strong personalities. Egos as big as the Hollywood sign, in fact. But Amanda's take on Ragnar Bruin was in another realm entirely.

And she was clearly convinced that he was responsible for her friend Savannah's murder.

"I think I'd heard that Ragnar Bruin was a bit of an egomaniac," I said, trying to sound casual. "But I've never heard anything about him being—well, as extreme as you make him sound."

Amanda snorted. "That's because he's so good at making money that no one wants to get on his bad side.

"That's how Hollywood works," she went on. "People can get away with pretty much anything as long as they're good at turning out movies that make everyone rich. That's certainly true for actors, and it's especially true for directors."

I thought about all the scandals in recent years concerning powerful people in Hollywood who had exhibited despicable behavior. But I'd always suspected that there were plenty more we never heard about.

"Ragnar is exceptionally lucky because his scandalous behavior never got into the news," Amanda went on. "Maybe it will finally come out." Bitterly, she muttered, "Now that it's too late."

"So he and Savannah were . . . friends?" I prompted, still not understanding.

She let out a contemptuous snort. "That's not the word I'd use, but they did know each other."

"What word would you use?" I asked, now even more cautious.

"How about 'stalker'?" Amanda replied. "Yeah, that'd work."

"Ragnar Bruin was stalking Savannah?" I repeated, even though that was exactly what she had just told me. The problem was that I was having trouble digesting this bizarre bit of news. "When did it start? How did they meet? What did he do, exactly?" I had lots more questions, but those were the ones that immediately came to mind.

"It started when he met Savannah at the Academy Awards last year," Amanda said.

"Savannah went to the Oscars?" Another question. But I was still trying to wrap my head around all this.

"She was working at the Oscars," she explained. She paused to eat another spoonful of ice cream. This time, she went for the Blueberry Pomegranate. "She was there as a seat filler."

"I think I've read about that," I said. "Aren't they people who sit in an empty seat whenever one of the celebrities or anyone else in the audience gets up to go to the bathroom or make a phone call or whatever?"

"Exactly," Amanda replied. "It's usually a really fun gig— hey, this ice cream flavor is amazing! It tastes so fresh and fruity! What is it?"

"Thanks," I said. "It's Blueberry Pomegranate."

"That's new to me," Amanda said, shaking her head. "Anyway, as you can imagine, Savannah was beyond excited. She got all dressed up for it—fortunately, she found a fabulous gown at a resale shop in Los Angeles—and she got her hair and makeup done at a salon near where she was staying."

"And where was that?" I interjected. "Did she have an apartment in L.A.?"

Amanda shook her head. "No. She would crash with friends whenever she had to go to L.A. Like for an audition or to meet with her agent or some other career-related business. But that girl was a New Yorker at heart. She lived in Brooklyn."

"But she was up here at the weekend house, too," I interjected.

"True," Amanda agreed. "But she spent most of her time in the city."

"So she met Ragnar Bruin at the Oscar ceremony?" I prompted, anxious to get back to what she'd been telling me.

"That's right," Amanda said. "Apparently she ended up sitting next to him when one of the nominees for Best Actress went to the bathroom. And during the ten or fifteen minutes they spent sitting together, Ragnar became obsessed with her.

"Of course, at the time Savannah thought it was the best thing that could possibly happen to her career," she went on. "I mean, she gets a once-in-a-lifetime opportunity to meet this fabulously important, ridiculously famous movie director, and within minutes he's clearly infatuated with her.

"She called me that night," Amanda said. "It was two AM on the West Coast, which means that in New York, where I was, it was five AM. But she was so excited that I wasn't the least bit angry about her waking me up. In fact, I was as thrilled as she was. She told me that Ragnar had wanted to know who her agent was, as if he had a project in mind for her. But then he asked her for her personal number so he could get in touch with her directly. Naturally she gave it to him. She was certain that she'd just made the most important contact of her career. And I suppose she had. It was just that from that night on, he barely left her alone."

Amanda stopped eating and put down her spoon. "At first, she was flattered," she said. "Who wouldn't be? There she was, one of hundreds if not thousands of aspiring actresses living in New York and L.A., with Ragnar Bruin calling her and sending her flowers and texting her night and day—"

"Were they dating?" I interrupted, realizing she hadn't said anything about the two of them ever actually going out anywhere.

She shifted in her seat. "Not dating, exactly. After all, there was the issue of Ragnar's wife."

Of course. I suddenly remembered his wedding being all over the news. He had married a famous actress who was almost twenty years younger than he was. The couple had flown a hundred of their "closest friends" to a small island in French Polynesia, someplace near Bora Bora. The festivities had lasted three days. Helicopters had hovered overhead the whole time as daredevil paparazzi snapped photos of the famous pair and all the other celebrities who had gathered together for the glamorous event.

"So even though, at first, all the attention Savannah was getting from Ragnar was flattering, it started to get . . . creepy," Amanda continued. "And she felt stuck. She wanted to tell him to tone it down, but she was afraid of messing up her career. After all, he's a pretty powerful guy." She glanced around the shop. Even though no one else was there but the two of us, Count Dracula, and the witch standing near the door, she lowered her voice. "And then he started acting weird."

"Weird how?" I asked, my voice equally quiet.

"He began sending her . . . photos," Amanda said softly. "Of himself. Um, naked. Or doing . . . strange things."

"I see."

"And sending her presents like sexy underwear," she added. "*Really* sexy underwear. With notes saying he couldn't wait to see her wearing it."

"How did Timothy feel about all this?" I asked, trying to sound casual.

Amanda jerked her head up. "How do you know about Timothy?"

"I've been doing a little research," I replied. "Because Savannah was murdered in my shop, I'm on the list of suspects even though I'd never even met her before Thursday. I figured that the more I knew about her and her life, the better position I'd be in."

I was being honest, but not quite coming right out and telling her that I was trying to find out who had killed her.

"Makes sense," she said with a nod.

"Timothy seems utterly devastated," I commented.

Amanda's eyes widened. "Are you kidding? Of *course* he's devastated! Those two were absolutely crazy about each other. In fact, just before . . . all this happened . . ."

She stopped, unable to go on for a few seconds. Then she took a deep breath. "Just before all this happened, Savannah told me that she and Timothy had decided to get married."

My eyebrows shot up. "So they were pretty solid."

"*Very* solid," Amanda agreed. "And I was so happy for Savannah. I mean, Timothy is the sweetest guy in the whole world. He's perfect for her, since she's the nicest person you can imagine, too . . ." Her voice trailed off. "She *was* the nicest person," she corrected herself, choking on her words.

"How did they meet?" I asked.

"Through acting," Amanda replied. "They were in a play together. This one was much better than the one I told you about. It was actually off-Broadway as opposed to off-off-Broadway."

"How long ago?" I couldn't resist asking.

"About a year and a half ago," Amanda replied, "not long after she moved to New York. Savannah's relationship with Timothy was one more great thing in her life." She let out a deep sigh. "Everything was going so well for her. She'd found the love of her life, her acting career was about to take off . . . not that she was someone who cared about the money or the fame or any of the glitzy stuff. For her, it was all about the work. She truly loved acting. It was what mattered to her most. And she figured that once she'd broken out in a big-name film like *Ten Days*, she'd have enough clout to do the roles she wanted to do. Shakespeare, Chekhov, all the great plays.

"She was finally in a position give up her day job, too," she added. "She hated working at that big corporate machine, doing boring, low-level stuff."

My ears pricked up. This was the first I'd heard about Savannah doing anything besides acting. "What did she do?"

"She was basically an administrative assistant," Amanda explained. "Pretty low-level stuff. But that was the kind of job she wanted: something that would pay the rent but wouldn't be too taxing. She also needed to be able to take off time for auditions and the occasional acting gig. It's not like she was looking to climb the corporate ladder or anything.

"But even though the job was supposed to be as undemanding as possible, it still seemed to be taking a toll on her. She'd only been there about a year, but lately she kept talking about how she couldn't wait to get out. Landing that role in *Ten Days* was her ticket out of there." She laughed, then said, "Although she still didn't quite believe it. In fact, she didn't even quit her job. She took a leave of absence, just to be safe."

"Where did she work?" I asked.

She paused to eat another spoonful of ice cream. "A company in New York called Alpha Industries," she finally replied.

"I never heard of it," I commented. "What does it do?"

"It's one of those big companies that's involved in lots of different things," Amanda said with a wave of her hand. "She wasn't interested in talking about her day job. That's how little it mattered to her."

She gobbled down the rest of her ice cream, then began gathering up her things.

Gesturing at her empty dish, she asked, "That was truly amazing, especially the pomegranate thing. How much do I owe you?"

"It's on the house," I said.

"Thanks," she said, rising to her feet. Her voice was choked as she added, "And thanks for letting me be here. It was important to me."

"I'm so sorry," I told her sincerely.

Even though I'd only met Savannah once, my heart felt crushed. I'd lost enough people who mattered to me to understand only too well what she was going through. And as Amanda walked away, her body language spoke volumes. Her shoulders were still slumped, her head was lowered, and she moved as if the very effort was almost too demanding.

Once she was gone, I lingered at the table, thinking. Amanda and I hadn't talked for very long, but I'd learned a lot about Savannah Crane.

Mainly about her relationship with Ragnar Bruin.

I wondered how far jealousy had taken the famous director.

And then something else occurred to me. Ragnar Bruin was married. Which meant that his wife was undoubtedly as distressed about his obsession with Savannah as she was.

But Amanda had given me a second important lead: Savannah's day job. That struck me as something that I should be able to learn more about. I resolved to go into the city the first chance I got to do exactly that.

But as I sat alone at the table, it wasn't the investigation or even the details of Savannah's life that hung over me like a dark cloud. It was the heartbreaking fact that she was gone.

In the end, Savannah Crane had turned into a tragic heroine, just like a character in one of the Shakespearean plays she longed to be in.

Chapter 6

Most of the vanilla used to make ice cream
comes from Madagascar and Indonesia.

—*www.icecream.com/icecreaminfo*

Over the next several hours, business continued to be unusually light. I hoped it was just a fluke and that Wolfert's Roost—and Lickety Splits in particular—weren't suffering from the horrific crime that had been exploding in the headlines for the past few days.

When the door of my shop opened after a lull, I glanced up anxiously, assuming it was another customer. Instead, I was surprised to see that Chelsea Atkins had come into my shop.

I hadn't expected to see her again. And her presence instantly made me uncomfortable, thanks to that stray hair I'd found in my cabinet.

She was dressed more formally than the other times I'd seen her, in sleek black pants, a fitted jacket made of olive-green suede, and a tailored white shirt that looked like silk underneath it. While in the past her red hair had been pulled back into a haphazard knot with plenty of flyaway strands, today it hung loose, brushed into a sort of halo around her face.

She ignored me, instead looking around my shop critically the way she had the first time she'd come into Lickety Splits.

It was hard to believe that that had only been three days earlier.

"Hi, Chelsea," I said. "I didn't realize you were still in town."

She grimaced. "Not my choice," she said sullenly, ambling over to the counter. "I'd much rather be back home in Los Angeles, at least until Skip DiFalco decides what's going to happen with *Ten Days* now that Savannah is gone. But your local police department suggested that it would be a good idea if I stuck around for a while."

She seemed different from the other times I'd seen her. And it wasn't only what she was wearing or the way she wore her hair. She seemed . . . distracted. She was acting as if she was in a daze.

Her eyes traveled around my shop again. "You've put everything back," she observed, vaguely gesturing at Count Dracula. "Sorry I didn't make good on my promise to have the crew do all that. It must have been a big job."

"My niece and I worked on it together," I told her. "It didn't take us that long."

"Good." She was silent for a long time before saying, "That scary detective spent a long time questioning me." I could tell by the look on her face that she'd found the experience extremely unpleasant.

Not that I blamed her. Going head-to-head with Detective Stoltz wasn't exactly my favorite thing, either.

"Everything about this terrible event is awful," I said. "He questioned me, too. And I'd never even heard of Savannah Crane until Wednesday, when you first mentioned her to me."

I expected her to make a comment about her own relationship to Savannah. But she said nothing.

"I'm sure Detective Stoltz considers you an important source of information," I commented. "After all, you knew the names of everyone who came into Lickety Splits before and during the shoot."

She nodded. "I gave him a list. They were all people I'd worked with before, and frankly, I'd vouch for the innocence of each and every one of them."

"And no one came onto the set who didn't belong there?" I asked. "Maybe someone who said they were friends with Savannah or one of the other actors, or someone who didn't identify themselves at all . . . ?"

Chelsea shook her head. "It's just like I told the police: The only people on the set who I didn't know were the people from your shop."

A heavy silence hung between us. I was still trying to figure out why she'd come back. A quick phone call to apologize for my store's unexpected involvement in this horrific episode would have worked just as well as a personal visit.

Detective Stoltz's claim that the murderer might come back to my shop loomed large in my mind.

"Is there anything in particular I can help you with?" I finally asked.

"Not really," Chelsea replied. "I guess I just wanted to see this place one more time.

"I didn't know Savannah Crane well at all," she continued. "I'd only met her a few times before we started shooting this film. And I remember running into her at a restaurant one night while she was having dinner with her boyfriend, Timothy. But what happened to her was so horrible. I guess I thought that coming back here might give me some sense of—I don't know, closure."

She seemed so sincere that my heart melted, at least a little. "Is it working?" I asked gently.

She shook her head. "Things are never that simple, are they? But there's something else: I'd also like to apologize in person for all the disruption this nightmare caused for you. I feel responsible, since I'm the one who got you involved in the first place."

I didn't know how to respond. Frankly, I was finding this whole interaction a bit awkward. I was back to wondering if Chelsea really was looking for closure—or if perhaps there was some other reason for her visit.

But before I had a chance to try to find out, the door opened again. A man and a woman in their sixties, wearing jeans and tie-dye, sauntered in. The woman had a long, gray braid hanging below her waist, and the man's curly white mane gave him a distinct Jerry Garcia look. The Hudson Valley was home to a lot of people who had come to the area in the 1960s, fell in love with it, and never left. I had a feeling that this couple fit into that category.

"I see you have customers," Chelsea said. "I won't take up any more of your time."

I was actually relieved when she left, given her strange demeanor. I was still unsure if grief was behind it—or something else.

I turned to the couple, who were oohing and aahing over the display case. The woman, I noticed, had a blue streak in her hair, just like Emma. I liked her immediately.

"What can I get you?" I asked, anxious to spread a little joy in the form of ice cream. There had been too much bad karma in my shop over the past several days, and I hoped that a few generous scoops and a little chocolate syrup would work their usual magic.

"How about stopping over at the high school gym before you go into Lickety Splits this morning?" Grams suggested over breakfast the next morning. "I'm interested in what you think about the progress we're making."

"I thought you'd never ask," I replied. "I've been wondering how Halloween Hollow was shaping up."

From the excited expression on Grams's face, I had a feeling it was shaping up just fine. And I could hardly wait to get a peek. It wasn't only the local kids I was thinking about, either, since Halloween had been such a highlight of my childhood.

I found myself remembering that every year, my two sisters and I would start planning our costumes during the summer, usually while camped out on the front porch on a hot, lazy day, armed with lemonade. I remember one time in particular, when I was seven. My sister Julie would have been fourteen and Nina twelve—so the fact that they actually chose to hang out with me, their little sister, made it a particularly special occasion.

I could still hear myself telling my sisters that that year I wanted to dress up as either a princess or a pirate.

"I have a better idea," Julie said. As the oldest of three sisters, Julie frequently had a "better idea." And because of her status, we usually ended up doing whatever she had come up with.

"This year, let's coordinate our costumes," Julie continued. "We can have a theme. The Three Musketeers or the Three Stooges—"

"How about the three fairy godmothers from *Sleeping Beauty*?" Nina suggested. "Flora, Fauna, and Merryweather?"

In the end, we'd gone as characters from *Peter Pan*. Julie, being Julie, got to be Peter, decked out in green tights and a green felt tunic that Grams made. Nina was Captain Hook. And I was Tinkerbell, which I absolutely loved because I got to wear both a green, ballerina-style skirt *and* wings. True, the wings kept falling off, especially since it was windy and drizzly that year. But I still loved parading around in that costume.

The three of us always went trick-or-treating together, since until I was close to starting middle school, I was considered too young to go alone or even with friends my own age. Julie, in particular, always acted as if she was doing me a favor. But I always suspected she loved having an excuse to go house-to-house begging for candy, something her teenage friends considered uncool. And sometimes we got something even better, like the time we were invited into a neighbor's house for hot apple cider and freshly made cinnamon donuts.

Once we got home, exhausted but exhilarated, the sorting and trading began. My sisters and I each got two big bowls out of the kitchen cabinets and began dividing up our loot. The first bowl was for the good stuff we planned to keep for ourselves or share with Grams or our friends at school. The second bowl was for the rejects we were willing to trade away.

Our taste was generally similar. Everything made with chocolate ended up in the "keepers" bowl: Milky Ways, peanut butter cups, anything with a Hershey label on it.

But the rejects were much more personal, which turned out to be a good thing. Julie loved anything green—lollipops, jelly beans, green apple Skittles. And Nina went crazy for anything sour, from Sour Patch Kids to lemon lollipops. As for me, I liked candy that was cherry-flavored. We traded our goodies so that each McKay sister was able to load up on her sugary favorites.

Given my love of Halloween, I couldn't wait to see what Grams and her helpers had come up with. And as soon as I stepped into the high school gym, lugging a big box of rainbow sprinkles and round silver pearls and assorted Halloween candies for the do-it-yourself ice cream station, I saw that I wasn't about to be the least bit disappointed.

An actual, full-size house was under construction, complete with every scary element anyone could think of. Directly behind it, I could see the beginnings of a gigantic foam pit. I could practically hear the children's gleeful howls as they jumped off the edge, plunging into what amounted to a huge bowl filled with clumps of dense foam that would cushion their fall.

"Wow!" I cried. "This is a huge production! I had no idea you were doing this Halloween thing on such a grand scale!"

"I told you it was going to be fabulous," Grams said proudly.

At the sound of our voices, the front door of the dilapidated house in the center of the gym opened. George Vernon emerged, dressed in jeans and sneakers and carrying a paintbrush.

"I see the boss is taking a break," he quipped. "I guess that means the rest of us can, too."

"Halloween is less than two weeks away," Grams returned, sounding a bit flirtatious. "No slacking off!"

"Who, me?" George replied, flirting right back. "I've been here since seven!"

"Only because I read you the riot act," Grams countered. "I hope I finally convinced you that making sure the children have a wonderful Halloween is more important than that golf game of yours!"

He shrugged. "What can I say? The other guys depend on me. But I've been making up for it. I just finished painting the ballroom, and now I'm working on the front room."

"A ballroom?" I repeated, startled. I had to admit that I was dazzled by the scope of this project. "I can't believe you're building an actual mansion here in the gym!"

"That's exactly what we're doing," George said. "Come on, we'll show you around."

As we neared the front door, Grams said, "This house is going to be fabulous both outside *and* inside. Emma's already working on making more of those life-size monsters out of papier-mâché and duct tape and paint and whatever else she uses. But that's just the beginning. One of our volunteers has a daughter who runs a party store, and she donated some great props."

"Like this fog machine," George said, pointing at a large cardboard carton that had yet to be opened. "The haunted house will be surrounded by fog. We'll have more fog inside, as well."

"What's in here?" I asked, peering inside another box, this one full of big white rectangles with curved tops.

"Tombstones," George replied. "We're going to set up a fake cemetery out front. They'll have funny sayings written on them like, 'Charlie Chicken. He forgot to look both ways.'"

"On one of them," Grams added with a grin, "there'll be a bony hand that suddenly comes up from behind and reaches over the top."

I shivered at the thought. "Great effect," I said. "I hope the kids can handle it."

"That one's not for the youngest children," Grams explained. "We're going to have different effects at different times of the day, depending on which age group is here."

"The high school kids will get all the really fun stuff," George said, rubbing his hands together. I could tell he was getting a kick out of all this.

"On the outside," he went on, "we'll have twisting trees with creepy faces painted on the branches. One of the front windows will be broken, and another will be boarded up. The shutters will be falling off . . . and there'll be signs that say 'Danger!' and 'Enter at Your Own Risk!'"

"And the house itself will have one of those Gothic towers, like the Haunted Mansion at Disneyland," Grams said. "And glowing jack-o'-lanterns with snarling mouths and jagged teeth. Of course, cobwebs will be hanging everywhere. We can make those by taking pieces of gauze and shredding it. And someone is making a fake wrought-iron fence—"

"And there'll be a skull hanging over the front door!" George said.

I laughed. "Goodness, you've thought of everything!"

"Wait until you hear about what we've got planned for the inside!" Grams exclaimed as we passed through the front door. The interior was still mostly under construction. "When the children first walk inside, there'll be a room with a black light. That will make their white clothes glow. Their teeth, too!"

"And a cabinet will suddenly fly open and a white ghost will fly out at them!" George said. "Or maybe a skeleton." Frowning, he added, "Actually, I still haven't figured out how to make that happen. But I'm working on it."

"This front room will also have a strobe light in it," Grams said. "And in this corner, one of the volunteers who's dressed as a witch will be stirring a bubbling cauldron. You can get that effect by putting dry ice in warm water. If we throw in some glow sticks, we can make it yellow or green or whatever color we like."

"This area over here will have hundreds of spiders hanging from the ceiling," George said, pointing in a different direction.

"There'll be eerie music playing, too," Grams added.

"And other scary sounds," George said. "Growling, low chanting, rattling chains, and of course the classic evil laughter."

"You really have thought of everything!" I exclaimed.

"I've got a few other ideas up my sleeve, too," he said. With a wink, he teased, "But I'm not going to tell you about all of them. I'd rather let you experience everything for yourself!"

I laughed. "I can hardly wait," I told them both sincerely. "I'm overwhelmed by what a great job you're both doing."

And I wasn't only referring to what they were doing in the gym. Even more, I was talking about what they were clearly doing for each other.

* * *

Given how quiet the shop had been the day before, I suggested that Emma take the day off. I was hoping she'd spend the time studying, but instead she started texting Ethan before I'd even finished my sentence. Not that I was worried. She had already gotten A's on the first two quizzes in her computer course. As for her ability to do well in her art class, all I had to do was look around my shop to see how talented and committed she was.

So I was alone in the shop early Sunday afternoon when Brody Lundgren came striding in.

And *striding* is definitely the right word. Not walking, not wandering, but striding. The man has the longest legs I've ever seen, so every step he takes is a stride.

In fact, Brody looks like he just got off a Viking ship. In addition to his impressive height, he's got an equally impressive head of curly blond hair, which is ridiculously thick and just long enough to make him look as if he's been so busy climbing every mountain and fording every stream that he hasn't had time to schedule a haircut. His eyes are a remarkable shade of green, and his big smile shows off teeth so white they practically sparkle.

Two months earlier, back in August, Brody had opened a shop directly across the street from Lickety Splits. The name of his shop, Hudson Valley Adventure Tours, was written on the brick-red T-shirt he was wearing, his well-developed pectoral muscles distorting the letters a little. He was in the business of selling adventure. The sign outside his shop said it all: KAYAKING, CANOEING, TUBING, HIKING, BIKING, ROCK CLIMBING, SPELUNKING.

"Hey, Brody," I said. I tried not to let on that merely being in his presence always caused my heart to beat a little too fast and my breaths to become a little too short.

"Hey, Kate," he replied. Flashing me that blinding smile, he added, "You're looking fine today."

"That's a surprise," I told him, "given what's gone on this week."

"Yes, I heard all about it," he said, his smile fading. "I saw the crime-scene tape, too. I'm glad you were finally able to open your store again."

I wondered if he'd heard that I was considered a suspect, since Savannah Crane's murder had occurred in my shop.

"But I'm here to talk about happier things," Brody went on. "I wondered if you'd be able to take some time off this week. I'd like to take you hiking."

A *date*? I thought, my mind instantly racing. Is Brody asking me on a date? Or is he simply concerned about the ill effects of a life of too much ice cream and too little exercise, aside from pumping up my right arm with endless scooping?

I was still trying to figure that out when he added, "The weather couldn't be better. Sunshine and cool temperatures all week. Perfect for enjoying the mountains! And the autumn leaves are at their best. Not quite at peak yet, which means there's still enough green to make the reds and oranges look even more amazing." He paused. "I was wondering if you could get away for a few hours on Thursday."

It did sound like fun. And good for my health.

I couldn't think of a single reason to say no. So I said, "Yes!"

"Great!" he said, awarding me with another dazzling smile. "I'll swing by at three."

"That should work," I told him.

Seconds after he had left, Willow breezed in.

"I just saw Brody," she said. Teasingly, she said, "It seems the man can't stay away. Or is it your Toasted Coconut Fudge that keeps him coming back?"

"Actually, this is the first time he's been in the shop for days," I said, averting my eyes so she wouldn't see how red my cheeks were.

"Then what's behind his sudden interest in ice cream?" she

asked, grinning. "Or should I say his sudden *passion* for ice cream?"

"He invited me to go on a hike," I mumbled, my voice barely audible.

Willow heard me anyway. "A date! The man asked you on a date! I told you! I've been telling you all along—"

"I'm not sure it's a date," I told her. I realized I sounded just like Grams on the issue of George and his invitation to dinner at Greenleaf. "I think he just wanted somebody to go on a hike with."

"Right," Willow replied dryly. "And you're the obvious person, since your idea of a hike is walking from the parking lot to the mall."

"That's not true!" I protested. But she was close to correct. Unlike her, I wasn't one of those people who made exercise a priority in my life. I wasn't much of an outdoors girl, either. I'd always preferred indoor pursuits—including eating ice cream—to activities that made me sweaty and out of breath. With a few exceptions.

"I think he's just being friendly," I insisted.

Suddenly, Willow grew serious. "Honestly, Kate, why are you being so coy about this? The man clearly likes you! Why won't you admit that?"

I let out a deep sigh. "Because I'm still so conflicted about my feelings for Jake," I admitted. "If I can't figure out how Jake fits into the picture, how can I complicate things even further by bringing in somebody else?"

"Good point," she said. She patted me on the arm. "You've got a good head on your shoulders, Kate. I'm sure you'll figure out what's best for you. In the meantime, if you need a good pair of hiking boots, I have a pair that might fit you."

Hiking boots? I thought, horrified.

I was really starting to wonder what I'd gotten myself into.

*　*　*

I wasn't the only one with a blossoming social life. Tonight was Grams's dinner date with George.

I decided to close Lickety Splits a bit early. Sunday evenings were always slow, and business had continued to be quieter than usual. So I was in the dining room having dinner with Emma as Grams came out of her bedroom, wearing the same stretchy black pants and cushy gray Skechers walking shoes she'd worn all day. She had put on a different top, however; instead of the faded pink QUILTING IS MY HAPPY PLACE T-shirt she'd worn while giving Digger a bath, she had on a plain turquoise T-shirt.

"I'm ready!" Grams announced.

Emma and I exchanged a look of horror.

"Is that what you're planning on wearing tonight?" I asked.

Grams frowned. "Why not? I love these pants. They're so comfortable."

"This is a *date*, Grams!" Emma exclaimed. "Not a trip to the post office."

"It's just dinner," Grams insisted.

"It's dinner at one of the finest restaurants in the Hudson Valley," I pointed out. "If not the entire New York metropolitan area."

"Besides," Emma said, "this is your big chance to get dressed up. How often does anyone get to do that anymore? Go back to your closet and see if you can find something more formal."

"How about that blue dress?" I suggested. "The one you wore to the art opening back in September?"

"And put on that silver necklace with the blue beads," Emma added. "That will go with it really well."

Grams opened her mouth to protest, then immediately snapped it shut. I guess she understood that Emma and I weren't about to take no for an answer.

She retreated to her bedroom, then reemerged five minutes

later. This time, she was wearing a cobalt blue silk cocktail dress that was simply styled and extremely flattering. Around her neck was the necklace Emma had insisted on. She had also put on a pair of low-heeled, black patent-leather shoes. They looked almost as comfortable as the slouchy loafers, but considerably more elegant.

"Much better!" Emma declared. "But I think you need a little eyeliner."

"I suggest a bolder lipstick," I added. "Do you have one in a darker color?"

"Honestly!" Grams cried. "The way you two are fussing over me you'd think no one had ever gone out to dinner with a friend before!"

"As if George Vernon is just a friend," I scoffed. "Besides, how long has it been since you've been on a date?"

"It's not a—!"

"Grams!" Emma cried.

Grams thought for a few seconds, then said, "So many years that I couldn't even give you an answer."

When it was five minutes before the time George was scheduled to arrive, Emma and I fluttered around her like two mother hens.

"Take a light jacket," Emma instructed. "It's not that chilly now, but it will be later on."

"Do you have everything you need?" I asked. "Is your cell phone charged? Do you have—let's see, a comb? Tissues for a runny nose? Extra cash, in case you run into some sort of problem?"

"I'm fine," Grams insisted. "George and I are only going about three blocks away!"

"Even so, I don't want you staying out too late," Emma warned. "And feel free to text either one of us with updates. Or to ask us any questions." She took a deep breath. "And there's one more thing."

"What's that?" Grams asked, checking her reflection in

the mirror in the front hall and adjusting one of her pearl earrings.

"I don't think you should kiss George good night," Emma said firmly.

Both Grams and I let out a cry of surprise.

"Why not?" Grams asked. "For goodness' sake, Emma, if I really like him—and I think I do—why shouldn't I kiss him good night?"

"It just sends the wrong message," she replied. "There's plenty of time for that later. You two are still getting to know each other, and there's no reason to move things along too quickly."

Grams cast me a wary glance. "And you, Kate? Any more advice you'd like to give me before I walk out the door?"

"Yes," I said. "Have fun tonight."

"Thank you!" she cried. "I think that's the best advice I've gotten from either of you."

As if on cue, Digger ran over to the front door and started barking at it, acting as if sheer noise was what was required to let our visitor in. A few seconds later, we heard a knock.

Grams was about to put her hand on the doorknob when Emma whispered, "Not so fast. He can wait. You don't want to look too eager."

Grams and I exchanged another look. I'm sure we were thinking the same thing: Where on earth did this Victorian lady come from?

When Emma finally nodded, Grams opened the door. George stood on the doorstep, dressed in a suit and tie. He was holding a big, lush bouquet of yellow roses.

I immediately grabbed Digger by the collar, wanting to spare Grams's gentleman caller the horror of paw prints on his lovely suit.

"Aren't I lucky!" George greeted us. "Not one but three lovely ladies!"

Grinning at Grams and presenting her with the flowers, he added, "Maybe I shouldn't play favorites, but there really is one of you that I'm happiest to see."

"Just don't keep her out too late," Emma told him.

"I promise," George replied seriously. "I will be on my very best behavior tonight."

Once they were gone, Emma sank onto the couch as if she was exhausted by the ordeal of getting Grams out the door.

"Isn't it nice that Grams has a boyfriend!" I said with a sigh, lowering myself onto the green upholstered chair.

"Now we've all got one," Emma said.

"No, we don't!" I corrected her. "I don't have a boy-friend!"

"You have Jake," Emma pointed out. "I can see the sparks flying whenever you two are together. So can everyone else."

"Jake isn't my boyfriend," I insisted. Squirming in my chair, I added, "In fact, there's a new wrinkle in my life I want your advice on."

She was looking at me expectantly as I jumped right in and announced, "Brody asked me out. I said yes."

When she didn't say anything, I babbled on.

"And I'm not sure that I should have. You just said your-self that Jake and I have kind of a—a thing going on. At least we're trying to decide if we still have the connection we had back in high school—"

"You definitely have that connection," she said. "The only question is what you both want to do about it."

"Okay, so we're still feeling our way," I said seriously. "Which makes the idea of me going out with someone else even more complicated. Doesn't it?"

I suddenly realized the absurdity of me, a thirty-three-year-old woman, asking an eighteen-year-old for advice on my love life. A clever, insightful, worldly eighteen-year-old, but technically still a teenager.

Surely this represented a new low.

But then she said something very wise.

"Kate," Emma told me seriously, "I think you owe it to yourself to explore every option. I know that you haven't yet decided how you feel about Jake. The stuff that happened fifteen years ago, your anger over the fact that he never tried to get in touch with you afterward, the shock of him being back in your life all of a sudden . . . You still need time to sort all that out.

"But in the meantime, here's Brody. Charming, handsome Brody, who's been totally into you since the first time he laid eyes on you. So what I suggest is that at this point, you reserve judgment. You don't have to decide anything at this point. Go out with Brody—and go out with Jake. Sooner or later, you'll know what to do."

She really *was* clever and insightful.

Not that she wasn't telling me anything I didn't already know. It's just that by saying it out loud, by presenting it in such a matter-of-fact way, she was giving me permission to do what I'd pretty much decided to do already.

"You're right," I told her.

"I know I'm right," she said.

"Now let's have some ice cream to celebrate Grams's date," I suggested. "I've got another idea about making the perfect *affogato*. How about adding espresso *and* chocolate syrup?"

After all, I figured, there was no reason why Grams should be the only one who was eating well tonight.

Chapter 7

California produces the most ice cream in
America—and has since 1990.

—*www.californiadairypressroom.com/Products/Ice_Cream*

"You were certainly out late last night," Emma said the
following morning as she and I sat with Grams over
breakfast.

"Was I?" Grams replied, slathering orange marmalade
over half an English muffin. "I hope I didn't miss curfew. The
last thing I want is to be grounded. Especially with the Halloween dance coming up so soon."

I was glad that Grams was finding Emma's Mother Hen
act as amusing as I was. Neither of us would have ever
guessed that the youngest member of our little household
would turn out to be so protective.

"I was just worried, that's all," Emma said archly. She
paused to sip the banana-strawberry smoothie she'd whipped
up in the blender. "I was starting to think that maybe
George's car had broken down or something."

"George's car worked just fine," Grams said, her cheeks
reddening.

Before Emma had a chance to reply, I pushed back my
chair.

"I'm afraid I have to run," I announced. "Emma, could you

please drop me at the train station? I imagine you'd planned to head over to Lickety Splits soon, anyway."

Today, my niece would be running the shop by herself. Tomorrow, too, since I was about to embark on a two-day trip into Manhattan.

I had told Emma and Grams that I was going to take care of a few things in the city, then have dinner and stay overnight with Becca Collins, a friend from my job in public relations. And that was all true.

What I didn't explain was that the "things" I intended to do in the city were all related to my investigation of Savannah Crane's murder.

Less than an hour later, I was on an Amtrak train into New York City. While the ride would take less than two hours, I knew the trip I was embarking on would be transporting me to an entirely different world.

Sure enough, as the train chugged closer and closer to the city, the view outside my window changed dramatically. The open fields, the charming villages that looked as if they'd popped off the pages of a calendar, the calming sight of the mountains and the wide Hudson River, the breathtaking swaths of brilliant orange, red, and gold leaves . . . Before long, the quaint towns were replaced by clusters of buildings crowded together, many of them covered with graffiti. Trees became increasingly scarce. The streets the train sailed past were congested, and the sidewalks I glimpsed were filled with people, nearly all of them appearing to be in a hurry.

Still, while pastoral serenity was no longer part of the view, I could already feel the city's energy charging through me. It was as if there was electricity in the air, and it had the power to convey its spark to whoever was breathing it in.

I was simply one of those rare individuals who loved and appreciated both the big city and country life.

By the time my train pulled into Penn Station, my heart

was pounding with excitement. I hadn't been back in New York since the summer, when I'd asked Willow to fill in at the shop so I could take Emma to the city for lunch and a Broadway matinee. Only now that I had arrived did I realize how exhilarating it felt to be here.

Glancing at the address I'd jotted down on a slip of paper brought me back to reality with a big jolt. I suddenly remembered the reason why I'd come.

I took the subway uptown, eagerly drinking in the city's noise and crowds and busyness as I came up the stairs, onto the street. Alpha Industries was on Sixth Avenue, not far from Radio City Music Hall and Rockefeller Center. Those were two of my favorite spots during the holiday season.

But today, I made a beeline for the office building in which Savannah Crane had worked.

Alpha Industries was located on the fifty-fourth floor. After checking in with the security guard sitting behind a big desk and being given a name tag with the word VISITOR printed on it in red, I floated up in an elevator that was so smooth it didn't even feel as if it was moving.

I sneaked peeks at the other people crammed inside. All of them were stylishly dressed. The men wore well-cut suits, while the women favored separates in inoffensive colors like black and gray. I caught sight of more than one set of pearls.

Given the feeling of formality, it was difficult to imagine Savannah fitting in here. Then again, she was an actress. Maybe her ability to turn herself into different people had played an important role here as well as on a stage or a movie set.

When we arrived at the fifty-fourth floor, the doors opened onto what looked like a movie version of a thriving company in Manhattan. The walls and carpets were pale gray, and the chairs in the waiting area were low and sleek and uncomfortable-looking. An entire wall of windows off to the right afforded a spectacular view of Midtown, the tall, serious-looking buildings interspersed with crisscrossing streets far below that were crowded with slow-moving cars and yellow taxis.

In the center was a high counter, with a woman's neatly coiffed head bobbing above it. On the wall behind her, ALPHA INDUSTRIES was spelled out in huge silver letters.

I was finding it more and more difficult to picture Savannah working here.

The receptionist, I saw, was as conservatively dressed as everyone else I'd encountered so far. Her meticulously tailored black jacket made her look like a banker.

She turned her attention to me immediately. "Can I help you?" she asked pleasantly.

"I'm here to see Savannah Crane," I told her.

The woman's expression immediately changed to one of controlled horror. "May I ask what this is about?" she asked.

"Catering," I replied. "I'm meeting with her to talk about the company's holiday party. We made this appointment months ago."

"Holiday party!" the receptionist exclaimed. "But it isn't even Halloween yet!"

I shot her the most disdainful look I could manage. "Most firms have their entire holiday event planned by the end of the summer," I told her haughtily. "Perhaps you're not aware of how much competition there is to grab one of the top caterers."

Savannah wasn't the only one with acting abilities, I thought, surprised by how authoritative I sounded.

And she bought it. "I guess that makes sense," she said, clearly humbled. "I've never had to plan anything like that, so I wouldn't know . . . But Savannah isn't here any longer. I'll have to find out who I should put you in touch with instead—"

"What do you mean, Savannah isn't here?" I said. Now I was using my annoyed voice. "We had an appointment. She specifically told me that this would be a good time to meet! I have a *very* busy schedule!"

The receptionist was clearly growing more and more agitated by my insistence, biting her lip and tapping her tapered, blood-red fingernails nervously on the desk. "I'm going to have to make a few calls," she said.

"Why don't you give me Savannah Crane's cell phone number, and I'll talk to her myself?" I suggested, really getting into my "impatient" act. "Maybe she misunderstood and thought we were meeting somewhere off-site."

"You don't understand," the receptionist said. "Savannah Crane is—gone. As in she's not working here anymore. She took a leave a while ago, but now—"

I let out a yelp, moving on to "irritated." "And she didn't even bother to let me know?" I cried. "I'd like to speak to her supervisor."

That was my ploy for getting my foot in the door. Or, to be more accurate, my ploy for getting my entire body past the reception area, into the place in which Savannah had worked and in the midst of the people who had known her.

"This is—complicated," the receptionist said. "I'm going to ask you to leave your business card, and I'll have someone get back to you."

"But I came all the way from the Hudson Valley!" I protested. "That's a train ride of over two hours. Each way!"

"I'm sorry, but it's the best I can do," she said, sounding truly apologetic.

As we were having this exchange, a woman sailed into the reception area from the offices in back. I instantly picked up on the fact that she was one of those people who was inherently attractive. She was pretty, but in a quirky way that made her much more interesting than your standard Homecoming Queen–style beauty. She had wavy, white-blond hair cut in one of those tousled, irregular styles that made it look as if she had just gotten out of bed. Her long, slender nose had a bit of a hook in it, and her lips were pouty, colored with a swipe of pale pink lipstick.

She also was tall and slender, and walked with a sort of swagger that seemed to come to her naturally. Her outfit was simple: a gray pencil skirt that showed off her slim silhouette, an oversized pale blue sweater cut so wide at the neck that it kept slipping off one shoulder, and low-heeled black pumps.

She was one of those women who just exuded confidence. I wondered if she could give me lessons.

"Hey, Deb," she said breezily, glancing at the receptionist as she headed toward the elevators. "Quiet morning?"

"Hi, Coo," the receptionist replied. "Yup. Pretty much."

"I'm going out for coffee," the woman named Coo called over her shoulder as she pressed the DOWN button. "Want anything?"

Was it my imagination, or did she actually cast me a meaningful look?

"No, thanks," the receptionist said. Then she mumbled, "There's plenty of coffee in the snack room."

Coo glanced back at her and smiled winningly. "I have a sudden craving for a Starbucks Hazelnut Mocha Coconut Milk Macchiato. I'm addicted. What can I do but give in to my bodily urges?"

Is that a real thing? I wondered. Maybe I should be researching new flavor combinations at Starbucks instead of ice cream shops . . .

But I forced myself to focus on the moment at hand. The woman who was apparently called Coo appeared to be about my age, which meant she was about Savannah's age, too. And she had clearly worked on the same floor, which meant there was a good chance she'd known her.

"Thanks for your time," I told the receptionist. I dropped

one of my business cards on the counter in front of her, then
trotted after Coo.

"That was so weird," I said to her as soon as the elevator
doors closed, leaving the two of us alone. "I mean, if a person has an appointment, you'd think that would mean something."

"I guess you haven't heard about what happened," Coo
replied. "And apparently Deb wasn't about to tell you."

"Tell me what?" I asked, playing innocent.

"Savannah Crane passed away last week," Coo said
somberly. "Under very suspicious circumstances."

I took a deep breath, my mind racing as I planned my
strategy. I decided to take a chance.

"Look, I know all about what happened to Savannah," I
told her. "She was murdered in my ice cream shop in the
Hudson Valley. In fact, she was poisoned by ice cream that
I'd personally put into the dish she was eating out of."

Coo looked at me appraisingly. "You don't look like a
murderer," she said.

"I didn't even know her!" I insisted. "Which is why I'm
trying to find out whatever I can about the people who *did*
know her. I'm doing everything I can to clear my name.

"That's why I came here today," I went on as the elevator's
doors opened onto the lobby. "I was hoping for a chance to
speak to some of the people she worked with. I thought
someone might be able to tell me something that would give
me some insight into what was going on in her life."

"Maybe I can help," Coo said. Gesturing toward the Starbucks across the street, she added, "Come on. The coffee's
on me."

"I haven't even introduced myself," I said after the two of
us grabbed a corner table with our coffee and a couple of
scones I'd been unable to resist. "I'm Kate McKay."

"I'm Coo Jameson," she replied. "It's short for Cooper."

She wrinkled her nose. "My real name is Cornelia Cooper Jameson. I think Mummy had a vicious streak, naming me after my grandmother. My family called me Cornelia when I was kid. But as soon as I went off to prep school, my friends decided I needed a better name."

I was already getting a sense of where this young woman's self-confidence had come from. I watched her dump a packet of sugar into her macchiato. Then a second packet. Then a third. And this was a coffee concoction that already had more sweet flavors crammed into it than I could fit into my ice cream display case. I couldn't imagine how she managed to keep those hips of hers slim enough to pull off that skin-tight pencil skirt she was wearing.

She had clearly caught me staring. "What, you're surprised that I'm a sugar addict?" she asked, looking amused.

"I'm just jealous that you can eat so much of my favorite substance and still stay thin," I replied.

She laughed. "I'm one of those lucky people with a crazy-high metabolism. But it'll probably catch up with me one of these days. I just hope I don't end up gaining fifty pounds overnight. My worst nightmare is that all the calories I've ingested over the years will pile up on me in one fell swoop."

I laughed. Coo was a woman I liked. More importantly, she was someone I trusted.

She paused to stir all that sugar into her coffee. Grinning slyly, she asked, "Do you really cater corporate events? Or is that something you made up to try to get information out of Deb the Devil?"

"I actually do cater events," I told her. "I kind of fell into it, but over time it's become one of my shop's specialties." I hesitated, then added, "But you're right. I wasn't really planning anything at Alpha."

"Where is your shop, exactly?" she asked.

"A town called Wolfert's Roost. Have you ever heard of it?"

"Oh, sure," she replied, waving her hand in the air. "It used to be called Modderplaatz, right? Mummy had friends with a place in the Hudson Valley. I spent lots of summers up there, swimming in their private lake."

Did people really have private lakes? I wondered. I supposed they did, at least in the circles Coo seemed to travel in.

I noticed that even though her coffee was full of sugar, she didn't touch either of the scones I'd bought to go with my cappuccino, either the raspberry or the chocolate chip. I had a sudden urge to force some of my magnificent ice cream on this woman the first chance I got.

Suddenly, Coo leaned forward. Lowering her voice, she asked, "So tell me more about why you're trying to figure out who killed Savannah."

"It's partly because I'm considered a suspect," I replied, "and partly because I'm worried about my shop's reputation. But I also feel a weird sense of responsibility since this terrible thing happened in *my* store, with *my* ice cream."

"All good reasons," she commented, sipping her coffee.

"I've talked to a few people about Savannah's acting career," I went on, "but I don't know a thing about the rest of her life. And this job might not have meant much to her, but she undoubtedly spent a good chunk of her days here." I paused to drink some of my own coffee. "I'm also trying to find out more about what she was really like."

"She was great," Coo said. "She was one of the nicest people I've ever met. Everyone at Alpha liked her. She made a point of being as nice to the mail room guys as she was to the executives. She was one of those people who just exuded warmth." She frowned. "Which is why it's so puzzling that someone wanted to—you know."

"I was hoping you'd know who some of her enemies were," I said.

"Enemies?" She blinked. "I can't imagine Savannah having any enemies. You never met such a sweet, genuine person in your life."

"But there was clearly *someone* who didn't feel that way," I pointed out. "I was hoping you might have some idea of who that person might be."

Coo's expression suddenly changed. It was as if a rain cloud had passed over her face.

"You know something," I said without thinking.

"No," she insisted. She sat in silence for a few seconds, staring at her coffee cup.

And then, raising her eyes to me, she said, "But I did know that something was wrong. Savannah had begun acting strange."

"Strange?" I repeated. "In what way?"

Shifting in her seat, Coo said, "I'm not sure. She just seemed . . . *troubled* somehow. Her usual spark was missing."

"Was that before or after she got the role in *The Best Ten Days of My Life*?" I asked, aware that my heart had begun beating a lot faster than usual.

"Before," she replied without hesitating.

"Do you think that whatever seemed to be bothering her might have been related to her boyfriend?" I asked.

"Timothy?" Coo thought for a moment. "I guess it's possible. Especially since the last few times I saw them together I did notice some tension."

My ears pricked up. Amanda certainly hadn't said anything about there being any tension between Savannah and Timothy. In fact, she had claimed the opposite, insisting that the two of them were ecstatically happy together. That they'd even gotten engaged recently.

"Are you talking about the usual disagreements couples have?" I asked. "Even people who are madly in love have arguments sometimes."

Coo shook her head. "It struck me as more than that. I remember this one time . . . I came down the elevator around noon to go grab lunch. I saw Timothy standing in the lobby, looking as if he was waiting for someone. As soon as Savannah came down the elevator, the two of them started fighting. I was standing too far away to hear what they were saying, but you could tell from their body language that something was very wrong."

Why would Amanda lie? I wondered, swirling the foam in my cappuccino with my wooden stirrer. Was it possible that she and Savannah weren't as close as she claimed? Or that Savannah had simply been a private person, at least where her difficulties with her fiancé were concerned?

But that was unlikely. After all, I knew perfectly well that when it came to matters of the heart, it was pretty difficult for women *not* to tell their friends about whatever was going on—especially if it was something that was troubling them.

"What about that director, Ragnar Bruin?" I asked.

I half expected her to look puzzled. Instead, she said, "I wasn't sure if you knew about that." She shook her head and added, "Savannah was totally shocked when this past summer he moved his New York office to a building that's right around the corner from Alpha."

That was a new piece of information. "Ragnar opened an office close by?" I exclaimed, surprised. "I imagine she was terrified!"

Coo's eyebrows shot up. "Why on earth would she have been terrified?"

"Wasn't Ragnar stalking Savannah?" I asked. I was doing my best to sound matter-of-fact even though my thoughts were racing.

"Hardly," she said. "If anything, it was the other way around. Well, not stalking exactly. I mean, Savannah wasn't the type to stalk.

"But she was certainly into him," she continued after

pausing to sip her coffee. "She was constantly texting him, sending him little presents, like boxes of chocolate or, this one time, a huge bunch of balloons." She shook her head slowly. "It was no wonder that Ragnar's wife, Delia, was so jealous."

I had been wondering about how Ragnar's wife fit into all this ever since Amanda had told me about their involvement. But I was still stuck on what Coo had said about Savannah being totally into him, rather than him being an unwelcome stalker as her supposed best friend had claimed.

Coo leaned forward, meanwhile glancing around as if to see if anyone was listening. "There was this one time that Delia came to the office, screaming her head off," she said, her voice low.

"What was she screaming about?" I asked.

Coo grimaced. "What do you think? She was yelling at Savannah about keeping her hands off her husband."

I nodded. But then another thought occurred to me. "Are you sure their relationship was sexual? Is it possible that Savannah was simply cultivating Ragnar because he was an important Hollywood director and she was trying to get ahead?"

"I'm afraid I can't answer that," Coo said. "I always got the feeling that Timothy and Savannah were really committed to each other. I knew for sure that she was always texting Ragnar, and there was definitely a flirtation thing going on. But whether they were actually, you know, doing anything about it . . . that was something Savannah never talked to me about."

At that moment, Coo took out her phone and checked the time. "Sorry I haven't been more helpful. And now I should get back."

"You've been *very* helpful," I assured her. And I meant it.

"One thing's for sure: you've motivated me to do something I was assigned but which I've been dreading," Coo said as she crumpled up her napkin and stuffed it into her empty cup. "I'm going to clean out Savannah's office. Since she was just on leave, everything had been left pretty much the way it was. But now that she's gone . . ."

I was startled. "You mean no one has done that yet?"

She shook her head. "Our office manager was supposed to do it. At least that's what I heard, that she'd been instructed to clear everything out and just throw it away. Files for work, personal items, her coffee mug, and the dumb little stuffed animals she kept lined up on a shelf . . . Handling the cleanup that way struck me as a little cold, but apparently that was the word from the top."

"But that hasn't happened?" I asked.

"Not yet," Coo replied. Grimacing, she added, "Our office manager is one of the laziest people you ever met. It's practically impossible to get her to answer the phone, much less deal with somebody else's stuff. So, do you know what I'm going to do? I'm going to grab some empty boxes out of the storeroom as soon as I get a chance and pack up all of Savannah's things."

Once again, she glanced around Starbuck's nervously. "And you can have it all, if you want. Especially since I wouldn't know where else to send it. It's certainly not anything her family or her friends would be interested in. But you might find something interesting in there. Something that will help you with—you know, what you're trying to do."

Her offer had sent my heart into overdrive. "That would be great."

"I'll ship the boxes to you as soon as I pack them up," Coo said. "Just give me the address you want me to use. And while you're doing that, I'll give you my cell phone number in case you want to get in touch with me again."

I jotted down my home address, 59 Sugar Maple Way.

Somehow, having the boxes delivered to my house seemed more private than having them show up at Lickety Splits.

Then something else occurred to me. "Do you happen to have Savannah's address?"

"I do," Coo said. "She had a party there a couple of months ago, so I have it in my phone. I'll text it to you . . ."

I lingered at Starbucks for a few minutes after Coo raced off, scraping the last of the foamed milk off the sides of the paper cup with my wooden stirrer. My head was spinning from the opposing stories I'd heard from two women who had known Savannah Crane well.

Amanda had insisted that Savannah and Timothy were the happiest couple on earth. But Coo had said that recently there had been tension in their relationship.

Amanda had claimed that Ragnar Bruin was stalking Savannah and that she was convinced that the director was her friend's killer. Coo, meanwhile, said she had witnessed Savannah texting him and sending him cute little presents.

I had already known that Savannah had had two men in her life, one of whom was married. But Coo's take on the murder victim's complicated relationships had cast them both in an entirely different light.

At this point, I didn't know who—or what—to believe. But that only made me more determined than ever to find out.

Chapter 8

First-class passengers on the *Titanic* were treated
to French ice cream for dessert, according to the
April 14, 1912, menu. Second-class passengers
had to settle for plain, egg-free American
ice cream.

—Everybody Loves Ice Cream: The Whole Scoop on
America's Favorite Treat, *by Shannon Jackson Arnold*

Even though it was close to lunchtime, my visit to Starbucks and my inability to resist scones had left me full. As I walked to the subway, I noticed that the delicatessens and takeout restaurants I passed were already buzzing with the office crowd. I found myself missing being part of the hustle-bustle of city living.

But that feeling only lasted about ten seconds. Instead, I found myself appreciating the freedom of my life in Wolfert's Roost. Nowadays, I could have lunch anytime I felt like it. And I could take as much time as I wanted, as long as Lickety Splits was taken care of.

Thanks to Coo, I had added one more destination to my list. And this one was taking me to Brooklyn. I got on the subway after consulting the New York City Transit app on my phone. Forty minutes later, I climbed up the station's concrete steps and found myself in a different world.

The buildings around me weren't towering high-rises, the way they were in Manhattan. Here, the streets were lined with shops, with just a few floors of apartments above them. You could tell you were in place where each neighborhood had its own personality.

Unfortunately, this particularly neighborhood's personality was that of someone who hadn't quite gotten his act together.

While most of the businesses I walked past were staples of everyday life, like hair dressers and small food markets, there were also several pawn shops and a check-cashing place. There were quite a few empty shops, too, boarded up tight and decorated with aggressive slashes of graffiti.

Savannah Crane lived *here*? I thought, anxiously checking the address Coo had texted me.

But I knew that neighborhoods could change from block to block, so I kept on walking. By the time I got to the address that Coo had given me, the buildings were a bit cleaner, and there were more bakeries and dry cleaners than pawn shops. But the area still wasn't what I'd expected.

I stopped when I spotted the number on the address on my phone screen: 304. It was stenciled on the glass door of a shop that sold ninety-nine-cent items, the kind of place I love to browse in. Next to it was a second door with the same number. To the right there were a dozen buzzers, along with handwritten or typed names next to them.

The buzzer for Apartment 5A had a strip of bright-green duct tape next to it. The name CRANE was handwritten on it in black.

I peered through the glass window set into the door. It would have benefited greatly from a good scrubbing. Inside, I could see a small foyer that was a far cry from elegant.

A woman came up behind me. She carried two plastic tote bags filled with groceries in one hand and a leash in the other.

At the end was a small, fluffy black dog that immediately began barking at me with the ferocity of a pit bull.

"Going inside?" the woman asked cheerfully.

"Uh, no," I said. "I was just . . . I'm on the way out."

She nodded. And then, gesturing at the bags she was carrying, she commented, "Boy, at times like this I really wish I lived in an elevator building. Anyway, have a good day!"

"You, too," I replied.

So this building didn't even have an elevator. Which meant that Savannah Crane had lived in what was commonly called a five-story walk-up.

I was more puzzled than ever. How could Savannah have owned a weekend house in the Hudson Valley, yet lived in a seedy neighborhood like this?

I supposed that Timothy could have helped. But he, too, was an aspiring actor, with even fewer credits than she had. He certainly wasn't enjoying an explosive career. True, it was possible that he had a lucrative day job. Then again, it would be difficult to go to auditions if you were a stockbroker on Wall Street.

I headed back to the subway, anxious to move on to the next place on my list.

Reaching the address I'd found online for Monarch Cinema Props required getting myself from Brooklyn to Queens. While these two boroughs actually border each other, with Queens directly above Brooklyn, traveling from one to the other required a seemingly endlessly long subway ride back through Manhattan.

When I finally emerged from the subway station in Long Island City, I found myself surrounded by large, flat industrial buildings. I walked several blocks, then finally spotted my destination.

I had thought Amanda was exaggerating when she'd said

that Monarch occupied a one-hundred-thousand-square-foot space. But as I stood outside the warehouse-like building, I could see that it sprawled across an entire city block.

As soon as I walked in through the main entrance, I noticed a big sign that listed five floors and what was on each of them. Drapery and linens were on the fourth floor. Pews, confessionals, and religious artifacts were on five, garden ornaments on three. There was also furniture on every one of the floors, arranged by period. Mid-Century modern, sixties, and seventies on the fourth floor; Colonial, Asian, and 19th-century French on the second.

As I peered beyond the sign and into the building, I saw a mind-boggling amount of stuff on display.

Neatly arranged inside the nondescript building were dozens of leather couches and chairs, a dozen statues of frightening Samurai swordsmen, and a cluster of at least thirty coatracks of different styles and sizes. Along the wall to my left were shelves that ran all the way up to the high ceiling. One eight-foot side section was crowded with clusters of artificial flowers. The one next to it held stacks of silver trays. Another was filled with old-fashioned toys, like wooden animals on wheels and metal wind-up toys. Another group of shelves was crammed with hundreds of ceramic figurines, ranging from a few inches high to almost two feet: ladies in long dresses, ballerinas, soldiers on horseback, dogs, lions, even little castles.

And from the long corridors that stretched ahead of me, I could tell that the display area extended far beyond what I could see. Directly in front of me were rows of office chairs. They were neatly lined up on two levels, with one platform right above the other. I spotted at least twenty padded, black office chairs, followed by another twenty white ones, and behind that a row of wooden ones. Carefully arranged in front of them were conference tables: ovals and rectangles, wooden and glass, small and large.

The place reminded me of a giant thrift store, one that was extremely organized and only carried items that were in perfect condition. Once again, I thought about how much Emma would love seeing a place like this. At the very least, I had to tell her all about it.

A receptionist sat behind a counter at the front, just like at Alpha Industries. Only this particular woman had hot-pink, spiky hair and glasses with thick, perfectly round black frames.

"I'm here to see Amanda Huffner," I told her.

"Do you have an appointment?" she asked automatically.

"Just tell her Kate McKay is here," I replied.

She nodded, then picked up the phone. "Amanda? Kate McKay is here to see you."

Less than two minutes later, Amanda emerged from behind the row of Samurai swordsmen. Her wavy, dark brown hair was pulled back into a loose ponytail, and she was wearing denim overalls.

"Kate!" she said, sounding a little out of breath. "This is a surprise! But such a nice one."

She glanced back at the receptionist, then turned back and loudly said, "Let me show you around, Ms. McKay. I'm sure you'll find that Monarch has everything you need."

Once we'd stepped away, she whispered, "Ella is such a busybody. For some reason, she's really weird about having friends come here during the workday."

She hit the elevator button, and we rode up to the fourth floor.

"There's nobody up here right now," she explained as we stepped out. "That'll give us a chance to talk without anyone overhearing."

We had just walked into the 1950s. In front of me were five television sets from that era, big hulking contraptions that were half the size of a refrigerator. Just past them were groupings of furniture arranged to create the feeling of a little room, just like in furniture stores. We sat down on a boxy orange couch, surrounded by two white leather lounge chairs, a blond coffee table, and several white plastic lamps that looked as if they had come from outer space.

"Do you recognize any of this?" Amanda asked, smiling as she gestured at the pretend room we were sitting in.

"I'm afraid not," I admitted.

"These were used in *Tom's Story*," she said. "Remember the scene where Marnie Merrill tells Alan Prescott that he's the father of her teenage son?"

"I do remember that scene," I told her. "But I don't remember the furniture at all."

She laughed. "It's funny; most people never even notice the props in a movie. But it's so important in setting the tone for each scene. Maybe the audience isn't aware of them when they're done correctly, but they sure would be if anybody got it wrong! Like in that scene, what if there had been a flat-screen TV? Can you imagine how strange that would have looked?"

"It makes perfect sense that everything has to belong," I said, nodding. "So I guess a big part of your job is to make sure that everything looks as if it should be there."

Glancing around, I joked, "The next time I want to buy furniture, I think I'll just come here and order up an entire room."

But Amanda was shaking her head. "Actually, Monarch doesn't sell any of its props. It's our policy.

"In fact," she went on, "Ragnar Bruin—" She paused to make a face. "That *monster* Ragnar Bruin wanted to buy one of the chairs that had been used in his movie *Pirates*. Apparently, he and the star, Jimmy Dorp, are great friends, and he wanted to give it to him as a birthday present." She shrugged. "My boss said no, and he refused to budge. Of course, I was secretly pleased, given how I feel about the guy.

"But enough Hollywood gossip," she said. She dropped her hands into her lap and looked at me expectantly. "What can I do for you?"

"It's funny that you brought up Ragnar, since that's why I'm here." I took a deep breath. "I was hoping you'd be able to help me come up with an excuse to meet with him."

A look of horror crossed her face. "No!" she cried. "That's not a good idea, Kate. The man is dangerous! I'm convinced that he's responsible for what happened to Savannah! And if he found out that you knew what was going on between him and her, I don't know what he'd do!"

"But I'd be meeting him at his office," I told her, still hoping I could change her mind. "I don't think he'd make a scene in front of the people who work for him."

Amanda shook her head hard. "Kate, you have no idea. I'm sorry, but I'm definitely against you having anything to do with that man. It's just too risky."

Her insistence that I keep away from him fueled my theory that when it came to the true nature of Savannah's relationship with Ragnar, Amanda was the one who was lying, not Coo. But I had no choice but to play along.

"I suppose you're right," I said. "It was just an idea."

"A *terrible* idea," she agreed. She must have figured that she really had convinced me to see things her way, since she stood up.

"Look, I should get back to work," Amanda said, still agitated. I wondered if being afraid of getting caught goofing off was the real reason. "You need to go."

"Of course," I said, gathering up my things. "Thanks for your time."

"You can let yourself out," she said. "I have a couple of things to do up here. But honestly, Kate? Stay as far away from that creep as you can. I'm serious."

As I rode down in the elevator, I was still mulling over Amanda's strong reaction to the idea of me talking to Ragnar. She was determined to keep me away from him, which made me more curious than ever to meet the man.

And even though she'd been unwilling to help me come up with a way of getting through the door of Ragnar Bruin's office, during our short conversation she'd inadvertently done exactly that.

It was late afternoon by the time I left Monarch and headed back to the subway. After my long day running around the city, I was glad I didn't have to get back on the train to go home. But in addition to being tired, I was also looking forward to seeing my work friend, Becca Collins.

Becca and I had worked at the same public relations firm for two years. While I'd been friendly with most of the people who worked there, she and I had developed a special bond almost from the beginning. She was one of those people who just *got* me.

Even so, I hadn't yet decided whether I'd tell her about what had really brought me to the city. Since Becca had been a work friend, there were some limits to what we told each other.

I figured I'd decide once we were together. I knew that sometimes it was possible to maintain a friendship after two people no longer worked together, and sometimes it wasn't.

At a small corner grocery, I plucked a bouquet from the dozens on display outside, a happy profusion of mixed blossoms in bright shades of yellow and orange. I also picked up a hunk of cheese and two boxes of interesting crackers. The tremendous selection that was available, even in a tiny place like this, gave me a pang of regret over no longer having access to the abundance of choices that city living offered.

But trudging down the street lugging my purse, my tote

bag, the groceries, and the bouquet reminded me that the urban experience had its negatives, too.

Becca's apartment building was a stark contrast to Savannah Crane's. It was a white brick high-rise, at least twenty-five stories tall, with a sleek lobby decorated in black and silver.

The doorman buzzed Becca's apartment, then nodded at me after she gave him the go-ahead. I shared my elevator ride to the fifteenth floor with a jogger and an old man with a slow-moving Westie on a leash. For a moment, I let myself pretend that I lived there and that I was still a city gal.

"Kate!" Becca squealed when she opened the door. She threw her arms around me even though my hands were both full, which made for a pretty one-sided hug. "It's so great to see you!"

Despite the fact that she'd probably gotten home from work only minutes before, she had already changed into stretchy black sweatpants and a faded Nine Inch Nails T-shirt. Her long, dark brown hair had been pulled back into a loose ponytail. I was a little taken aback since I was used to seeing her in business clothes and more eye makeup than I had ever felt comfortable wearing.

I handed her the flowers and the snacks. "I figured we could talk for a while before we went out to eat."

"I've already ordered in," she announced. "I got Thai food from that place you told me about on Second Avenue. They have a new owner, but the food is just as good. And they still have the same red curry dish you put me on to!"

"Sounds great," I said sincerely.

"How about some coffee while we wait?" she offered. "Or tea? Or a glass of wine?"

"Tea sounds great," I said. "Do you have any herbal tea?"

Five minutes later, Becca and I were sitting in her small living room, nursing mugs of tea and admiring the flowers, now standing tall on the coffee table in a cylindrical glass vase. She was settled on the couch with her bare feet tucked under her. I was curled up in a comfy upholstered chair that took up a good twenty-five percent of the compact room. I was surprised by how the rooms in a New York City apartment suddenly struck me as so absurdly small.

"So tell me how you are!" Becca demanded. "I was thinking today that just about everything in your life changed—let's see—not even a year ago! You must be totally overwhelmed! I mean, you moved from the most fabulous city in the world to a teensy little town upstate, you went from living alone in a cute apartment to living with your *grandmother* in a big old house, you gave up your glamorous PR job and opened a *store*, of all things . . ."

"It's true," I agreed. "A lot *has* changed in my life."

I wondered if I was simply being too sensitive or if Becca's pronouncements really did border on criticism. Or at least sounded a lot more judgmental than they needed to be. But I'd certainly reached a decision about whether or not to tell her the truth about what had brought me to the city today. The answer was no.

"My niece Emma has come to stay with Grams and me, too," I added. "She's my older sister Julie's daughter. She's eighteen, and she's taking some time off before going to college. She wants to figure out what direction she wants to go in."

Becca nodded. "That's right," she said. "I remember you emailing me something about that. So even more has changed! Now you're also living with a *teenager*! That must be . . . well, interesting!" She paused to sip her tea. "But I guess what matters is whether you're happy with the changes you've made. Are you?"

I thought for a few seconds. "You know, Becca, I really am."

"But you must miss the city!" she insisted.

I drank some of my tea as I gave her question some thought. "I don't, at least most of the time. I certainly thought I would. I also expected that I'd be coming back every chance I got. But I'm finding that small-town life suits me better than I ever would have expected."

"Tell me more about what it's like," Becca demanded. "I mean, honestly, living in your hometown again? That's something I can't even imagine. Do you feel like you're in high school again? Do you wake up in a sweat in the middle of the night, worried about a math test—or about having to play field hockey again?"

I laughed. "Surprisingly, no. It feels . . . comfortable. Yeah, I guess that's the best way to describe it. When I look back at my years in the city, I realize it was much more work than living where I am now. Standing in the rain waiting for a bus, crowding into the subway every morning, carrying groceries and everything else I needed blocks and blocks every day . . ." I shrugged. "Maybe I'm just getting lazy in my old age."

"I get that," Becca said earnestly. "But really, going back to the same place where you grew up? I bet there are still plenty of people around from your childhood. That must be weird. Old friends, old enemies . . ."

"Sure there are," I replied. "But I'm actually finding that that's one of the nicest things about being back. My best friend from high school, Willow Baines, still lives in town. She runs a yoga studio now, but she works in my shop from time to time. She's helped out at a few catering events, too.

"And I've run into some other people that I grew up with," I continued. "Like Pete Bonano, who used to be our star football player. He's our local friendly police officer now."

I paused to take another sip of tea. Given the way this conversation with Becca was going, I was debating whether to bring up the other old friend who lived in town.

But even before I'd decided, the words popped out of my

mouth. "And then there's Jake. Jake Pratt. You may remember me mentioning him. He and I have actually . . ."

I let my voice trail off, not certain how to finish that sentence. Gotten back in touch? Struck up a friendship? Nervously entertained the idea of picking up again where we left off?

"Wait a minute." Becca banged her mug down on the coffee table and stared at me intensely. "Jake? Jake, the old high school flame? The one you never got over, the one you talked about endlessly—"

"I didn't talk about him endlessly," I said crossly.

"Maybe not *endlessly*," Becca said. "But he definitely came up in the conversation from time to time. Especially when you'd had a cosmopolitan or two."

"Really?" I said, blinking. I wasn't playing dumb. I honestly didn't remember.

Becca rolled her eyes. "I love you dearly, Kate, but sometimes I felt that if I had to listen to you go on and on about how blue his eyes were one more time . . ."

"They're amazingly blue," I commented. "The bluest I've ever seen."

"Or about how the two of you were soul mates," Becca said, grinning. Then she grew serious. "And then there was that awful thing that happened when he stood you up at—what was it, the homecoming dance?"

"The prom," I told her. I swallowed hard. "At the end of our senior year. The very end."

"That's right. Now I remember." Becca's face lit up again. "So you two are back in touch?"

"Yup." I suddenly pretended to find my mug so fascinating that I couldn't take my eyes off it.

Becca sighed impatiently. "Tell me!" she demanded. "What's going on exactly?"

"Nothing," I replied with a shrug.

"Nothing?" Becca repeated, sounding incredulous. "*Nothing*? Here you two were the Romeo and Juliet of Wilbur's Rooster, or whatever that town of yours is called, and you both find yourselves living in the same place fifteen years after you were torn apart like—like, well, like Romeo and Juliet . . . You've got to tell me more about what's going on with that, girlfriend."

I grimaced. "I'm not sure what's going on. I mean, I think he wants to pick up where we left off."

Becca let out a loud groan. I blinked, not sure if she was thrilled or horrified.

"That is so-o-o-o romantic!" she cried.

Okay, so she was thrilled.

"That is like something in a movie," she went on. "Here's this guy who you considered the love of your life, and then you lost him, and now he's in the picture again, so you two can go right back to where you were before—"

"It's not that simple," I interrupted. "At least, not from my perspective."

"Meaning?"

"Meaning I'm not sure how I feel about him," I told her.

Becca cast me a strange look. "You mean you're not sure how you feel about Jake, the person? Or you're not sure how you feel about getting back together with someone who broke your heart once upon a time?"

"Both," I told her. "And there's a third thing, too. I'm not sure I want to be involved with anybody right now."

Becca let out another loud noise, this one more of a moan. And this time, I was pretty sure it was meant to express being horrified, not thrilled.

"Kate McKay, what is *wrong* with you?" she demanded. "Here's this guy, who from the way you've always talked about him is *perfect* for you if not perfect in the absolute sense. He's nice, he's normal, he's stable, he's got those incredible blue eyes . . . and he's crazy about you!"

"But—"

"And you're crazy about him!" Becca went on. "Or at least you were once. And now you get a chance to see if you're still crazy about him, if even after fifteen years you two still feel that you were made for each other, and you're not jumping right in to find out?"

I frowned. "If you put it *that* way—"

"What other way is there to put it?" Becca cried. "Kate, I don't think you have any idea how hard it is to find a nice guy these days. All the guys I meet are boring or nerds or workaholics or chronically unemployed—or else they have something else seriously wrong with them. Have you forgotten how hard it is to find somebody you have real chemistry with?"

I was about to answer, but she kept going. "Do you really not remember all those horrid blind dates you went on? And what about the time you tried that dating service where you have lunch with a bunch of guys, like an assembly line, and all you got out of it was indigestion?"

"True," I told her. "But—"

"You have got to take the word 'but' out of your vocabulary," Becca insisted. "This Jake guy is definitely someone you have to take seriously. How can you just walk away from what could turn out to be the most important opportunity of your life? At least, your personal life. Your 'and they lived happily ever after' life?"

"No one lives happily ever after," I pointed out.

"Of course not," Becca agreed. "But you want to do everything you can to increase the odds of keeping the word 'happy' in the equation."

"Okay, I'll think about what you're saying," I told her.

Ready to change the subject, I glanced around her apartment and said, "Hey, that's a great lamp. I love the turquoise shade. Where did you get it?"

And then we were off on Becca's second favorite topic, after my love life. And that was her favorite web sites for shopping online.

Chapter 9

Rainbow Sherbet was invented by Emanuel
Goren while working at Sealtest Dairies,
Philadelphia, Pennsylvania, during the early
1950s. He is credited by them in conceptualizing
the three-nozzle design to fill the containers
simultaneously with three flavors, thus creating
the 'Rainbow' effect of the confection.

—*https://en.wikipedia.org/wiki/Rainbow_sherbet*

Spending the night on Becca's fold-out couch meant listening to a never-ending lullaby of honking horns, groaning trucks, and the occasional siren. When I woke up in the middle of the night, my head thick with sleep, for a few seconds I thought I was still back in my old apartment, living my old life.

But as I turned over and pulled my pillow over my head, I knew that as much fun as that old life had been, I felt more comfortable than ever in my *new* life.

I stayed at Becca's until mid-morning. I actually experienced a sense of relief when she went off to work and I had the luxury of lingering in her apartment for another couple of hours. As I savored a second cup of coffee, I plotted out my surprise visit to Ragnar Bruin's office.

By late morning, as I trudged up the stairs leading out of

the Midtown subway station that was closest to his office, I was pretty sure that I'd be able to carry off the scheme I'd come up with. Just like the day before, it was going to require a bit of acting. But I was growing increasingly confident about my abilities in the theater arts.

The building that housed the famous director's office was as different from Alpha Industries' building as I could imagine. Just as Coo had said, it was located mere steps away. But while Alpha Industries stood on a busy corner of Sixth Avenue, a major thoroughfare that was lined with towering office buildings, Ragnar Bruin's New York headquarters were located in a quaint, five-story brownstone on a much quieter side street.

In fact, it appeared that his offices occupied the entire building. That was pretty impressive, given the price of New York real estate. Then again, the man had had a ridiculously impressive career. That point was driven home by the giant movie posters covering every inch of wall space. As I walked into the front entryway, I immediately spotted posters for three of the films I knew he'd directed, *Pirates*, *The Hartford Trilogy*, and *Too Much Time*. But there were also posters for half a dozen other films I knew of but hadn't realized were his.

The furnishings were as funky as the building itself. They appeared to be deliberately mismatched: a burgundy-velvet Victorian couch paired with a glass-and-chrome coffee table straight out of the 1980s, a Noguchi-style floor lamp with a crinkled paper shade at the edge of a lush, deep-red Oriental rug that looked like a souvenir that Marco Polo had brought home. Then there were the fun touches: a jukebox, an old-fashioned movie camera that looked like it dated back to the 1920s, and a neon sculpture that spelled out "Go Away."

The receptionist was similarly unique. She was dressed in a salmon-colored suit with a 1940s look, complete with wide shoulders and a peplum waist. Her bright-red lipstick, a startling contrast to her espresso-brown skin, was another 40s touch. But she had several piercings on her face, and her head was shaved. An homage to the punk era, I assumed.

Trying not to stare at the safety pin jutting out of her nose, I took a deep breath and said, "Good morning. My name is Kate McKay, and I'd like to see Mr. Bruin."

"Do you have an appointment?" she asked, barely glancing up from her computer screen.

I'd had a feeling that that would be her first question, and I was ready with an answer. "I won't need one when he hears the reason I'm here."

She looked up, her expression skeptical. "And what exactly is the reason?"

"Just tell him it's about the Jimmy Dorp chair," I replied. "The one at Monarch Cinema Props."

Her face lit up. "The Jimmy Dorp chair?" she repeated excitedly. She was already pressing one of the buttons on her phone. "I'm sure Ragnar will want to talk to you about *that*."

Two minutes later, she was ushering me into the famous director's office. I knew it had to be his because it was huge, with a tremendous window that overlooked the street.

The room was so sparsely furnished that I couldn't tell if the various pieces were intentionally mismatched or not. A clear Lucite table that served as a desk was at one end of the spacious office, and a lime-green couch and two matching chairs were at the other. Hanging on the stark white walls were more framed posters for movies Ragnar had made.

Interestingly, I didn't see a picture of his wife on his desk. In fact, there was nothing on his desk but a small laptop computer.

And sitting at that desk was the man himself. He was tall; that was apparent even though he was seated. His nose was unusually long and crooked, and despite his Scandinavian first name—a name I recognized as a legendary Norse hero from watching the TV series *Vikings*—he had a wild mane of long dark hair and piercing dark eyes.

Partly because of his size and partly because of his status, he had an air of importance about him. Somehow, he managed to exude power.

I breezed into his office, doing my best to present the picture of self-assurance.

"I'm Kate McKay," I said, sitting down even before being invited to, "and I have good news, Mr. Bruin."

"Good news about the Jimmy Dorp chair?" he asked eagerly. "Is that what I heard you two talking about?"

I could already see that my ploy was working.

"As you know, Monarch has a policy of not selling any of its props," I went on, trying to give off the same air of confidence. I took care not to say anything about me actually *working* at Monarch or even about me representing the company. "But Monarch came up with another idea: the craftspeople there can make you a chair that's identical to the one you wanted. Would that work?"

He thought for a few seconds. "It's not quite the same thing, is it? So, of course, I wouldn't be willing to pay as much."

I started to panic. I hadn't anticipated talking about money. But I quickly came up with a good answer: "No one has gotten as far as determining a price," I told him. "At this point, Monarch just wants to find out if you're interested."

"I'm interested," Ragnar said, running his long fingers through his mane of dark hair excitedly.

"Wonderful," I replied. "In that case, the designers will figure out the cost. Someone will get back to you as soon as that's been done."

"Excellent!" he said. "Thank you so much for coming in."

We were done, as far as he was concerned. Which meant I had to do some fast thinking.

"Is the chair going to be a gift for your wife?" I asked.

I was surprised when he laughed, a loud, throaty guffaw that made me jump.

"My wife!" he repeated. "You obviously don't read the tabloids."

In response to my confused look, he added, "My wife left me. It's been two months now. In fact, she's already engaged to a French actor. And she's telling everyone who'll listen that divorcing me is the best thing that ever happened to her."

"I'm so sorry," I said.

So much for my theory about Ragnar's wife being a suspect. If she'd left the man and already moved on to someone else, it was hard to believe she'd be jealous enough to want to do away with his paramour.

But I still wanted to find out more. "I suppose couples simply grow apart some times," I commented.

"Or one of them finds their true soul mate," he said, his voice thickening. "The way I did."

I had a feeling I knew where he was going with this. But I wanted to make sure.

"Aren't you lucky!" I exclaimed. "That's something I'm still working on myself. Is it someone else in the industry?"

His expression darkened. "She *was* in the industry. She passed away recently." He swallowed hard before adding, "Savannah Crane. A terrible thing happened to her. It was in all the papers and all over the Internet."

"I did read about that," I told him. "And I'm so sorry."

I found it interesting that he was being so open about his feelings for Savannah. I would have expected that if he really had been stalking her, the way Amanda had insisted, he wouldn't want everyone to know that he had been, well, stalking someone. Which lent credence to Coo's claim that he hadn't been stalking Savannah at all.

"I'm devastated," he went on, his voice thick with emotion. "I had to take down all the photos of her I had here in the office. They make me too sad. I even had to put this away."

He reached into his desk drawer, pulled out a flat sheet, and handed it to me. I studied what looked like a handmade collage consisting of photographs, construction-paper hearts, and other items that had been artfully arranged on a big piece of cardboard.

"Who made this?" I asked, glancing up at him.

"Savannah made it," he replied, his eyes shiny with tears. "She gave it to me for my birthday, back in April. She was extremely creative."

He was right about that. The person who made this had taken half a dozen photographs of Ragnar and Savannah posing together and scattered them across the page. In one photo, they were sitting on a yacht, wearing bathing suits and sun visors. Their arms were wrapped around each other's waists, and they were both beaming. In another, they were dressed in evening clothes, dancing. Their bodies were pressed together tightly. Savannah's head rested on Ragnar's shoulder, and the expression on her face was one of pure bliss.

Interspersed among the photographs were the cut-out paper hearts. Scrawled across them were sayings like, "Love you forever!" and "So glad you're mine!"

If Savannah had actually made this, there was no way that Ragnar had been stalking her. This struck me as concrete evidence that the two of them had been involved in a genuine love affair.

Which meant one of two things. One was that Amanda had been lying when she'd told me about Ragnar and Savannah. The other possibility was that Savannah had been lying to her best friend.

It wasn't until the train that would take me home was pulling out of Penn Station that I realized how exhausted I was.

Simply being in the city had been tiring, I realized. True, I loved all the stimulation: the people hurrying by, the congested traffic, the honking horns and the screeching buses and the rumble of the subway under my feet. Then there was the visual excitement, things I'd paid special attention to over the past thirty-six hours: buildings with ornamentation I'd never noticed before, cafés with signs advertising foods I wasn't familiar with, enticing displays of shoes and fashionable clothes in the shop windows.

When I'd lived in Manhattan, somehow it had all become background noise. But now that I was a country girl again— or at least a Hudson Valley girl—I was shocked by how demanding I had found the city. I had changed. I wasn't used to walking on crowded sidewalks, having to veer around people who were moving too slowly or else being jostled by someone passing me because this time it was me who wasn't fast enough. I jumped every time a car horn bleated angrily. When a fire truck raced by, the shrieking siren was so loud and so shrill that I covered my ears.

As I settled back in my seat and closed my eyes, I could feel myself relaxing. The city was starting to feel farther and farther away. But the information I'd gathered during my two days there began coming into sharper focus. Thanks to what I'd learned, I was starting to put together a list of suspects in Savannah Crane's murder.

Timothy Scott was at the top. Even though he'd come across as someone who had sincerely cared about Savannah, the simple fact that he was her boyfriend meant that he was someone worth looking at. Crimes against women were too frequently perpetrated by the men in their lives. Then there was Coo's claim that things between Timothy and Savannah had been anything but smooth as of late. Given the fact that she appeared to have been honest about Ragnar and Savannah's relationship, I tended to believe her about Timothy, as well.

As for Ragnar, the director's name was the second one on my list. He, too, had been an important man in Savannah's life. But the question of what was really going on between them remained unanswered in my mind, even after seeing the handmade tribute to their love. For all I knew, she hadn't been the person who made it. It was still possible that Amanda had been right about their relationship. Which would mean he could even have made it himself.

Chelsea Atkins was next on the list. Despite her contention that she barely knew Savannah, she had had the most access to the dish of ice cream that had killed her. And I had found her hair in the cabinet, which raised the question of whether she had been tampering with the dishes minutes before Savannah had eaten the ice cream that had killed her.

At this point, I also had to include Amanda Huffner's name on the list. And that was mainly because it seemed possible that she had lied to me about Savannah's relationships with one or both of the men in her life, Timothy and Ragnar. It was possible that Amanda was trying to protect Timothy, mainly by pointing a finger at Ragnar. While I didn't know her motivation, I did know that it was possible that she hadn't been honest with me.

The last name on my list of suspects was Jennifer Jordan. She was a long shot, I knew. But I trusted Emma's instincts, and her insistence that Savannah's rival was worth looking at was something I couldn't ignore.

As the train chugged along toward the Hudson Valley and home sweet home, I began drifting off. Not into sleep, exactly, but more into a meditative state. Yet as I did, I found it more and more difficult to think about Savannah Crane. Instead, I found myself going back to my conversation with Becca.

The one about Jake.

And how I'd be crazy not to give the relationship another chance.

"Have you forgotten how hard it is to find somebody you have real chemistry with?" Becca had said, clearly exasperated over my inability to see what she found so obvious.

What about Brody? I thought. How does he fit into all this—if he fits in at all?

I hoped that my date with him, or whatever it was, would help me resolve that issue.

I guess I really did fall asleep, because I was suddenly jolted awake by the ringing of my phone. As I pulled it out of my purse, I was so disoriented that it took me a few seconds to comprehend the fact that it was Jake who was calling.

I hesitated for a moment, feeling guilty that not long before I'd been thinking about Brody. When I finally answered, my voice was groggy.

"Hi, Jake," I mumbled.

"You and I have a date tomorrow, Kate," he announced. "Well, not a date, exactly. More like an appointment. Wait, that's too formal. Let's just say there's someplace I'm taking you tomorrow. How does four o'clock sound?"

"Wait," I said, still not completely awake. "Where are we going?"

"It's a secret," he replied, sounding positively impish.

"But what should I wear?" I asked. "Should I bring anything? A bottle of wine, a warm jacket . . . a pint of Dark Chocolate Hazelnut?"

He laughed. "Wear whatever you want. And don't bring anything. Should I pick you up at home or at the shop?"

"At home," I told him. That way, I figured, I'd have a chance to freshen up after a long, grueling day with an ice cream scoop.

"Great," Jake said. "See you tomorrow." Then he hung up.

Another mystery, I thought, as I dropped my phone back into my pocketbook. But somehow, unlike the one surrounding Savannah Crane, this mystery made me feel good.

I don't remember the first time I saw Jake Pratt, or even the first time I spoke to him. Our high school was small enough—and our star baseball player was well-known enough—that I, like everybody else, just sort of knew who he was.

Our first serious interaction, however, was wonderfully dramatic.

At the beginning of my junior year, probably in early October, I was standing by my locker at the end of the day when my longtime nemesis, Ashley Winthrop, wandered by. Two members of her entourage were in tow.

But as Ashley sashayed down the hall with two members of her fan club, she stopped at the water fountain a couple of feet away from my locker and loudly said, "Would you believe that I've got not one, not two, but *three* invitations to the Halloween dance? And sadly, I'm sure that some people don't have any! Isn't that the saddest thing you've ever heard? My heart positively *bleeds* for the unpopular girls!"

I could feel her two sidekicks staring at me as Ashley leaned over to take a long sip of water. I could also feel my blood boiling.

I hate you, Ashley Winthrop, I remember thinking, trying to keep my cheeks from turning bright red as I pretended to reorganize my textbooks. I truly hate you.

As if that wasn't bad enough, Ashley then came right over to me and said in a nauseatingly sweet voice, "Why, hello, Kate. I didn't notice you standing there. Are you going to the Halloween dance?"

Just then, out of nowhere, Jake Pratt appeared. Popular Jake Pratt. Gorgeous Jake Pratt.

Independent Jake Pratt, one of the few hot boys at school who refused to get corralled into Ashley's group of popular kids, the ones who ran the school and tormented everyone who wasn't part of their clique.

"Hey, Kate," he said breezily, stopping right behind me and Ashley. "I was wondering if you'd like to go to the Halloween dance with me."

I was certain that my cheeks were the same shade of crimson as the history book I happened to be holding in my hand. But Ashley's nastiness had little to do with it.

"I'd love to, Jake," I said.

"Wow, that's great!" he exclaimed. "You just made my day! My entire week, in fact!"

And he actually sounded as if he meant it.

I turned to Ashley. "So I guess the answer to your question is yes, I *am* going to the Halloween dance."

She just stared at me, her expression one of total shock. This appeared to be one of the few times in her life when she couldn't think of anything to say.

"See you there, Ashley!" I called after her as she and her two ladies-in-waiting slunk away.

I turned to Jake. But instead of feeling grateful, I was furious.

"You didn't need to do that!" I cried. "You don't have to—to feel *sorry* for me! It's not your job to bale me out just because you think I'm—I'm *desperate* or something!"

He just blinked. "I don't think you're desperate," he replied calmly. "And I certainly don't feel sorry for you. I just want to go to the dance with you."

Now it was my turn to be at a loss for words. "You do? I mean you *really* do? You weren't just trying to make a point?"

He laughed. "I must admit that I did overhear what Ashley said. And the timing of me asking you to the dance had everything in the world to do with that. But I've wanted to ask you for days, and, well, I just haven't had the nerve."

"Really?" I croaked, too astonished to handle this moment any more gracefully. "But I didn't even think you knew who I was!"

"Of course, I know who you are," he said. Now *his* cheeks were turning pink. "I've been trying to get up the courage to ask you out ever since—well, ever since Kathy Norwood and I broke up last month."

With a shrug, he added, "I guess I have Ashley to thank for finally presenting me with just the right moment. My intention wasn't to put her in her place, but doing it sure felt good!"

Jake and I went to the Halloween dance. He dressed as a pirate, complete with a colorful stuffed parrot on one shoulder and a fake black mustache. I was a tiger, wearing a fuzzy orange-and-black one-piece suit that Grams whipped up on her sewing machine. We attached some of the fabric to a black headband for ears, and I carefully painted whiskers on my face. But my long tail was the best part, even though I did end up holding onto it most of the evening to keep it from banging into people.

Ashley came as Cleopatra, wearing a flowing white skirt that revealed her bellybutton. With it, she wore a low-cut, gold-sequined bra that prompted Mr. Ambrosiano, a curmudgeonly math teacher and one of the chaperones for the evening, to insist that she wear a Modderplaatz High School sweatshirt over it for the entire evening.

Yet even having her costume ruined didn't stop her. She made a point of flirting with Jake every chance she got until he finally told her, "Look, Ashley, I'm here with Kate. And Kate's the only person I want to dance with. And talk to. And drink that horrible sweet punch with. So why don't you go spend some time with your own date? I'm actually starting to feel sorry for that jerk Tommy Barrett, something I never thought would happen."

That night, Jake kissed me for the first time. The two of us were standing on the porch at Grams's house, saying good night after an absolutely lovely evening. All around us were the glowing jack-o'-lanterns that Grams and I had carved together. They all seemed to be smiling at us, and it was one of those moments I knew I'd remember for the rest of my life.

Which is exactly what it turned out to be.

Chapter 10

Iced dairy products made from the milk of horse,
buffalo, yak, camel, cow, and goat first appeared
during the T'ang Dynasty in China (618–907 AD).
King T'ang himself relished an iced-milk dish
called kumiss. The frosty concoction included
rice, flour, and 'dragon's eyeball powder,' better
known today as camphor, a chemical taken from
the wood of an evergreen tree.

—We All Scream for Ice Cream!
The Scoop on America's Favorite Dessert, *by Lee Wardlaw*

Wednesday morning, when the alarm clock in my bedroom went off, I had to remind myself that during my
stay in the city I'd developed a new appreciation for the life
I'd made for myself in Wolfert's Roost. And that included
getting up with the sun to make ice cream.

Ice cream can sure be a cruel mistress, I thought grumpily
as I dragged myself into the bathroom and turned on the
shower.

But within half an hour, the steaming hot water and two
cups of strong coffee had turned me into a new person. In
fact, I was feeling energized enough to walk to Lickety Splits,
rather than driving.

As I stepped outside onto the porch, the early-morning air

was crisp, and the sun was shining brightly. It was hard to believe the weather forecaster's gloomy prediction that rain clouds would be moving in by afternoon.

In honor of the upcoming holiday, I decided to whip up a batch of a new flavor I'd been thinking about. I planned to call it Bag o' Tricks and Treats, inspired by my memories of my own haul every Halloween. I started with a rich chocolate ice cream, mixing in chopped-up pieces of the candies that trick-or-treaters love most: Milky Ways, Snickers, M&Ms, and Reese's Peanut Butter Cups.

I was afraid it might be too much. But as I scooped up a small amount and cautiously tasted it, a wave of pleasure immediately rushed over me. For a while, I was transported back to my childhood. Or at least a *fantasy* from my childhood.

This one is going to be a winner, I thought.

And I was right. Bag o' Tricks and Treats turned out to be a big hit with my customers, too, at least my more adventurous ones. While plenty of people came in to Lickety Splits for the usual chocolate, vanilla, and strawberry experience, there were quite a few who stopped into my shop expressly to try whatever new concoction I'd just dreamed up.

Elton Hayes was one of these people. Elton, who owned and operated Let It Brie, the gourmet cheese shop a block or so away, was passionate about food.

He also happened to be one of my first customers that day.

"It's only eleven-thirty, but I'm already on lunch break," he exclaimed as he bustled into my shop. He was short, with chubby cheeks and a waistline to match. Even though he was only a few years older than I was, probably around forty, he had already lost most of his hair. "And I decided that ice cream was on the menu today."

He leaned over the glass display case and studied the tubs of ice cream lined up inside. Rubbing his pudgy hands together, he cooed, "And I can't wait to hear about the extra-special goodies you have in store for your loyal fans today, you ice cream goddess, you!"

I laughed. "How does Bag o' Tricks and Treats sound? It's chocolate ice cream with four kinds of candy mixed in."

Elton rolled his eyes appreciatively. "It sounds like you've brought the ice cream experience to a ridiculous new level. I need some. *Pronto!*"

"Coming up," I said, still laughing. "Cone or cup?"

"I'm going to have to take that in a waffle cone and eat it on the run," Elton said. "I've got a delivery from the Cow Girl Creamery in California that's due any minute. Getting a package from them always feels like Santa arriving on Christmas morning, so I don't want to miss it!"

Even though he insisted on rushing back to Let It Brie, Elton tasted my new concoction as soon as I handed it to him. His eyes grew big.

"Oh, my, Katy McKay," he said breathlessly. "You truly are a genius. If there's an ice cream hall of fame, you deserve to be in it."

I was still chuckling over Elton's appreciation of my ice cream fantasies and fine food in general when the door opened once again. I glanced up, expecting to see another customer. Instead, I encountered a familiar face.

"George!" I exclaimed. "How nice to see you! What brings you into town today?"

"I was doing some errands, so I thought I'd stop in and say hello," he replied congenially. With a wink, he added, "And possibly avail myself of some of your ice cream. I hear it's amazing."

"You mean you haven't tasted any yet?" I asked, surprised.

"Nope," he said. "But as the old saying goes, there's no time like the present."

"In that case," I told him, "you're welcome to sample as many flavors as you'd like. All of them, in fact. And, of course, it's on the house."

"That's certainly the best offer I've had in a long time," he said. He came over to the display counter and earnestly studied the rainbow of three-gallon tubs neatly lined up under the glass. "Let's see," he mused. "Cherry Cheesecake sounds amazing. So does Kahlua and Chocolate. Bag o' Tricks and Treats? I've never heard of that one, but I have a feeling you've come up with something inspired. I can see that I should take advantage of your offer to try as many of these as I have room for!"

He sampled four different flavors, declaring each one the best thing he'd ever tasted.

Finally, he said, "I'd treat myself to a Hudson's Hottest Hot Fudge Sundae made with Chocolate Almond Fudge and Cappuccino Crunch," he commented, "but I shudder to think of what my doctor would say if he ever got wind of it."

So he settled for a scoop of each of those two flavors. I still couldn't resist pouring on a little hot fudge sauce, to which I'd added a touch of cinnamon. It complements both flavors so well that it just seemed wrong not to.

George was grinning like an eight-year-old boy as I set down the oversized tulip dish on the table he'd chosen.

"If you don't mind, I'll join you," I said after scooping myself a much more modest dish of Peach Basic Bliss sorbet. It's one of my Lickety Light selections, a line of frozen treats I developed for people who wanted a snack that was a little less sinful. I sat down in the chair opposite his. "I've already had a few customers, even though it's still early. But as you can see, we're in a bit of a lull right now."

"I'm glad for the company," he said. "Now that I'm retired, I'm finding life a little—well, I hate to use the word 'dull,' so let's just say it's a lot less exciting than it used to be."

"I'm sure it's a big adjustment," I said, savoring a spoonful of the delectably light fruit sorbet with the surprising touch of basil. "What exactly did you do?"

"I sat in an office and did boring things with numbers," he said. "Which I suppose is a good reminder that maybe I shouldn't miss it so much, after all."

I smiled. "It seems to me that building foam pits and haunted houses is a much more fun way to spend your time." Gesturing toward his dish, I said, "And eating ice cream, too, of course. It's my personal belief that there's no better way for anyone to spend their time."

"I'm with you on that," he agreed, chuckling.

Then he grew serious. "So you've had a tough few days," he said. "Are you doing okay?"

"I think so," I told him. Glancing around, I added, "I sure am glad I was able to open the shop again."

"It must feel strange," he commented, glancing around. "Being back in here, I mean. Now that this . . . *thing* has happened here."

"I'm trying really hard not to let it affect my feelings about Lickety Splits," I told him. "And I'm doing okay with that. I adore this place, and that helps a lot."

His expression grew tense. "It didn't happen at this table, did it?"

"No," I assured him. "Savannah Crane was sitting at the table behind us."

He looked relieved.

"Besides, when the movie people were here, the whole place looked different," I said. I gestured at Emma's fabulous Halloween-themed creations. "They had taken all these decorations down. Those paintings of ice cream that Willow made, too. So it wasn't Lickety Splits as I know it." I shrugged. "That helps, too."

"Good," George said. "You seem to be a pretty strong person, Kate. It looks like you've weathered this whole thing just fine."

"I think so," I agreed. I was more than ready to change the subject. "So how's the ice cream?"

"As good as people say it is," he said. "But I actually came by today for another reason. Aside from finally trying your ice cream, that is. And, of course, having a chance to see you again, too."

"What's that?" I asked.

"I wanted to ask you about your grandmother," he said.

"Okay," I said, not sure where this was going. "What about her?"

His cheeks turned the slightest bit pink. "I was just wondering if she'd said anything. About me, I mean."

"Why, George!" I exclaimed. "I do believe you've got a crush on Grams!"

By now his cheeks were definitely pink. "I'd say that's pretty obvious," he said. "But I wondered if she'd said anything about how she feels about me. Or at least what she *thinks* about me. The kind of person I am, whether I'm, oh, I don't know, fun or boring or—or . . ."

I was finding this conversation absolutely charming. "George, I think it's pretty obvious that Grams likes you, too."

"So she hasn't told you anything specific?" he asked.

"Not in so many words," I said. "But I can tell she likes you. In fact, I can't remember the last time I've seen her so happy."

A look of relief crossed his face. "So she thinks I'm okay," he said.

I laughed. "I'd say she thinks you're *very* okay."

"I was hoping that was why she invited me over for dinner tomorrow night," George said, looking relieved. "I wasn't sure if she was just being nice because of all the time I've been putting in on her Halloween Hollow project."

"I'm sure she's grateful for that, too," I said. "But I do think there's more to it."

George grinned. "I'm glad we had this little talk. And I think I'm going to enjoy this ice cream even more."

With that, he dug his spoon into the scoop of Chocolate Almond Fudge and stuck it in his mouth, looking more like that contented eight-year-old boy than ever.

Late that afternoon, Emma came to Lickety Splits for her usual shift, right after her computer class. The two of us usually work side by side, but given her passion for playing the role of matchmaker, today she was more than happy to take over by herself.

I hurried home and changed into nice pants and a rose-colored sweater that Grams had hand-knit and given to me as a Christmas present. Deciding what to wear was tricky since I still had no idea where Jake was taking me or what we were doing. I hoped the outfit I had finally decided upon would be suitable.

I perched on the living room couch and played with my phone while I waited for Jake. Sure enough, at exactly four o'clock, Digger started barking his furry little head off. A few seconds later, I heard the usual creak made by a footstep on the wooden front porch, followed by a knock.

"You're right on time," I greeted Jake. I was relieved to see that he wasn't particularly dressed up, either. He was wearing jeans and a light jacket over a dark blue knit shirt that made his eyes look even bluer than usual. His light brown hair was neatly combed, as if he'd made a point of getting spiffed up for little old me.

"Are you kidding?" he said. "I've been watching the clock all day, waiting for this."

"Then I guess you don't want to come in first," I said, "either for coffee or my standing offer of ice cream. I tried out something new today, and it seems to be a success. It's my own personal tribute to Halloween, called Bag o' Tricks and Treats. It's made with chocolate ice cream, Snickers bars, Milky Ways, M&Ms . . ."

Jake laughed. "It sounds like heaven on earth, but even that can't tempt me. Not today."

"My goodness," I said. "You really are a man with a mission."

As soon as I walked out the front door and saw the car that was parked in the driveway behind Grams's gray Corolla, I froze.

"What is *that*?" I demanded.

"That," he replied, "is my new toy." He was wearing a grin that would have put the Cheshire cat to shame.

"It *looks* like a toy," I told him.

And it did. The Miata sports car in my driveway, which was the same brilliant shade of red as an M&M and at least as shiny, was about the size of a Hot Wheels number a child would find in a Christmas stocking.

"Is this the surprise?" I asked, still shocked. "What you wanted to show me, I mean."

"Nope," he said. "This is the just the chariot that's transporting you *to* the surprise. And I promise that you're going to love riding in it."

I was skeptical. Tootling around in a vehicle that wasn't much bigger than a three-gallon tub of ice cream had never been a top priority for me.

Yet once we were on our way to wherever we were going and Jake began taking the curves in the road just a tad faster than I would have, I had to admit that driving around in a sports car really *was* fun. Especially with the top down.

It didn't hurt that the weather that afternoon could have been expressly ordered for an exhilarating ride in a sporty convertible. Despite the forecaster's prediction of rain late in the day, the sun was still holding its own, shining its heart out with that slightly golden color it takes on in October. The sky was shadowed with gray but could still rightfully be considered blue. And the air was supercharged with the crisp coolness that makes autumn in the Hudson Valley feel as if something magical is about to happen.

Then there were the leaves. All along the road, the trees were decked out in brilliant shades of orange that reminded me of flames, yellows that bordered on gold, and patches of crimson that looked as if they'd been scribbled by a super-creative child with a red Crayola. The Hudson Valley is beautiful at any time of year, but in the fall, the intensity of the colors at every turn make it look like something Walt Disney created rather than a real place.

All in all, I'd have to classify this as a close-to-perfect autumn day.

"Having fun?" Jake asked, turning to me and wearing that big grin again. Or I should say wearing that grin *still*, since I didn't think he'd stopped smiling since he'd climbed in.

"I am," I told him. "And here I'd always thought one car was as good as the next."

"Ah, but this isn't just a car," he corrected me. "This is a *lifestyle*."

I laughed. "So you're a person who has a gleaming red sports car, and I'm somebody who has a red truck," I said.

"And what do you think that says about each of us?" Jake asked.

"I'm not sure," I said, considering his question seriously. "Maybe that you're better at having fun than I am?"

"Or maybe that you're more practical," he said. "Of course, I have a truck, too. More than one. But that's business. This is pleasure. So maybe it just means that I'm more of a car person than you are."

"I'm definitely not a car person," I assured him. Casting

him a sly smile, I added, "But I can see myself turning into one."

Jake threw back his head and laughed. "In that case, I've
already gotten my money's worth out of this baby!"

And then another aspect of Jake's new "lifestyle" occurred
to me.

"Did you just win the lottery or something?" I asked him.

"I'm not that lucky," he replied, "though business has
been good lately. Really good. And something did happen recently: I picked up a great new account. I'm going to be supplying organic dairy products for several local branches of a
big national supermarket chain."   ·

"Congratulations!" I said sincerely. "That's wonderful,
Jake. So is that what's behind this mystery outing? Are we
going somewhere to celebrate?"

He looked over at me and, with one hand, made that locking-
my-lips-with-a-key motion.

"You are such a man of mystery," I teased. "I feel like I'm
going for an afternoon drive with James Bond."

"I don't think this outing will be quite as thrilling," he
said. "Then again, it's pretty exciting for me."

"*More* mystery," I said, pretending to be exasperated. But
I was secretly enjoying this. The sense of embarking on an
adventure, the pleasurable drive . . . and simply being with
Jake.

As soon as he turned off the road, I understood what this
was about. He had pulled into the driveway of an abandoned
store, a low brick building that looked unloved but which
definitely had good bones. It was a good size and had large
windows. It also had a wide, welcoming front door and
plenty of parking. A big FOR SALE sign was out front, along
with the name of a local realtor. Directly underneath it was a
smaller sign that read IN CONTRACT.

"So this is it," I said, climbing out of the car. "The future home of the Flying Frog Farm Stand."

"I'm still not convinced about the 'Flying Frog' part, but otherwise, you're exactly right," Jake replied.

"This place has incredible potential," he said as we stood in the parking lot, studying the building. Pointing at the boarded-up windows, he said, "I'm going to replace the shutters, of course. And I'm thinking of painting them a bright color, something that'll be hard to miss if you're driving by."

"Emma could help you decide on a color," I commented. "She's great at that kind of thing."

"And at some point—maybe not right away—I'd like to add on a wooden porch," he went on. "That would give it a homier look. Maybe paint that a bright color, too, although I might be better leaving off leaving it natural. I'd run hanging baskets of flowers all along it, except in winter when I'd put up tons of Christmas lights—"

"You could hang wreaths along that front wall," I suggested. "Christmas wreaths in the winter, but the rest of the year, maybe you could find a local craftsperson who makes wreaths out of branches and dried flowers." Thoughtfully, I added, "Grams makes those. I wonder if she'd like to start her own cottage industry."

"That's a great idea," he said. Glancing at me, he continued, "I was counting on you to have plenty of those."

"Can we go inside?" I asked.

He reached into the pocket of his khaki pants and pulled out a key. But before we went in, he grabbed something out of the trunk. It turned out to be a big tote bag. It was zipped up so I couldn't see what was inside it.

When we stepped through the front door, I gasped. Even though the exterior had looked as if needed plenty of TLC, I still wasn't prepared for what was inside. The walls had no sheetrock, only wooden studs. The floor was bare concrete with a few cracks. And strewn around the place were planks of wood, empty cardboard boxes, and enough dust and debris to make me sneeze. Which is exactly what I did.

"Whoa," I said. "This place needs a lot of work."

"Yes, but that's not necessarily a bad thing," Jake said. The expression on his face was one of total excitement. He reminded me of that little kid I'd pictured finding the Hot Wheels Miata in his stocking on Christmas morning. "That way, I can start from scratch, making the space exactly the way I want it."

He proceeded to dash around, gesturing with both arms as he explained his vision. "The first thing I'd like to do is build a really attractive shell. Paint the walls a nice color, redo the floor, of course, probably using wood to give it that old-fashioned feeling I want . . . I thought I'd put the counter over here. The refrigerators and freezers will go along that back wall. And back here, I'll put shelves. That's where I'll keep the local food products, like the jams and jellies. And on tables, over here, I'll display the crafts made by local artisans—"

"Wow, I can see you've already put a lot of thought into this," I commented.

His cheeks turned pink. "I have. I've also had a few conversations with Hayley Nielsen. You remember her from school, don't you? She became an interior designer, of all things. And she had a bunch of amazingly good ideas."

I was surprised that I actually experienced a flash of jealousy over Jake's mention of one of the prettiest, most popular girls from our high school days.

"And I've talked to Johnny O'Hare and Danny Melski," Jake went on. "You probably remember them from school, too, right? They were always getting into trouble. But these days, they have a construction company. They've kept it pretty small, and they mainly do local projects. Jobs this size are exactly the kind of thing they specialize in."

"So you're already pretty far along in this process," I observed.

"Yes and no," Jake said. He suddenly seemed overcome with awkwardness. "That depends on you. And whether you're interested in becoming my business partner.

"But we can talk about that later," he went on before I had a chance to say anything. Picking up the tote bag he'd retrieved from the trunk of his car, he added, "For now, I'd like you to join me in celebrating this new venture."

I looked around at our chaotic surroundings. "There's no place to sit."

He held up one finger, as if to say, "Wait." He unzipped the bag and pulled out a red plaid wool blanket dotted with moth holes. "A picnic blanket for m'lady."

So *that* was what was in the bag. A picnic. I could feel the color rise in my cheeks.

With a flourish, he spread the blanket out on the floor. I lowered myself onto it, sitting cross-legged. Jake sat down opposite me with the big bag between us.

"This floor is kind of hard," he said with a frown, rocking from side to side as if to prove his point.

"It's fine," I assured him. I was so tickled by all the effort he'd gone to that I didn't want to say or do anything to ruin the moment. Peering inside the bag, I said, "So what else have you got in there?"

He grinned at me slyly, then pulled out two champagne flutes.

"I hope there's champagne to go with those glasses," I teased.

"Of course there is," he replied.

"I was joking!" I insisted. "And please tell me that those glasses are plastic."

"Crystal," he said.

"I'm impressed."

"Hey, this is an important celebration!" he insisted. "I'm about to—I believe the expression is 'expand my business vertically.' "

I groaned. "And here I thought I'd left the world of big business behind when I gave up my big-city job in public relations!"

"In this part of the world," Jake replied, pushing the champagne bottle stopper with both thumbs, " 'big business' means selling organic half-and-half in quart containers instead of just pints."

Laughing, I said, "I can deal with that."

A loud pop echoed through the room. Jake immediately filled the two glasses.

As he handed me one, I asked, "Should we toast your new venture?"

"Not yet," he insisted. "First I have to set everything up."

"Can I help?" I asked as he began pulling more items out of the tote bag.

"Nope," he said as he took out several slabs of cheese, a baguette and a long knife, and a plastic container of fresh fruit, cut up into bite-size pieces. "Today you are my guest of honor. In fact," he continued, "you're the first person I've brought here."

"Really?" I said. "Then I do feel honored."

Jake pointed to the wall behind him. "See that space over there? That's where I picture the ice cream freezer. Horizontal or vertical—your choice."

"Definitely vertical," I said. "It's much easier for customers to see all the flavors that way. And I've already started thinking about what flavors might make sense."

"I was thinking basics—like chocolate, vanilla, and maybe coffee—that would be available every day," Jake said. "But I

LAST LICKS 165

hoped you'd be willing to add a few of your more creative
flavors, too. Two or three at a time, maybe. That way, people
would get to try them, but they'd still have to go to your
shop to get refills. To try your other flavors, too."

"That sounds like a good plan," I said. I took a deep
breath. "Jake, at some point we really do have to discuss
your idea about me becoming your partner." Quickly, I
added, "I mean, going into business with you."

"Yes, but right now there's something more important we
need to do," he said.

"What's that?"

"Eat some cheese," he said. And he handed me a napkin.
A *cloth* napkin, the rich yellowish-white color of organic
cream.

"The cheese is from Let It Brie," he said. "Elton picked
these out for me himself. He promised me that the 'piquant
bleu' would be the perfect complement to the fresh strawberries. And if anyone knows cheese, it's Elton."

Jake reached back into the tote bag again. This time he
took out two packages of crackers, one with cracked pepper,
the other with rosemary.

"Elton also swore on his life that I simply had to get these
to go with the cheeses he selected," Jake said.

"I can just hear him," I said, laughing. "I imagine he
threatened not to sell you the cheese unless you took the
crackers."

"That sounds about right," Jake said. "But I picked these
out myself." He brought out a series of small containers: cashew
nuts in one, dried cranberries in another, tiny chunks of dried
mango and pineapple in a third.

"This is lovely," I said with a sigh. "I'm so glad I didn't eat
lunch today. Or much ice cream. At least by my standards."
Holding up my glass of champagne, I asked, "*Now* can we
make a toast?"

"That moment has arrived," Jake agreed.

I was about to say something bland like, "To your new business." But Jake beat me to it.

"To new possibilities," he said, raising his glass, "and the wonderful fact that life never stops bringing us exciting surprises and unexpected opportunities. None of us ever really knows what amazing experiences are just around the corner. So let's drink to that."

As we clinked our glasses, Jake locked his eyes on mine. "I can't think of anyone I'd rather be with right now."

I didn't know how to respond, so I pretended to be too busy tasting the champagne to talk. It was delightful—crisp and cold and deliciously dry. I took another sip, then another. I could already feel myself relaxing.

"Did Elton instruct you in which cheese we should eat first?" I teased. "I wouldn't want him to sic the cheese police on us."

"I think we have free rein with that," Jake replied. "Of course, he might have strong feelings about which cheese goes with which type of cracker."

"I'm surprised he didn't include written instructions," I joked. "Explicit ones."

"Hey, remember that math teacher we had who'd give an exam and he'd start by saying, 'Take out your pen. Take off the top. Turn over the page. Now begin!'"

"I *do* remember!" I squealed. "Mr. Miller!"

"That's right, Michael Miller." Jake laughed. "What a character! Like we didn't know we were supposed to take the top off our pens before we started writing!"

"And that's something that's a lot easier than knowing what cheese goes with what cracker," I said. "But Mr. Miller wasn't nearly as quirky as Mr. DeMarco. Do you remember all those long stories he used to tell about his kids? What was his son's name?

"Frank David!" Jake replied. "I remember him going on and on about Frank David setting the trash pail on fire. He acted like it was some amusing prank. I wonder where that kid is now!"

"Probably doing ten to fifteen upstate," I said.

I realized I felt warm inside, as if I was glowing. And I was pretty sure it had nothing to do with the champagne. It felt so good, being with Jake again. Someone with whom I had so much shared history, someone who knew me so well . . .

Someone who *used* to know you well, I corrected myself.

But either the champagne or the blissful feeling that had come over me made my usual arguments feel far, far away.

And then I became aware of the rhythmic tapping of rain against the roof.

"That's one of my favorite sounds," I said, glancing upward, as I took another sip of champagne.

"Rain on the roof?" Jake asked.

I nodded. "It always feels so nice and cozy being inside while it's raining. It makes me feel like I'm holed up in a comfortable cabin somewhere, all safe and secure."

"That's because you don't have cows to worry about," he said, smiling.

"True," I said. "No cows in my life."

"But I have to admit that I like that sound, too," Jake said. "It reminds me of when I was a kid and I'd go camping with my uncle. I really loved those trips. The problem was that for some reason, it seemed to rain every time we went! But I came to associate the sound of rain falling against the tent with that same feeling you're talking about, the feeling of being safe and secure."

He was quiet for a few seconds, then added, "My uncle was like a father to me. My real dad was usually passed out on the couch with an empty bottle in his hand, so it was Uncle Steve who did most of the stuff a regular father would do. I don't know if my mom asked him to do it or he took it upon himself, but we did all kinds of cool stuff together."

"I'm so sorry you lost your uncle," I said quietly. "I remember you talking about him a lot, but I never realized he was like a father to you."

"Did I talk about him?" he asked. "I don't recall doing that. But I'm glad I did. I hope I appreciated him enough while he was still around."

With a meaningful look, he said, "We don't always take time to appreciate the people who matter to us while we still have them in our lives. We don't always tell them how much they mean to us. And we should. We should tell them every day. We shouldn't let time slip away without letting them know that they're the most important thing in our lives."

His eyes were fixed on mine. As intense as the moment was, I couldn't bring myself to look away.

"Hey, Kate?" he said softly.

"Yes?"

"I really like the idea of you and me being partners," he said.

I could hear the sound of my own breathing as he reached across the tattered wool blanket and took my hand.

I didn't pull it away.

I knew what was coming next. And I was ready for it to happen.

My heart was racing as Jake leaned forward and gently pushed a strand of hair away from my face. When his lips touched mine lightly, it was almost as if he was asking a question. And I answered it. I kissed him back.

I thought it would be the same, but somehow all the years apart had erased that feeling of first love, as delicious as it had been. We weren't seventeen anymore. We weren't two kids who were in a constant state of giddiness, unable to believe we'd actually found someone who could elicit such strong feelings.

I understood in that moment that the idea I'd been wrestling with, that I'd be going back into the same relationship I'd had with Jake before, dissipated like a burst of smoke.

This time, it all felt brand-new.

Chapter 11

The top-selling Ben and Jerry's flavor is Half-
Baked, chocolate and vanilla ice creams mixed
with gobs of chocolate chip cookie dough and
fudge brownies. Cherry Garcia is next, followed
by Chocolate Chip Cookie Dough.

—*http://www.benjerry.com/whats-new/2016/top-
flavors-2016*

The following morning, I woke up with butterflies practic-
ing their gymnastics routines in my stomach. Today I
had another challenge to confront: my hike with Brody.

I was nervous about it for two reasons. First of all, the
word *hiking* was simply not a part of my working vocabulary. In fact, if there was ever anyone who could best be described as indoors-y, that was me. I'm someone whose idea of
an adventurous vacation is staying at a hotel that has a rating
of four stars instead of five. Who thinks the only boots worth
owning are the ones that are made of Italian suede. Who
once stayed inside the house for a full week after spotting a
man-eating-size raccoon going through the trash can.

Okay, so maybe that's a bit of exaggeration. But the point
is that I'm not exactly a nature lover unless I'm viewing it
from the inside of a car. Or, better yet, a movie theater.

Yet here I was, about to go hiking. In the mountains.

Second, there was my lingering ambivalence about doing anything at all, indoors or out, with Brody. Especially after yesterday. That kiss had been pretty special. *Jake* was special. Or he at least had the potential to be special.

I reminded myself that going hiking with Brody wasn't necessarily a date. The man was a positive fanatic about the outdoors, so I still believed it was possible that he was just looking for someone to keep him company. Or even someone to turn on to the wonders of being outside simply because he felt that gaining converts was his mission in life.

And even if it *was* a date, Emma had been right about me owing it to myself to explore—well, whatever it was she had said. It had certainly sounded reasonable at the time.

Which left me with the problem of what to wear. I dragged myself out of bed and stood in front of my closet, wondering if I even owned anything suitable for trekking around in the so-called Great Outdoors.

It took me about two seconds to decide on jeans. If there's anything that cowboys and other people who spend lots of time breathing fresh air like, it's jeans. I'd always assumed the reason they were so popular was because they looked good on pretty much everybody. But now that I was thinking about it, I realized it was probably because they were made of rugged fabric that didn't tear easily, they had a little stretch in them, and they had plenty of pockets.

For the top half of my body, I decided on layers. October was unpredictable in the Hudson Valley. It could be pretty warm during the day, especially in the sun. But once the sun got low, it could be positively chilly. Especially in the woods. Not to mention the mountains.

So I pulled a thermal undershirt out of one drawer, a long-sleeved T-shirt out of another, and a fleece vest out of a third. With my bra, I was wearing more layers than a fancy birthday cake.

The last part was the hardest. And that was footwear.

Of course, I'd heard the term "hiking boots," but I didn't own anything that came even close to what I imagined those to be. In the end, I opted for sneakers with thick socks.

I had just put everything on and was studying my reflection in the mirror when Emma walked by and glanced through my open door.

"This is a new look for you," she observed, sounding surprised. "Modeling for the L.L.Bean catalog?"

"I wish," I replied. "I'm going hiking later."

Her eyebrows shot up to the ceiling. "You? Someone who sprays on bug repellent every time she walks by a newsstand that sells *National Geographic*?"

"Ha, ha, very funny," I told her. "It's never too late to explore new horizons."

Emma thought for about two seconds before her face lit up. "Brody!" she cried. "Today's your date with him!"

"Bingo," I told her.

"Whoa," she said, folding her arms across her chest and leaning against the door frame. "If I were you, I'd be ready for some pretty serious trekking."

"I can always insist that we turn back," I told her. "Or pretend that I twisted my ankle."

"Just hope he doesn't decide that you're too heavy to carry and that he has no choice but to leave you behind for the wolves," she teased.

I stuck out my tongue.

Growing serious, I told her, "I'm thinking about canceling."

"Kate," she cried, sounding exasperated, "Brody is probably the nicest, sexiest, handsomest man in town! I thought I'd talked you into give him a chance. Why would you change your mind?"

"Jake," I replied simply. I took a deep breath, then said,

"Yesterday he took me to see this new roadside farm stand he just rented. And, well, we ended up kissing."

I expected sympathy. Instead, she looked impatient.

"For goodness sake, Kate, a kiss isn't exactly an engagement ring. Have some fun! Explore your options!" Her expression became grave. "But I do have one piece of advice."

"What's that?" I asked.

"Don't eat too many protein bars on that hike," she said with mock seriousness. "Those things can wreak havoc on your guts if you're not used to them."

I tossed a balled-up pair of socks at her, and she ran away, laughing and shrieking.

For the next several hours, I was busy enough scooping ice cream that I forgot all about my upcoming adventure. But those annoying, super-athletic butterflies returned a few minutes before Brody was due.

When Emma arrived at Lickety Splits around then, ready to take over at the shop, she was upbeat and encouraging. But I still wished I could spend the rest of the day filling cones, drowning sundaes in hot fudge sauce, and making stomachs happy instead of hanging out with Mother Nature.

Brody arrived right on time. I was relieved to see that, like me, he was wearing jeans and layers. The man was a professional, after all, so he knew all about appropriate attire. But I was unnerved by his boots, which looked a lot more substantial than my wimpy Skechers. In fact, his footwear looked suitable for climbing one of the lesser Himalayas.

"All set?" he asked. He flashed his sparkling smile. That alone was enough to ease my anxiety. Emma had certainly been right about him being nice and sexy and handsome. In fact, his eyes looked particularly green today, and his curly blond hair seemed even thicker than I remembered it.

"I'm ready," I told him. I sounded almost convincing.

"Have fun, you two!" Emma called as we headed out the door, toward his truck. "And don't forget what I told you about those protein bars!"

"Have you done much hiking?" Brody asked as we drove out of town, toward the Great Beyond.

"Only in Manhattan," I told him. "I've been known to walk from Fourteenth Street to Times Square in under a half hour."

He laughed. The man had no idea that I was serious.

We road into the Mashawam Preserve, as I expected. But when we reached the parking lot, instead of pulling into one of the spaces, he continued on toward a dirt road at the very back. One that was marked with a sign that read KEEP OUT!

He completely ignored the sign and just kept going. The ride suddenly got very bumpy. "I don't think we're supposed to go in here," I said nervously.

"You mean because of that sign?" he said. "That's only there to keep amateurs from getting hurt."

But I *am* an amateur! I wanted to cry. And not getting hurt is one of my key goals for today!

But it was too late.

We bumped along for another quarter of a mile before we finally stopped. And once we did, there were no parking lots in sight. No people, either. Or signs. Or any traces of civilization. We were, to use a cliché, in the middle of nowhere.

I guess the look on my face was pretty telling because Brody chuckled. "Don't worry, Kate," he said. "I've been here before. There's a great trail right around that bend." Thoughtfully, he added, "Well, maybe not a *trail*, exactly . . ."

By this point, scenes from a PBS documentary about the Donner Pass I'd recently seen were playing through my head. It's only October, I told myself. The snow won't be coming for months. Or weeks, anyway.

We hopped out of the truck. Actually, Brody hopped. I

kind of dragged myself out, gazing at it longingly and wondering if I'd be seeing it again. Next, he grabbed a heavy-looking backpack and shrugged it on. I hoped there was water in it. Lots of water.

But before I had a chance to ask, he reached into his pockets. His eyes glittered impishly as he said, "I brought snacks! There's no reason why we shouldn't enjoy a little fun food while we're hiking!"

He held out both hands so I could inspect his offerings. In his right hand was a bag of those protein snacks Emma had warned me about. The packaging boasted that these were made with chick peas, quinoa, *and* chia seeds. Just seeing those words in print was enough to make my stomach churn. In his left hand was a bag of kale chips.

This, I thought, for a woman whose idea of "fun food" is something that includes whipped cream, a few dozen carbohydrate grams of sugar, at least as many grams of fat, and chocolate.

Still, if there was anything that I'd learned over the past week, it was that I was a pretty good actress.

"Yum!" I cried. "Can't wait!"

I only hoped I'd find some ancient M&Ms or some dry-roasted peanuts in one of the many pockets in my jeans, just in case I got light-headed from all the physical exertion I knew lay ahead.

"All set?" Brody asked. His cheeks were flushed, and his eyes were practically glowing.

He truly loves this! I realized. Lugging heavy equipment through the woods in order to pretend we're squirrels is his idea of a good time!

"I'm as ready as I'll ever be!" I said. I reminded myself that for a few years, back when I was in elementary school, I had been a Girl Scout Brownie. True, we had mainly sold cookies, sung "Kumbaya," and made Thanksgiving centerpieces out of branches and plastic chrysanthemums. But surely some of that group's spiritedness and can-do attitude had sunk in.

We headed into the woods. I was dismayed to find that the "trail" Brody had mentioned turned out to be nothing more than patches of dirt about six inches wide that were scattered here and there. As we trudged through the dense growth, I was pretty sure I could feel the bears watching us. I could even hear them licking their chops.

And Brody, being very tall, had ridiculously long legs. Keeping up with him was a challenge, especially given all the nasty rocks and malicious roots that kept jumping in front of me.

"I should probably have made this clear earlier," I called to him in a wavering voice, "but I'm not exactly what you'd call an outdoor girl. Not that I don't love adventure, but I'm more into adventure that involves maps and vending machines."

Brody laughed. "You are so funny, Kate. I've never met a woman with such a great sense of humor."

Soon afterward, he stopped, looking around and letting out a deep sigh. I, meanwhile, was happy that I was finally getting a chance to catch my breath.

"Isn't this amazing?" he said, his voice filled with reverence. "I feel like I'm truly alive when I'm in the woods like this."

And I'm hoping to get *out* alive, I thought.

Still, I had to admit that he had a point. It *was* beautiful out here. Peaceful, too. No honking cars, no buzzing cell phones . . . maybe this business of being in the middle of nowhere really did have its good points.

"Listen!" he said, his voice dropping to a whisper. "Did you hear that?"

"No, what?" I cried, glancing around. Terror instantly gripped every cell of my body.

"I think that was a blackpoll warbler," he said. "Yes, I'm pretty sure it was."

At least birds don't maul you to death and eat your vital organs, I thought, relieved. Unless they're the ones that starred in Alfred Hitchcock's movie.

We walked on. I did my best to appreciate my surroundings, but I had to admit that they were starting to look pretty much the same. I mostly saw trees. And, of course, those sadistic rocks and roots. I encountered some spiteful vines, too, but I managed to step around them before they had a chance to lunge at me.

"We're almost at the lake," Brody finally said, glancing at me over his shoulder.

"There's a lake up here?" I asked, surprised.

Sure enough, after only another twenty minutes of plodding through the woods, the trees suddenly cleared, and we stepped out onto the shores of a lake.

"Isn't this the most amazing spot you've ever seen in your life?" Brody half-whispered, sounding awed.

I had to admit that it was indeed gorgeous. The lake's calm blue waters glistened in the low afternoon sun, and surrounding it was a spectacular view of mountains, trees, and the clear blue sky.

I found myself wondering if I could find it in myself to share this man's love of communing with nature, making it a major part of my life. I'd actually enjoyed reading about Thoreau's *Walden* when I was in middle school. I'd even gotten an A on the five-page paper I wrote about it. Maybe I was capable of embracing Thoreau's appreciation of the simple life, even if it involved bugs and ugly footwear.

"The sun is getting low in the sky," Brody said after we'd admired the lake for a few minutes. "We should probably start back. Let's take a different route."

"Whatever you say," I said affably. While I'd ended up enjoying this outing more than I'd expected, I was starting to miss the strangest things about civilization. Not only my bed, my bathroom, my coffeepot, and Trader Joe's. But also things like donuts. And I've never even been that big a fan of donuts.

Still, as we headed back into the woods and continued on our way, I tried to remain in the moment. I breathed in the fresh air, raised my face toward the smudge of yellow that was the late-afternoon sun, and tried to remember the lyrics to "The Happy Wanderer." Aside from the "val-de-ree, val-de-rah" part, most of them seemed to have vanished from my head.

We walked a bit farther and suddenly seemed to be on an actual trail. Not Brody's idea of a trail—the Parks Department's idea of a trail, which was more in line with mine. Beneath our feet was a wide pathway that had been put there deliberately. There were even markers, small wooden arrows indicating which way to go as well as an occasional sign indicating the direction of the parking lot.

"We're almost back to civilization," Brody said, sounding a little sad.

Sure enough, there was the parking lot we'd driven past, a few hundred yards in front of us.

But as we walked past it, something odd caught my eye. One of the main paths leading off the paved parking lot was marked with a big sign reading PINE TREE TRAIL. But a high metal fence had been put up across the entryway, along with another sign that warned DO NOT ENTER. Given our natural surroundings, it looked extremely out of place.

"I wonder why that path is closed," I said, thinking aloud. Glancing around, I added, "Especially since it looks as if all the other paths are open."

Brody shrugged. "There could be lots of reasons," he said. "Maybe a tree fell across the path and they're still in the process of clearing it away. Remember that big rainstorm we had last month?"

"Maybe," I said. And, of course, he was right. There could be a lot of reasons why one of the paths in a preserve would be closed off to the public. After all, we ourselves were guilty of ignoring the park's warning, heading down a dirt road that was officially off-limits.

And then, as sudden as a slap, my ears were assaulted by the loud roar of an engine. It seemed to be coming from somewhere beyond the fence, cutting through the silence of the forest. I was beginning to appreciate the sound of that blackpoll warbler.

"Sounds like I was right," Brody observed. "They're obviously doing some kind of work in there."

Maybe it was just as well that we'd hiked along a quieter route, I thought. Even though it meant breaking a few rules.

As we drove back to Wolfert's Roost, the sun was low in the sky. I was tired, I realized, but in a way that felt good. I had enjoyed the workout. And in the end, I had appreciated being in such a spectacular and peaceful setting.

And what about Brody? I asked myself. Did you enjoy being with him, too?

The man must have been reading my mind, because at that very moment he glanced over at me and, with a big smile, said, "That was great. We'll have to do it again sometime soon."

"Definitely," I agreed.

Deep down, I wasn't so sure. But the reason for my uncertainty had nothing to do with hiking. Or even chia-laden protein bars.

After Brody dropped me at my house and I let myself in, all I could think about was a long, hot bath and a big mug of peppermint tea.

"Is that you, Katydid?" Grams called from the kitchen.

"It's me, all right," I called back. "I've made it back from the wilds of the Hudson Valley."

She came out, wearing an apron and drying her hands on a dish towel. From the tantalizing smells coming out of the kitchen, I could tell she'd been baking something delicious.

"How was your hike?" Grams asked eagerly.

"Not bad," I said, surprising myself. "It was actually kind of—fun."

"I'm so glad," she said. "I want to hear all about it, but my Russian tea cookies will be ready in about two minutes. By the way, UPS dropped off some boxes for you this afternoon. I asked the nice delivery man to put them in the living room."

Sure enough; three big cardboard cartons were stacked up next to the coffee table. As soon as I saw them, my heartbeat speeded up. I didn't even have to look at the labels to know what they were: the boxes of Savannah Crane's possessions from work that Coo had packed up for me.

Chapter 12

Ben and Jerry's employees get to take three pints
of ice cream home with them every day.

—*http://www.benjerry.com/whats-new/2017/09/ice-cream-
useless-facts*

As I distractedly gave Digger his usual stomach scratching, I knelt down to check the mailing labels. Poor Chloe stood by, looking irritated over being neglected.

As I expected, the return address on the boxes was Alpha Industries. The bath and the tea would have to wait.

"I'm going to take these into my room," I called to Grams.

I carried the three boxes through the hallway one at a time, forgetting all about my aching muscles. Then I folded back the handmade quilt that served as my bedspread and deposited them on my bed.

I opened the first box using the sharp edge of my house key. As I pulled back the flaps, my heart was pounding as hard as if it was Christmas morning and I'd just received a very special gift.

But as soon as I saw the three Beanie Babies on top, I felt deflated. In fact, my eyes filled with tears as I was struck by the fact that I was doing more than trying to solve a mystery. I was delving into someone's personal life—a life that had ended much too soon and much too tragically.

Still, I knew I had to go on. I pulled out the floppy stuffed animals, wondering what they had meant to Savannah. I got a partial answer when I noticed that written on the tag that was attached to the furry orange tiger was, "Love you forever! Timothy."

I took out some more items that were typical of what you'd find in anyone's work space. A mug that said, INSTANT HUMAN! JUST ADD COFFEE! A nail file. Coffee stirrers and packets of artificial sweetener. A folding umbrella. Finally, a framed photograph of Savannah and Timothy standing on a beach with their arms around each other, both of them grinning.

That was all there was in the first box. I went on to the second, wondering if I'd find something more meaningful. I was heartened when I saw that it was stuffed with files, dozens of manila folders filled with papers.

I was hopeful as I pulled out the first few folders. But that feeling dissolved as I looked at one after another. Inside the folders there were just forms, lists of numbers, printouts of emails, and other documents that meant nothing to me.

The third box was more of the same. I scrutinized the labels on these folders, too, but I still didn't see anything useful.

Still, I knew that if I was going to uncover anything from Savannah's job that was related to her murder, chances were good that it would be somewhere in these files. And combing through them, page by page, was going to take some serious time.

I immediately felt overwhelmed by the task ahead of me. Could I really figure out enough about what Savannah's job was all about—and what Alpha Industries was involved in— that I could understand if the goings-on at the company where she worked might have been behind someone's decision to kill her?

That task suddenly struck me as impossible.

* * *

Having Grams's gentleman caller over for dinner was a welcome distraction from investigating Savannah Crane's murder. But it suddenly felt as if there was a lot to do.

Instead of a long hot bath, I settled for a shower. Then I gulped down a cup of mint tea as I blow-dried my hair and put on my version of a nice outfit: black slacks instead of jeans and a shirt that wasn't bubble-gum pink and didn't have LICKETY SPLITS ICE CREAM SHOPPE embroidered on it.

Emma seemed as excited as I was. When I went into the kitchen, I found that she was already bustling around, taking masses of fresh vegetables out of the refrigerator. She had put a black-and-white-checked Lickety Splits apron over her jeans and T-shirt, and her cloud of black-and-blue hair was pulled back into a bushy ponytail. Grams stood at the sink, scrubbing potatoes and humming.

"Grams, let me do that," Emma insisted. "Why don't you go lie down for a while before George gets here?"

"I don't need to lie down!" Grams insisted, laughing. "Goodness, Emma, I may not be eighteen anymore, but I'm still capable of washing a few potatoes."

"If you insist," Emma said with an exasperated sigh. "In that case, I'll start chopping these veggies. I'm going to mix them with olive oil and garlic and a few other magic ingredients and roast them. Yum!

"And I'm pretty sure everything else is under control," she added thoughtfully, as if she was checking a mental list. "The roast, the biscuits . . . and, of course, I'm leaving dessert up to Kate, since she's our resident Empress of Ice Cream."

Emma glanced up then, noticing for the first time that I'd come into the room.

"If it isn't the bachelorette herself!" she joked. "I can't wait to hear all about your date with Brody!"

I just sighed.

Emma grimaced. "I think I can guess. The man is simply too outdoorsy for you, right?"

"It's not even that," I said. "It's more like . . . there's no real chemistry between us."

"Maybe you're expecting too much, too soon," she suggested. "These things take time. Don't they?"

"I don't know," I said thoughtfully. "With me, it's always been an instant thing. Like I knew from the beginning."

At least, that was how it had been with Jake. By the time our first date at the Halloween dance had ended and he kissed me good night, I knew. That spark had been there since the very start.

And I kind of felt as if that spark was still firing away.

"If you want my opinion, I think you should give it more time," Grams commented, glancing up from the sink.

"I agree with Grams," Emma said. "If I were you, I'd go out with both Jake *and* Brody. Sooner or later, I'd think it would be pretty clear which one of them makes your heart go pitter-pat."

Once again, my niece sounded so logical. Even so, I wasn't so sure I agreed with her.

But before I had a chance to ponder the issue any longer, Grams said, "Goodness, look at the time! George will be here in half an hour. Kate, would you mind setting the table?"

"Not only will I set it," I replied, "I'm going to make it Martha Stewart–worthy. I'm going to use your 'good' china, along with that gorgeous hot-pink-and-orange jacquard tablecloth you bought in the south of France. I'll get out the matching napkins, too."

"And I insist on exiling Digger to the backyard," Emma added, glancing up from the brussels sprouts she was hacking away at with a sharp knife. "I love that doggie to death, but we don't want to overwhelm poor George, especially since this is the first time he's having dinner here."

"You two!" Grams cried. "You're acting as if royalty was coming over!"

"That's because we see you and George as the new Prince Harry and Princess Meghan," Emma said, grinning.

I've always found that preparing for an event is as much fun as the event itself. And tonight was no exception. Between the teasing, the tasting, and the enjoyment of the three of us simply being together, adding George to the mix was just—well, the cherry on top of the ice cream sundae.

Still, Grams seemed pretty excited when he showed up, snappily dressed in a sports coat, a red-and-blue-striped tie, khaki pants, and black shiny loafers. Especially since he'd brought her another bouquet, this time an explosion of blossoms in every color imaginable. Glancing out the window, I saw that he'd pulled up in a sleek black sports car. With the top down, of course.

I'll have to tell Jake about that, I thought, smiling. Maybe the two of them can race sometime—or at least compare notes on horsepower or spark plugs or whatever else sports car enthusiasts like to brag about.

"Thanks for inviting me, Caroline," George greeted Grams. He handed her the flowers, then leaned over and gave her a quick kiss on the cheek. Grams immediately turned pink.

"We're glad you're here!" she replied. And she leaned forward and gave him a kiss on *his* cheek.

The two of them were pretty darned cute together.

Next George handed me a white bakery box.

"I assume that you're in charge of dessert," he said. "And I'm pretty sure that dessert involves ice cream. So I brought these cookies from a fancy bakery. I hoped they'd be a good accompaniment to whatever's on the menu."

"They're perfect," I assured him. I peeked inside the box and found an assortment of butter cookies that would, indeed, go well with the baked Alaska I planned to serve. In honor of Halloween, underneath the baked meringue crust, I was using the Smashed Pumpkins ice cream Emma and I had dreamed up—luscious, pumpkin-flavored ice cream dotted with pecans and pralines. The ice cream was a beautiful pale orange that I thought would look gorgeous with the white meringue shell.

By the time dinner was ready and the four of us sat down at the dining room table, I felt as if we had all known each other for years. George fit right in, making wry observations about our inside jokes and our comfortable banter. He didn't seem the least bit intimidated by the three of us fluttering around him, treating him like—well, like Prince Harry.

We had just begun eating when Emma's phone buzzed. Naturally, she couldn't resist checking it. Her eyes instantly grew as big and round as two Oreos.

"You won't believe what just happened!" she cried, cutting into our chatter about the various Halloween costumes we'd worn when we were children.

Grams and George looked at her expectantly. I also glanced over at her, although I'm sure that my expression was more along the lines of skeptical.

"It's Jennifer Jordan!" Emma went on excitedly. "She's been spotted in the Hudson Valley!"

That *was* interesting.

"Who's Jennifer Jordan?" George asked, spooning himself a generous portion of roasted vegetables. "And why is it important that she's here?"

"You probably don't know about this," Emma explained, "but Kate has been investigating Savannah Crane's murder."

"She's the actress who was killed in Kate's shop," Grams interjected.

Emma nodded. "And Jennifer Jordan is one of the prime suspects."

George looked surprised. "I didn't know Kate was an amateur sleuth."

Grams and Emma exchanged a meaningful look.

"Kate is too much of a risk-taker," Grams said at the exact same time Emma said, "Kate is so amazing!"

Proudly, Emma added, "Kate has already helped with two other cases."

"You mean this isn't the first time Kate has investigated a murder?" George asked, sounding incredulous.

"Let's just say that I've had reason before to look into some local crimes," I muttered, reaching for a biscuit and wishing we could change the subject. I didn't feel comfortable being the center of attention, at least not when people were talking about my past involvement with something so unsavory.

"Kate also happens to be really, really good at snooping around," Emma said.

"But isn't that dangerous?" George asked, his eyes clouded with concern. "If you ask me, dealing with murderers is something that's better left to the professionals."

"Thank you, George," Grams said meaningfully. Turning to me, she said, "See, Kate? I'm not the only one who's worried about you getting messed up in this case."

"But it affects me directly!" I protested. "The horrible thing occurred in *my* shop! And poor Savannah Crane was eating *my* ice cream!"

"It's not the best thing for Lickety Splits' reputation, either," Emma added. "I'm with you, Kate. The sooner this case is solved, the sooner people will forget all about it and we can focus on more important things—like coming up with more fabulous new flavors."

"So who are the suspects in this case of—what's the actress's name again?" George asked.

"Savannah Crane," Emma and I replied in unison.

"I'm putting together a list," I told him. "It includes her boyfriend, a famous movie director, and a few other people who knew her."

"I still think Jennifer Jordan is behind this," Emma insisted. "She's an actress, too, and she and Savannah have been rivals for years. And according to what I read online, Jennifer really wanted this part."

"It sounds as if you've already put a lot of time into this," George observed. "But I'm afraid I'm with Caroline on this. It sounds as if you're treading into dangerous waters. If I were you, I'd put my efforts into making more of that delicious ice cream of yours."

"Here, here," Grams agreed. "Now who's ready for more potatoes?"

I fell into bed as soon as Emma and I finished cleaning up. George had left early, around ten. But even though it wasn't that late, it had been a long, tiring day.

I was sure I'd drift off to sleep immediately. Instead, I lay with my head propped up on the pillow, staring at the shadowy tower of cartons I'd stacked up in the corner.

Finally, I couldn't stand the suspense any longer. I threw back the covers, turned on a light, and hauled one of the two boxes that was stuffed with files back over to the bed.

Just like before, I pulled a bunch of folders out of the carton. But this time, I forced myself to look through the pages inside them, one by one. It appeared that Savannah had created a file for each property Alpha was developing, with all the forms related to every aspect of it from start to finish: its original architectural drawings, its construction, and its financing. And the projects themselves ranged from strip malls to apartment buildings to office complexes.

It was a miracle that it didn't put me to sleep.

But as tedious as it was, I kept looking through files. When I finished that batch, I moved on to another. And another. I was starting to get a feel for the paperwork that went along with each building Alpha Industries was involved in.

But I still had no idea how any of it could have been related to Savannah being murdered—if there was even any connection in the first place.

It was midnight when I finally glanced at the clock. I could hardly believe that I'd spent so much time going through all these pieces of paper. And I could hardly believe that I had absolutely nothing to show for it.

I was ready to give up. In fact, I was squeezing the last wad of paper back into the box when I noticed one more manila file folder.

Up until that moment, I'd missed it completely. That was probably because it was so skinny. Unlike the other folders, which were all at least a half-inch thick, this one appeared to be empty. And it had slipped down to the bottom of the box so that only the top corner was visible. I pulled it out.

Instead of being labeled in the same manner as the others—with a tab that said something like SYLVAN APARTMENTS or FOUR SQUARE OFFICE PARK—the label on this folder was a hand-drawn emoji.

An emoji of a frowning face.

I opened it and found that inside was nothing but a single sheet of paper. A date was handwritten in the top left-hand corner, August 12 of that year. Written in the right-hand corner were the initials HH.

There were two words scrawled across the top, as well. They were written in a different color ink, as if they'd been added at a later date.

Savannah had written MASHAWAM PRESERVE, then underlined each word twice and added two exclamation points.

I was still puzzling over what that could possibly mean as I zeroed in on what was written below. I let out a gasp, feeling as if I'd just been slapped in the face.

It was a handwritten list of five names: Timothy Scott, Amanda Huffner, Chelsea Atkins, Ragnar Bruin, and Jennifer Jordan.

I blinked hard, trying to comprehend the fact that in my

hand was a list of names that was identical to the list of suspects I'd put together. And according to the date on top, Savannah had made this list a little over two months before she was murdered.

I didn't sleep well that night. Gone was all the fatigue from my demanding day of hiking, then helping prepare dinner and entertaining Grams's new beau. Instead, I lay in bed as rigid as a wooden plank, replaying everything that had happened in the past week over and over again.

Finally, after breakfast and before heading into Lickety Splits, I put in a call to Coo. It had occurred to me at around three AM that she was the one person I'd talked to who was most likely to know what this list referred to.

I was surprised that a real person answered, rather than a machine.

"Alpha Investments," a woman greeted me pleasantly. I recognized her voice. She was the receptionist I'd met on Monday.

It took me a few moments to remember Coo's real name.

"May I please speak to Cornelia Jameson?" I asked politely.

"I'm sorry, Ms. Jameson is out of the office today," the receptionist replied. "Would you like her voice mail?"

Darn, I thought. Here I'd been hoping for immediate results. Instead, I said yes.

"It's Kate McKay," I said after the formal, business-y recording, followed by the usual beep. Trying to be as cryptic as I could, I added, "I came across something I'd like to talk to you about. Call me as soon as you can!"

Next, I tried her cell phone. I wasn't surprised that she didn't answer. But when I tried to leave her a message, a recording informed me that her voice-mail box was full.

For the rest of the day, as I scooped out ice cream and

made small talk with customers, I desperately waited to hear back from Coo. All I could think about was that list of names and what it could possibly mean. I must have checked my phone a hundred times.

No response.

Finally, I couldn't stand the suspense anymore. Waiting for the phone to ring—especially when it refused to do so—was simply too frustrating.

So I texted Emma, who I knew was spending the evening with Ethan. I asked if there was any chance the two of them could fill in for me for the rest of the evening. Twenty minutes later, they burst through the door, ready to take over the shop.

It was time for me to do a little more sleuthing.

Emma and Ethan plied me with questions about what I was doing and where I was going. But I remained secretive, partly because I didn't know if I was embarking on a fool's errand.

And that errand was trying to talk to Timothy again. Over the past week, since I'd gone to his house the day after Savannah's murder, his name had popped up again and again.

Yet there was still so much I didn't know. What had his relationship with Savannah been like? Lovey-dovey, as Amanda had insisted, or turbulent, which was Coo's take on it? Had Timothy known about Ragnar Bruin being in her life—and, if so, did he have any insight into what the true nature of their relationship had been?

Then there was the fact that his name was on the mysterious list I'd come across in Savannah's files. Did he know what that list meant—and why his name was on it?

I was hoping that meeting with him again would help me answer some of those questions.

As I drove up to the house in Cold Spring and parked on

the street in front of it, my anxiety level began to climb. I was starting to wonder if I should have told Emma and Ethan where I was headed tonight. Maybe I was taking more of a risk than I realized by coming to Timothy's house. Especially since I was alone.

It didn't help that it was a strangely dark evening, with no stars in the sky. Even the moon was unusually pale, giving the impression that it simply wasn't trying very hard. It was also pretty late by then, almost ten o'clock. There didn't seem to be anyone else around. In fact, the neighborhood felt positively eerie as I got out of my truck.

As if that didn't do enough to create a creepy mood, a few of the houses around me were decorated for Halloween. Tonight, the smirking jack-o'-lanterns looked strangely spooky, their grins evil rather than whimsical. The next-door neighbors had hung rubber vampire bats along their front porch, and I jumped when out of the corner of my eye I noticed them swinging.

Jack-o'-lanterns and fake bats never hurt anyone, I reminded myself, trying to quiet my pounding heart.

Besides, now that I was here, I still wasn't sure whether or not it would be foolhardy to ring the bell. Turning around and leaving was still an option.

I was still trying to decide as I slowly started up the front walkway toward the house. Someone had pulled down the louvered blinds on the living room's big picture window. Even so, I could see that there were lights on inside.

But as I got closer, I noticed that the garden gnome I had damaged the week before was still perched on the windowsill, right where Timothy had deposited it. Next to it was the chunk of his hat that had broken off. When the blinds had been lowered, the bottom slats had gotten caught on the two ceramic pieces, creating a gap that allowed me to see inside.

I suddenly felt my eyes growing as big and round as those sneering pumpkins.

Through the window, I could see Timothy lying on the couch, his shirt off and his hair tousled. There was someone else there, as well. Someone who had also taken off some of her clothes.

Their bodies were intertwined in a way that immediately told me they weren't just watching a movie together.

Timothy sure didn't waste any time, I thought, suddenly angry. And here I thought he was such a nice guy. I'd believed that, even though he and Savannah may have been arguing, he was still in love with her . . .

And then he stood up, smiling at the woman and gesturing toward the kitchen, as if indicating that that was where he was now headed.

Which allowed me to get a good look at his companion.

I had to clasp my hand over my mouth to keep from crying out. The woman who was lying on the couch with Timothy was Amanda.

Chapter 13

Pecans are the most popular nut chunk in the US, and strawberries are the most popular fruit chunk.

—*http://www.benjerry.com/whats-new/2017/09/ice-cream-useless-facts*

I felt as if someone had punched me in the gut.

Timothy and Amanda? I thought, feeling dazed. Savannah's boyfriend and the woman who claimed to be her best friend . . . they've been having an *affair*?

I turned and raced back down the front walkway, taking care not to trip. I was trying not to make any noise, either. I was out of breath by the time I reached my truck, but I was pretty sure that at least I'd managed to sneak off the property without being spotted.

But as I started to drive off, I glanced over my shoulder, for some reason taking one last look at the house. And what I saw made my stomach tighten even further.

The blinds in the living room had been pulled all the way up, exposing the silhouettes of two people standing at the window, watching me drive away.

They *saw* me! I thought, instinctively stepping harder on the gas. They know that *I* saw *them*—and that I now know their secret!

As I careened back to Wolfert's Roost, I struggled to sort through all the noise in my head. I started by replaying every word I could remember Amanda saying about Savannah's relationship with Timothy.

She had insisted that the two of them were madly in love, echoing what Timothy had told me. She had said they had even gotten engaged recently. She had sounded so convincing that it had only been Coo's version of recent events, her claim that the two of them had been fighting constantly, that had made me question what Amanda had said.

Then another thought occurred to me: that Detective Stoltz had said there was a good chance that the murderer would return to the scene of the crime. And Amanda had come to Lickety Splits. In fact, she hadn't even pretended to have any reason for coming besides wanting to see the place where Savannah had died.

Were Amanda and Savannah really friends? I wondered. But even if they had been, or at least appeared to be, what I had just discovered proved that Amanda hadn't been a very good friend to Savannah at all.

Amanda also had a good reason to protect Timothy, I realized. That could certainly have been why she had made up that story about Ragnar Bruin stalking Savannah. She could have been trying to shift suspicion away from the victim's boyfriend—always an obvious focus—to the director.

All this told me that what I had learned tonight had three possible implications. One was that Amanda had killed Savannah. Her intention could well have been to get rid of her rival for Timothy's affections. But it was also possible that she had murdered her for some other reason entirely, a reason I hadn't yet identified.

The second possibility was that Timothy was the murderer. He could have killed Savannah for two reasons: either because he was jealous of her affair with Ragnar or because he wanted her out of the picture so he'd be free to continue his relationship with Amanda.

The third possibility was that Timothy and Amanda had acted together.

But as I drove on, winding along Route 9 and noticing how quiet the usually busy road was this late at night, I pondered another issue that had been bubbling along on the back burner of my mind. And that was the question of how either Amanda or Timothy had managed to get into Lickety Splits to put poison into the dish of ice cream right before Savannah ate out of it.

And then a realization popped into my head like a bolt of lightning.

Amanda worked for a props company. While she'd told me that Monarch hadn't handled the props for *Ten Days*, she could easily have been lying.

Which meant she would have had easy access to the set.

I wanted to check with Chelsea Atkins about whether or not Amanda had been telling the truth about that. I made a mental note to send her a text as soon as I got home, asking her to call me the first chance she got.

But as I drove on, I realized that even if Amanda's company, Monarch, hadn't supplied the props for *Ten Days*, the woman *did* work in the movie industry. Which meant it was quite possible that she knew some of the people at the film shoot simply because that was the world she traveled in. She could easily have stopped in, claiming she was there to see how the filming was going or to say hello to a friend.

And maybe no one on the *Ten Days* set had thought to mention it merely because, in their eyes, Amanda popping in to say hello was a non-event.

The same went for Timothy. Since he was Savannah's boyfriend, he, too, could have stopped into Lickety Splits just to say hello. No one would ever have suspected that the reason he was there was not to wish his girlfriend good luck—but, instead, to make use of the poison he had sneaked in.

I was starting to think that the names of the two people who were closest to Savannah both belonged at the very top of my list.

I was still lying in bed early the next morning, going over the same points I'd been ruminating about as I'd driven home the night before, when my cell phone rang.

My first thought was that it was Chelsea, responding to the text I'd sent her the night before. But when I grabbed my phone off the night table and glanced at the screen, I saw a number I didn't recognize.

Still, the area code was Manhattan's 212. I answered immediately.

"Hey, Kate," Coo greeted me breezily. "Sorry I didn't call back sooner. I was in an all-day training seminar yesterday. In fact, since it ate up the whole day, I actually had to come in this morning, on a Saturday, to finish up a couple of things. So I just got your message. Did the boxes arrive?"

"They did," I told her. "Thank you so much for sending them."

"I figured that was what you were calling about," she said. Lowering her voice, she added, "Which is why I'm calling you from my cell phone, rather than Alpha's landline. In case you came across something interesting." She hesitated, then in the same soft voice said, "And it sounds as if you did."

"I'm not sure if I did or not," I replied. "I'm hoping you can tell me if what I found means anything."

I described the list I'd found in Savannah's files, explaining that it had been written two months earlier yet included the names of all five of the suspects I'd identified.

"I'm afraid I have no idea what that list means," Coo said,

sounding frustrated. "I don't even know who Chelsea Who-ever is."

"She's the assistant director on *Ten Days*," I told her. "She claims she'd only met Savannah a few times before filming began. Yet there she is, on the list."

"Timothy, Amanda, Ragnar . . . They're all people Savannah was close to, of course," Coo said, sounding as if she was thinking out loud. "But aside from that, I don't know what they have in common. As for Jennifer Jordan, I'm pretty sure she knew her, but it's not as if they were close friends."

She paused, then asked, "Was there anyplace else where those five names were listed together? Another file, perhaps?"

"Not that I found," I said. "Are you sure you got every-thing out of Savannah's office?"

"I'm positive," she assured me.

"Is it possible that somebody else went into the office be-fore you did and took something out?" I asked. "Maybe another file that would have shed light on what the list Sa-vannah made was all about?"

Coo was silent for several seconds. And then I heard her gasp. "Timothy!" she cried. "Of course. I don't know why I didn't think of this sooner. He could have taken something out of Savannah's files."

"Timothy?" I repeated, confused. "Isn't it unlikely that he would have been able to get into her office?"

"Why not?" Coo asked. Now *she* sounded confused.

"Because I would think that most companies wouldn't want an outsider coming in and going through their files—" I started to explain.

But she interrupted me.

"An outsider?" she said. "What do you mean, an out-sider?"

This conversation seemed to be getting more and more muddled. "I just mean that having someone like Timothy who's not an employee—"

"But Timothy *is* an employee," Coo declared.

I was still trying to understand. "Timothy works at Alpha, too?"

"Of course," Coo replied. "You didn't know that?"

"No, I didn't," I said. My mind was racing as I tried to wrap my head around this new piece of information. "But I thought he was an actor."

"He *is* an actor," Coo said. "Or at least he's trying to be an actor. Which is why it made sense for him to work at his family's firm. That way, he has all the flexibility he needs. After all, when your father is the CEO of a billion-dollar company, it's no problem if you want to take a day off here and there to memorize a script or go to an audition."

"Timothy's father is the CEO of Alpha Industries?" I was still having trouble piecing all this together.

"That's right," Coo said, still sounding surprised that she had to explain all of this to me. "I'm sorry. I just assumed you knew.

"I guess I also figured you knew that Timothy got Savannah her job at Alpha," she continued. "All he had to do was pick up the phone and ask his father to hire her. Savannah and Timothy met through acting, but like everyone else who's trying to break into the business, they both needed a way to pay the bills. Once they were seeing each other, he was more than happy to help her out with that."

My thoughts were reeling. Timothy not only worked at Alpha Industries; he was the boss's son. My earlier suspicions about Timothy's involvement in Savannah's death were growing stronger every second. But I still didn't have a grasp of what had been going on that might have motivated him to kill Savannah.

"There was something else written on that sheet of paper with the list of names," I told Coo. "The initials HH and the name of a local preserve."

Coo was silent for a few minutes. "The only thing I can

think of is Hudson Hideaways. I suppose that could be what the HH stands for."

My heart suddenly began to pound wildly in my chest. "What's Hudson Hideaways?"

"One of the properties Alpha has been developing," Coo replied.

That made sense. After all, nearly every one of Savannah's files had been dedicated to a different property. And if the Hudson Hideaways file was conspicuously absent, it could have been because Timothy had made a point of grabbing it out of Savannah's office.

And I had a hunch about why.

"Is it near the Mashawam Preserve?" I asked, picturing the underlined name of the preserve scrawled at the top of the list, along with two exclamation points. I was beginning to feel as if the pieces of the puzzle I'd been agonizing over were finally starting to fit together.

"Sorry, but I'm afraid I don't know anything about it," she replied. "But I'll see if I can do a little nosing around. It looks like I'm the only person here in the office this morning. Maybe I can find something that'll be useful to you."

The sick feeling I suddenly had in my stomach told me that while Coo didn't have a sense of what all this pointed to, I did. But there was still a lot more I had to find out.

Despite the sense of urgency that engulfed me, the reality was that I had an ice cream shop to run. And because it was a Saturday, I didn't feel comfortable leaving Emma to run Lickety Splits all by herself. On a crisp, sunny autumn weekend like this one, there were bound to be hordes of leaf peepers who hopefully liked ice cream as much as they liked beautiful scenery. In addition, with Halloween growing close, I figured there would be plenty of customers putting in orders for parties and other holiday-related events.

So I spent the entire day at Lickety Splits. Business was as bustling as I'd anticipated, and Emma and I worked nonstop. Smashed Pumpkins turned out to be as popular as we'd hoped it would be. As for Creepy Crawlers, it turned out that Emma had been right. Plenty of people were eager to eat gummy centipedes, candy spiders, and powdered cocoa that looked like dirt. And it wasn't just ten-year-old boys, either. Even a woman I recognized as the head librarian at the Wolfert's Roost Public Library was eager to try it. In fact, she giggled like a little girl as she pulled one of the wriggly candy centipedes out of her scoop of ice cream and stuck the whole thing in her mouth.

It wasn't until late afternoon that things quieted down and I felt I could leave the shop entirely in Emma's hands. As I drove toward the Mashawam Preserve, I was dismayed to see that the sun was already getting low in the sky. Finding my way around in the woods in the dark wasn't exactly something I was likely to be very good at.

But I didn't want to wait any longer. I was too anxious to find out if my hunch was correct.

The sky was rapidly growing darker as I pulled in to the preserve's parking lot. And from the looks of things, in another few minutes I was going to be the only person there. The park closed at sundown, and the three or four cars that remained had their trunks open, with hikers packing away their gear and getting ready to leave.

I climbed out of my truck, dismayed as I watched the last car drive off. I was suddenly all alone in the parking lot, accompanied only by long, eerie shadows and the occasional cry of a bird. The trees rustled ominously. I reminded myself that there was bound to be a breeze up here. Nothing strange about that.

I didn't waste any time. I walked right up to the chain-link fence I'd spotted two days earlier during my hike with Brody.

And I realized that it was probably just as well that no one else was around. I was about to break the law. Or at least do something I wasn't supposed to do.

I glanced around, but I didn't spot any security cameras. So I took a deep breath and began to climb.

Even though I'm not particularly athletic, I'm pretty strong. Maybe hours of standing behind a counter, scooping out ice cream, has helped build the muscles of my arms and legs. But whether or not I had ice cream to thank, I was surprised at how easy I found it to scale that fence. Grabbing the metal with both hands, sticking my toe in, and hauling myself upward brought back childhood memories of having done this before, even though I couldn't remember the exact circumstances.

I'd just reached the top and was about to sling my right leg over the top when I heard a loud *snap*.

I froze.

A few seconds later, as my heart pounded away wildly, I finally dared to look over my shoulder. I expected to see a uniformed park ranger standing below, scowling.

Nothing.

I must be imagining things, I thought, sharply breathing in some fresh air. Or maybe I'd just heard an animal. Or the wind.

I climbed over the top and made my way down, jumping off the fence and onto the dirt path below. Tall trees surrounded me, casting more of those long, creepy shadows ahead of me.

I really should have researched bears, I told myself as I began to walk. As in whether or not there are likely to be any lurking in the woods around here.

But part of me felt that bears weren't the only thing I had to worry about.

And then I heard another unexpected noise. This one was

different. It was more like a cry. A human cry. As if someone had tripped or encountered something unexpected . . .

No one is following you, I told myself firmly. You're just nervous, being out here in the woods all alone, with the sun going down and you sneaking into an area of the park where no one is supposed to go . . .

I quickened my pace. By now I was nearly jogging along the path. Finishing my mission before it got completely dark was starting to feel more and more urgent.

And then I heard another snap.

I whirled my head around, certain this time that this wasn't merely something I'd imagined. And whatever had made that noise wasn't some innocent woodland creature.

Either my imagination was playing cruel tricks on me or someone was following me.

"Who's there?" I called.

The only response was silence.

You're just imagining things, I scolded myself. And who wouldn't, walking around the woods all alone like this? You really have to cut down on the caffeine, young lady. Perhaps even start eating less Cappuccino Crunch. Or maybe create a decaf version.

I walked on, even though I was beginning to wonder if I'd made a mistake in coming here. The farther I got, without any results, the more this mission of mine was starting to seem like a waste of time.

And then I stopped. My mouth had suddenly become dry, and my heart had begun racing again. And this time, my reaction had nothing to do with imaginary sounds.

Directly in front of me was a sign that said, FUTURE HOME OF HUDSON HIDEAWAYS.

Hudson Hideaways—*here*? I thought. On public land? Land that's supposed to be preserved for, well, for forever?

I walked a little farther and let out a gasp. Just beyond the sign was a construction site.

Not just any construction site, either. This one was on such a tremendous scale that it would have seemed horribly out of place anywhere in the Hudson Valley, much less in the middle of a preserve.

There must have been a hundred condos under construction. Spread out before me were row after row of half-built brick town houses, each one two stories high. There was a driveway in front of each, along with a small yard. Dirt roads connected them, but to judge by the size of the trucks parked nearby, I got the feeling that they'd be paved roads before long.

I felt sick. The fact that the gears were turning in my head, putting together all the pieces of the puzzle, did little to alleviate the fact that what I had found was so ugly that I could barely process it.

Alpha Industries had been involved in an illegal construction project. The company must have paid off local officials or engaged in some other type of corrupt practices, unethically gaining the right to build a housing development smack in the middle of a preserve.

And Savannah Crane had found out about it.

I was about to take my line of reasoning to the next step when I heard another strange noise. This time, it was a rustling, followed by a thump that was definitely a human foot landing hard on the dirt-covered road.

And it sounded as if it was right behind me.

I whirled around, instinctively balling my hands into fists. Then I let out a cry as I found myself face-to-face with a tall lean figure dressed entirely in black, including a ski mask that completely concealed my stalker's face.

Chapter 14

The Klondike bar was created by the Isaly Dairy
Company in Mansfield, Ohio, which was founded
in the early 1900s by William Isaly, the son of
Swiss immigrants. It was made by hand-dipping
square pieces of homemade ice cream into Swiss
milk chocolate. In 1922, the company released
five flavors of the chocolate-covered bars: vanilla,
chocolate, strawberry, maple, and cherry.

—https://www.klondikebar.com/about .

"Get away from me!" I yelled, feeling the adrenaline
shooting through my veins like a drug.

Every one of my muscles was tense. I was poised to run.
But the terrifying ninja standing in front of me was blocking
my way.

I was also ready to fight, even though I felt fairly helpless
since I had nothing to use as a weapon. I looked around,
frantically searching for a stick or a rock.

But before I had a chance to either fight or flee, the figure
in front of me whipped off the ski mask.

She was a woman. A tall, thin, beautiful woman who shook
out a thick mane of long, jet-black hair.

"I'm sorry if I scared you," she said, flashing me a brilliant
smile.

As soon as I saw that smile, I knew who she was. In some remote part of my brain, stored away with other useless bits of information like my old gym locker combination and Grams's foolproof recipe for perfect cornbread, was the image of this face and the name that went with it.

"You're Jennifer Jordan, aren't you?" I said, feeling as if I was finally emerging from the state of shock I'd been in.

"That's me," she replied. Grimacing, she said, "Which is why I'm wearing this ridiculous getup. You're not the only person who's likely to recognize me. I was afraid I'd run into a bunch of hikers or a Girl Scout troop who'd start hounding me for pictures or an autograph."

With a sigh, she added, "It's the price of fame. It turns out that being a celebrity isn't all it's cracked up to be."

My momentary sense of relief faded as I remembered that Jennifer Jordan was a suspect in Savannah Crane's murder. She was also someone who had followed me deep into the woods, secretively trailing me as I headed into an isolated place.

Not a good sign.

"I'm not alone," I said, raising my chin defiantly. "I'm here with a group of people. In fact, I'm sure they're looking for me—"

"Of course you're alone," she interrupted. "I've been following you since you got out of your car." With a shrug, she said, "But by now I hope you've realized that I'm not exactly someone you should be afraid of."

I had to admit that she had a point. Even here in the woods, with she and I the only people around for miles, it was hard to believe that this disarming woman was a cold-blooded killer. Then again, I'd misjudged people before.

"I thought you'd gone into hiding," I said boldly. "Everyone is saying you've disappeared."

She raised her eyebrows. "Me—disappeared? What are you talking about?"

"The tabloids are saying that you vanished right after Savannah Crane's murder," I explained.

"I didn't *vanish*," she said, sounding even more exasperated. She thought for a few seconds. "I did make a point of staying out of sight, though. I was afraid that those ridiculous supermarket tabloids would drag out those silly stories about us hating each other."

"Do you mean it's not true that you two were archenemies?" I asked.

"It's true that Savannah and I have known each other since our days together in acting school," Jennifer said, sounding frustrated. "And, of course, she and I ended up auditioning for some of the same roles. But so did a hundred other actresses. Sometimes she got the role, sometimes I got it, and most of the time someone else entirely got it. That doesn't mean we hated each other. No one could survive in show business if people took things like that personally."

"But what about the starring role in *Ten Days*?" I demanded. "I heard that you desperately wanted that part."

"Are you kidding? Savannah was *made* for that role," she insisted. "The willowy blond ingénue? That's her to a T. And not me at all." With a sigh, she added, "She would have been amazing in it. It would have turned her into a megastar, and she totally deserved it."

"So if you're not in hiding because of Savannah Crane's murder," I asked, "what are you doing in the Hudson Valley? And why are you in a preserve, following me?"

"Because I wanted to find out for myself if this horrendous housing development had anything to do with what happened to Savannah," Jennifer replied, her big brown eyes filling with tears.

"So you knew about Hudson Hideaways," I said.

She nodded. "I was one of the earliest investors."

The wheels in my brain immediately started to turn. In my mind, as big as a movie screen, I could see the list I'd found in Savannah Crane's files.

So Coo had been right. HH stood for Hudson Hideaways, this sprawling condo complex that was being built illegally in the middle of a preserve. As for the list of names, since Jennifer Jordan was one of the investors, I suspected that everyone else on that list was an investor, too. And every one of those people was someone Jennifer knew personally.

Wanting to confirm what I'd just concluded, I said, "So you invested in Hudson Hideaways, like Savannah's friend Amanda Huffner and the director Ragnar Bruin . . ."

"That's right," Jennifer agreed. "A bunch of people who knew her invested back when we were still operating under the delusion that this was a legitimate development project."

Thoughtfully, she added, "It wasn't until Savannah got in touch with me a few weeks ago that I found out the ugly truth. Alpha had been working with local politicians to gain access to preserved land, bribing them to get them to quietly change its status. Needless to say, it was all done behind closed doors. I knew what a serious risk Savannah was taking by telling me. The whole idea was that no one would find out until Hudson Hideaways had already been built and it was too late."

She paused, then said, "I guess Savannah felt partly responsible since she worked at Alpha. And because of Timothy, too, of course."

"Timothy?" I asked, my ears pricking up. "What did he have to do with Hudson Hideaways?"

Jennifer looked surprised by my question. "He's the one who pitched it to all of us."

"So Timothy was involved in the corruption behind Hudson Hideaways," I said breathlessly, thinking aloud.

"He was up to his ears in it," she replied angrily. "He'd invested tons of his own money, for one thing. And then he'd apparently asked Savannah for the names of her friends, figuring they'd be more likely to go in on something if it was her boyfriend who was pitching it."

So Timothy had used Savannah to get people to invest in what *he* undoubtedly knew was a shady land-development project.

And then *she* found out.

Savannah had made a point of telling all the investors who were friends of hers. And given my sense of her, I had a feeling she had intended to tell a lot more people as soon as she got a chance. Which was why someone who was deeply involved in the project had felt motivated to keep her from doing exactly that.

And that someone, I fully believed, had been Timothy.

I noticed that Jennifer had gone on a few steps farther and was gazing out at the huge construction site that stretched just beyond the spot where we were standing.

"So this is it," I heard Jennifer say mournfully, breaking me out of my reverie. "This is the crummy housing development that cost Savannah Crane her life."

"We don't know that for sure," I said. "I mean, nothing has been proved yet . . ."

But Jennifer looked over at me, and our eyes met as a moment of understanding passed between us.

We were both silent for a few moments, staring at the ugly construction site in front of us. Dozens of tall, magnificent trees had been chopped down and now stood in haphazard piles next to bright yellow tractors and cranes. There were huge, gaping holes behind the houses that were already half-built, marking the places where more buildings would be put up. The ground looked raw, as if it was wounded.

The image was made even worse by the long shadows draped

everywhere like shrouds. Which jolted me back to the reality that the sun was on the verge of setting.

"We should get back," I said. "It's almost dark, and I don't know my way around this place very well."

"The trail is pretty decent," Jennifer said. "My phone has a great flashlight app. But you're right: we should head out." Sadly, she added, "Besides, we're done here. We both saw what we came to see."

"Would you like to come back to my house?" I offered as we started back along the trail. "You could join my family and me for dinner. We even have a guest room where you're welcome to spend the night. But I'm warning you that my grandmother and my niece will both make a terrible fuss over you. You'll have to pose for photos, give autographs—"

"Thanks, but I'm heading back to the city," she said. "I've got to get home. I'm actually in the middle of negotiations for a new movie. The project is just getting off the ground, so the trade papers haven't even written about it yet."

"That sounds exciting," I commented.

"It truly is," she said. "It's an independent movie that focuses on an issue I care about deeply. I'm pretty sure it's going to make a big difference in the way people see things." Grinning, she added, "It's also a once-in-a-lifetime role. Perhaps even one that's Oscar-worthy."

"So your career is about to get back on track," I observed. And then I realized what I'd just said. "Sorry! It's only that I read something online—"

She laughed. "Believe me, I'm used to not having any privacy. And it's true that my career has been in a slump lately. But I really think this new film is going to turn things around for me."

"I'm glad," I told her. And I meant it.

"But can I ask you for one small thing?" I asked as the parking lot came into view. "Could I please get your autograph for my niece? It would mean so much to her."

"It sounds as if you and I should take a selfie together, too," Jennifer said. "You don't want this niece of yours to stop speaking to you, do you?"

A few minutes later, as I watched Jennifer ride away in the taxi that had brought her to the preserve an hour earlier, I was warmed by what a nice person she had turned out to be.

She had also given me some valuable information.

Information that had fully convinced me that it was Timothy who had killed Savannah.

He certainly had a strong motivation. It was very likely that she was about to ruin him. And the fact that she was on the verge of being catapulted to national and even international fame was part of it. While his corrupt dealings were likely to have caught up with him at some point, perhaps even sending him to prison, Savannah's new celebrity status would have enabled her to blow up the story and smear his name on an even larger scale.

The fact that their personal relationship had deteriorated so badly convinced me of his guilt even further. The man had been having an affair, which meant that there was no reason for him to feel protective toward her any longer. His loyalties had clearly shifted elsewhere.

Only one piece of the story was still missing: how he had managed to do it. And at this point, I was hungrier than ever to figure that out.

Which meant getting in touch with someone who was likely to have that information—whether she realized it or not.

Chelsea Atkins was the one person who I knew had been in Lickety Splits the entire time before Savannah's death, which meant she had to have been there when the murderer put poison in the ice cream dish. It was true that she'd been busy, coordinating all the chaos that went along with turning my shop into a movie set. But she was *there*, and she had therefore seen everyone else who had been there.

If someone who wasn't part of the regular crew had been in Lickety Splits for even a few moments, she would know about it.

I tried texting her as soon as I climbed into my truck. Not surprisingly, my phone informed me that there was no service up here in the mountains.

I made a mental note to get in touch with her as soon as I got to my shop. By the time I drove into Wolfert's Roost, I had decided what the text would say. It would definitely include the word "urgent" and it would contain several exclamation points.

It was completely dark by then, with a handful of stars and only a sliver of a moon. While Hudson Street was lit up by streetlights, the fact that it was a Saturday night meant that most of the shops I drove past were closed. All the lights were out at the cheese shop, Let It Brie. The quilt shop, Stitchin' Time, looked positively spooky. The same went for the florist, Petal Pushers, and the hair salon, Lotsa Locks. At least Brody's shop, right across the street from Lickety Splits, was open. But from the looks of things, not much was going on in there.

Things in town seemed so sleepy tonight that I wondered if Lickety Splits was getting any customers. Saturday night usually brought out quite a few people: teenagers hanging out downtown, couples who had just had dinner at one of the restaurants, dog walkers, even day-trippers in search of one more bit of fun before heading back to wherever they'd come from. But tonight, for some reason, downtown felt strangely still.

There were lots of free parking spots, and I spotted one a few doors down from Lickety Splits. As I headed toward it, I rode past my shop.

As I did, I suddenly let out a sound that was a cross between a gasp and a scream. Abruptly, I slammed on the brakes, then rolled down the window as I tried to get a better look at what I thought I was seeing.

Sure enough; it was exactly what I'd thought it was.

Lying on the sidewalk in front of Lickety Splits was the body of what appeared to be a large man. And protruding from his chest was a dagger.

Chapter 15

August 6 is National Root Beer Float Day, honoring the treat consisting of a scoop of vanilla ice cream floating in a mug of ice-cold root beer. The root beer float, also known as a "Black Cow," is believed to have been invented in a mining camp by Frank J. Wisner, the owner of the Cripple Creek Cow Mountain Gold Mining Company.

—https://nationaldaycalendar/national-root-beer-float-day-august-6/

Stay calm, I told myself, aware that my heart was pounding away at jackhammer speed. *Before you deal with this, you have to park the truck.*

Doing my best to remain in control of my vehicle—and not cause any accidents—I pulled into the parking space I'd been heading for. My hands were shaking as I switched off the ignition. Part of me thought that the next thing I should do was call 911. But another part of me wanted to investigate before taking any action at all.

So I climbed out of my truck, my cell phone in hand. As I walked toward my shop, I switched on its flashlight. But when I was still a good thirty feet away from Lickety Splits, I suddenly understood what I was looking at.

The man who was lying on the sidewalk was the Frankenstein monster that Emma had created.

But even though *he* wasn't real, the knife that was sticking out of his papier-mâché chest appeared to be *very* real. I leaned down to get a better look, taking care not to touch it, and saw that it was a kitchen knife. From the clean incision it had made into the dummy's paste-and-newspaper chest, it was a very *sharp* kitchen knife.

If this had been any other Halloween season, I might have found it humorous. Clever, even.

But not this Halloween. Not when the sick feeling in the pit of my stomach bore out the first thought that came to mind: that this was meant to be a warning.

Suddenly, I remembered that Emma was alone inside Lickety Splits. I rushed inside, a wave of panic rushing over me.

But it faded as soon as I spotted her standing behind the counter. She was cheerfully chatting with two women who were about Grams's age, meanwhile scooping up a generous amount of Honey Lavender and pushing it down into a sugar cone.

I resisted the urge to ask her if she was all right—at least, until the two customers left, exclaiming over the deliciousness of the Honey Lavender and Cashew Brittle with Sea Salt cones they were carrying out.

"Emma, are you okay?" I demanded.

She looked surprised. "Why wouldn't I be?"

"Did you hear anything strange going on outside?" I asked. "Did you see anyone who was acting funny? Did any of the customers say anything about Frankenstein—?"

"Frankenstein?" Emma repeated, clearly puzzled by all the bizarre questions that were flowing out of my mouth, one after another. " 'Anything strange?' Kate, what are you talking about?"

I took a deep breath. "Someone vandalized your Frankenstein monster."

"Oh, no!" she cried, already dashing toward the door. "Is he okay?"

Something about her question struck me as ridiculously funny. Maybe it was a reaction to all the tension of the day or maybe it was simply because I was so tired, but I burst out into uncontrollable laughter.

"Emma, he's not real!" I cried. "Of course, he's okay! Or at least he will be as soon as you patch him up with a little duct tape!"

The look on my niece's face told me she still didn't understand what was going on. Also, that she thought her aunt had lost her mind.

But she hurried outside. I heard a yelp of dismay, and a few seconds later she was back in the shop.

"What does this mean, Kate?" she cried. "Is someone playing a practical joke?"

"That's probably all it is," I told her, realizing that there was no point in frightening her. Especially since I was feeling much calmer now that I was standing in my brightly lit shop, surrounded by multiple tubs of ice cream and one of my favorite people in the entire universe.

And I told myself that that really could be the case. After all, it *was* possible that someone who had wandered by had simply thought that stabbing Frankenstein with a knife would be a good practical joke, a special touch that would carry the horror-themed decorations of my shop to a new level. After all, the young man who'd come into Lickety Splits right after Savannah Crane's murder had assumed that the crime-scene tape was part of my store's tribute to Halloween.

But would that random person happen to have a kitchen knife with him or her? I immediately wondered, that uneasy feeling coming right back. Not very likely. And it wasn't much more likely that the prankster would have been motivated enough to go home to get one, come all the way back, and then carry out what he or she thought was nothing more than a lighthearted bit of theater.

While I would have liked to believe that an attempt at humor was all that was behind this, deep down I knew that Frankenstein had been used to send me a warning. Someone wanted me to know that it was time to abandon my unofficial investigation of Savannah Crane's murder.

If not, that person was telling me, I might end up in the same sorry state as Frankenstein. The difference, of course, was that *I* wasn't made of paper and paste.

In the end, I decided not to tell Detective Stoltz about this incident. At least not yet.

After all, by this point I was fairly certain that I'd identified Savannah's killer. But before I went to Stoltz with my theory, I wanted to talk to Chelsea Atkins. I needed to find out if she'd spotted Timothy Scott at Lickety Splits in the hours before the murder.

I went ahead and texted her, using the word "urgent" and the three exclamation points I'd already decided to include. Then, all I could do was wait.

Since it was a Saturday night, I knew it was unlikely that I'd hear back from Chelsea right away. But that didn't keep me from checking my cell phone every two minutes as Emma and I dragged poor Frankenstein into the shop.

Watching Emma pull that knife out of him was wrenching. Even though she was chattering away, explaining that all she needed to do to fix him up was glue a few strips of painted newspaper over his chest, I couldn't stop thinking about the fact that whoever had done this had the ability to do the exact same thing to me.

I was actually glad that we didn't have many customers that night. And I let Emma handle most of the ice cream seekers who wandered in. I was so preoccupied that I was afraid someone would order Mint Chocolate Chip and instead I'd give them Pistachio 'n' Almond 'n' Fudge Swirl.

My agitated mood continued for the rest of the night. I barely slept, instead wrestling with my sheets and blanket and even my poor pillow. And the few times I did manage to doze off, Timothy's face loomed large in my nightmares.

I was obsessed with proving that he had come into Lickety Splits before the shoot. And I desperately hoped that Chelsea would be able to verify that he had been there, even if only for a minute or two.

The next morning, instead of feeling groggy, I was pumped up with adrenaline from the moment the sun peeked in my window. I jumped out of bed, threw on some clothes, and made a big pot of coffee. As soon as I fueled up, I went off to Lickety Splits. It was still ridiculously early, and given my agitated state, I didn't think I could be quiet enough to keep from waking Emma or Grams way too early on this Sunday morning.

Once I was in my shop, I didn't feel like whipping up fresh batches of ice cream or doing paperwork. Instead, I sat at one of the tables, just thinking.

And trying to will Chelsea to call me back.

When my cell phone finally did buzz, I grabbed it before the first ring had ended. I assumed it was Chelsea. So I was disappointed when I recognized the number as Coo's cell phone.

"Is it too early to call?" she asked anxiously.

"It's fine," I assured her. "I've been up for ages."

I was about to tell her about what I'd learned from Jennifer Jordan—and that I was now convinced that Timothy had killed Savannah. But before I had a chance, she jumped right in with, "I'm sorry, Kate, but even though I scoured the office yesterday, I couldn't find out a single thing about Hudson Hideaways. I even brought home a bunch of files to look through, which is why it's taken me so long to get back to you. I'm here at the office again this morning, still looking. But I'm coming up empty."

She let out a frustrated sigh. "And it doesn't make any sense at all! I know for a fact that it was a property Alpha was developing. I heard people talking about it all the time. But it's as if every shred of paper mentioning it has suddenly vanished."

"Are you sure you looked everywhere?" I asked.

"Absolutely," she insisted. "I even looked through the big boss's files. Or at least I tried to. His secretary's cubicle is right outside his office, and she's got a couple of big file cabinets where she meticulously files every single paper that crosses her desk. I looked through every drawer, but I couldn't find a thing about Hudson Hideaways. It just doesn't make any sense."

"I suppose he could have kept his files in his own office," I said, thinking aloud.

"Good point," Coo agreed. "But that's one place I couldn't look. I'm afraid that good old G.V. keeps his office locked, at least over the weekends."

"G.V.?" I repeated, even though I pretty much knew she was referring to the head of Alpha.

"That's what we call him around the office," she said lightly. "G.V. for George Vernon."

All the blood in my body had turned to ice. "George Vernon?" I repeated, barely able to get the words out.

"That's right," Coo said. "George Vernon Scott. He's the CEO of Alpha Industries. Of course, he's not in the office much these days, since he's in the process of retiring. Not that he's ever been that involved with the day-to-day workings of the company. He's got his minions to do that. Like me," she added with a chuckle.

But I wasn't laughing. "You're telling me that George Vernon is the name of the CEO of Alpha Industries?" I repeated, saying the words aloud as a way of trying to understand them.

"Yes, that's right," Coo said, sounding puzzled by my question. "George Vernon Scott."

"And the man is Timothy's father," I said, still attempting to digest what I'd just learned.

"Right . . ."

I felt both a rush of understanding and a wave of confusion rushing over me at the same time, something I never would have thought was possible.

Everything about George Vernon had been a lie—starting with his name. He had used only his first and middle names to keep Grams and me and everyone else from knowing his true identity.

Then there was his claim that he was retired. Another lie. While he'd pretended to be playing golf a few days a week, in reality he had been going into the city to run his company, Alpha Industries.

And at Thursday night's dinner, he had acted as if he'd never heard of Savannah Crane. Yet she had been an employee he had hired himself, as well as his son's girlfriend—perhaps even his fiancée.

One more lie. A really *big* lie.

That same evening, he had also learned that I was investigating the crime. Which could have led him to vandalize Frankenstein as a warning to me.

My head was spinning. Was it possible that George Vernon Scott had been involved in Savannah's murder? Here I had been so certain that Timothy was responsible. But George was Timothy's father, which only muddied the waters even further . . .

"Coo, I have to go," I said abruptly.

"Sorry I couldn't be more helpful," she said.

I didn't bother to explain that she had been more helpful than she could imagine.

After I hung up, I put down my phone and buried my face in my hands, struggling to focus on the hurricane of thoughts whirling around in my head. But before I had a chance to calm down enough to even begin to sort through them, the door to my shop opened. And in walked Chelsea Atkins.

Chapter 16

The first cookbook in history devoted entirely to
ice creams and sorbets was M. Emy's *L'art de Bien
Faire les Glaces d'Office* (The Art of Making
Frozen Desserts), published in France in 1768.
The title page from the book illustrates a common
opinion of the day that ice cream was a "food fit
for the gods."

—We All Scream for Ice Cream! The Scoop on America's
Favorite Dessert *by Lee Wardlaw*

"You didn't have to come to the shop," I told her. "A
phone call would have been fine."

Chelsea let out a cold laugh. "As if I have anything else
to do. Until this case is cleared up—or until that creepy Detective Stoltz tells me I can leave—I can't go back home to
California. I'm just twiddling my thumbs up here in the
boondocks." Glancing around my shop, she added, "Coming
here actually gave me something to do this morning."

She plopped down at a table. "So tell me: What's so urgent?"

I decided to jump right in. "Chelsea, are you sure no one
came onto the set who didn't belong there?"

"Positive," she replied without hesitation. "Kate, I've been
over this with you before. The police, too, more times than I
care to think about."

"What about Savannah's boyfriend, Timothy?" I asked. "Maybe he stopped in just for a minute . . . ?"

She shook her head. She was clearly growing exasperated as she said, "I'm telling you, Kate, I didn't see anyone who wasn't part of the crew. And Stoltz has questioned them all and concluded that he doesn't have reason to suspect any of them."

I thought for a few seconds, then asked, "Who handled the props for *The Best Ten Days*?" I held my breath as I waited for her answer. Amanda had claimed her company hadn't been involved with this film. But I now knew that she had a penchant for lying.

But I discovered that this time she had been telling the truth when Chelsea replied, "A company called CineProps. They're based in New Jersey. Why?"

"It's a long story," I told her. "But let me ask you something else: do you know Amanda Huffner?"

Chelsea shrugged. "I've never heard of her. Who is she?"

"She was, or at least she says she was, Savannah Crane's best friend," I said. "She also happens to work at a props house, which is why I wondered if she had an excuse to be involved with this film. I thought she might have come onto the set the night before the shoot or early that morning. But the company she works for is called Monarch."

"I've worked with Monarch plenty of times in the past, but not on this film." Scowling, she added, "Honestly, the only people who were there besides the crew members were the people who work for you. All those cheerful people dressed in those bright-pink polo shirts . . ."

Even though I knew that no one from my 'Cream Team had had anything to do with any of this, I said, "Tell me exactly who you remember being there." I knew the answer to this question was beyond obvious, since I had been myself

there with Emma, Ethan, and Willow. But I wanted to be absolutely certain I was covering every possible angle.

Chelsea scrunched up her face thoughtfully. "Okay, let
me see if I've got this right. You, of course. Then there was
the young woman with the curly black hair and the blue
streaks . . ."

"My niece, Emma," I told her.

"Right. Then there was another woman, probably around
thirty," Chelsea went on. "She had short hair. Really light
blond, like almost white."

"That's Willow," I said.

"Right. Then there were the two men—"

I froze. "Two men?" I repeated.

"Yes," she replied. "The young one and the old one."

My heart had begun pounding, and the room suddenly felt
very warm.

"Can you describe them?" I asked, trying to sound matter-
of-fact.

"Sure," Chelsea said. "The young one—he was probably
eighteen or nineteen—had straight black hair that kept
falling in his eyes."

"That's Ethan," I said. "Emma's boyfriend."

"Then there was the older guy," Chelsea went on. "He was
only here Wednesday night for the setup, though. He didn't
show up again on Thursday morning for the actual filming."

"But *I* was at Lickety Splits Thursday night, too," I reminded her, confused. "Only the four of us were there. Emma,
Willow, Ethan, and me."

Chelsea shook her head. "He wasn't here the same time
you were. He came in afterward. Right after you left, in fact."

"What did this man look like?" I asked, still struggling to
keep my voice even.

"Let's see," Chelsea said thoughtfully. "He was nice-looking.
Tall and lean, without that paunch that a lot of old men get.

Gray hair, or more like silver maybe . . . and he had this cute habit. It struck me as kind of old-fashioned, but in a charming way."

"What habit?" I asked. By this point, my heart was threatening to burst out of my chest.

"He winked at me," she replied. "Twice. It wasn't flirtatious or anything. It was his way of punctuating what he was saying. Like we were both in on some inside joke."

By that point I thought I really *was* going to explode.

The man she was describing was George Vernon.

Or, more accurately, George Vernon Scott, the CEO of Alpha Industries. The man Savannah Crane had been on the verge of destroying by going public about the corrupt land-development deal he and his company were involved with.

"So this man with the silver hair and the wink came to the shop after the rest of the Lickety Splits employees were gone?" I asked, trying to reconstruct what had happened.

"That's right," Chelsea said. "A few minutes after you and the other three people you mentioned left, he came into the shop. He was wearing a pink shirt, just like I'd seen you and your employees wearing. He said he had to do something with the ice cream or it would all go bad. I didn't want that to happen, so I let him do whatever he had to do."

"Did you see what he did?" I asked.

"No," she said. "I didn't see any reason to pay any attention to what he was up to. I figured he worked for you and that he was simply taking care of business as usual."

"And you're sure he was wearing a pink shirt?"

"That's right," Chelsea replied. "I'm positive about that, since I was thinking about how unusual it was for a dignified older man like him to wear a shirt that was the color of bubble gum—even if it was part of a uniform." She added, "That's why I figured he really must be a Lickety Splits employee."

I was still puzzling over how George had gotten hold of a Lickety Splits shirt when another thought occurred to me.

"By any chance, do you remember if the shirt he was wearing actually had the Lickety Splits logo on it?" I asked.

Chelsea shrugged. "I have no idea. There was so much going on that there was no way I would have noticed a detail like that."

By now, I was able to picture the entire scenario in my mind. George had staked out Lickety Splits, watching the door of the shop from a distance. Once he saw me leave with Emma, Ethan, and Willow, he had come into the shop, pretending that he worked for me. And in order to carry off that little charade, he had worn a pink shirt that was similar in color to the real Lickety Splits T-shirts.

I found myself replaying the conversation I'd had with Amanda when I'd stopped in to see her at work. After she'd pointed out the importance of the props fitting in with the time and place in which the scene was set, I'd commented, "It makes perfect sense that everything has to belong. Part of your job is to make sure everything looks as if it should be there."

Which is exactly what George had done. He had taken great care to make sure he looked as if he belonged at Lickety Splits.

Once he had access to the shop and everything in it, it would have been easy for him to put poison into the ice cream dish that Savannah Crane was going to eat out of. The dish was already out on the table, so he would have had no trouble identifying it. And everyone around him would have been too involved in what they were doing to pay attention to what George was doing.

He was also someone who had returned to the scene of the crime, which was exactly what Detective Stoltz had told me the killer was likely to do. George had come into Lickety Splits a week after Savannah's murder, pretending to ask me about where I thought his relationship with Grams was going.

Now I knew that wasn't the real reason he had come to my shop.

I had been silent for a long time as my mind clicked away. Chelsea must have been growing concerned because she said, "Kate? Are you okay?"

"I'm fine," I assured her, even though at the moment I was feeling anything but fine.

"Do you know who this man is?" she asked anxiously. "It sounds like maybe he wasn't really someone who worked for you."

"I know exactly who he is," I told her.

"Do you think he had anything to do with—?"

But I didn't answer her. I was too busy calling Detective Stoltz.

Even though the age of technology is supposed to make communicating a breeze, it doesn't always play out that way.

Detective Stoltz didn't answer his phone. Instead, I got an annoying message encouraging me to leave a detailed message. I did.

"Detective Stoltz, this is Kate McKay," I said, doing my best not to speak too quickly. "I just found out something really important about what happened at Lickety Splits the night before Savannah Crane's murder. There's a man in town that I'm sure you haven't even considered a suspect. His name is George Vernon Scott, and he's the CEO of a company called Alpha Industries. Savannah worked at his firm. I learned from another employee that Savannah had found out something terrible concerning George's business dealings and she was going to go public with it.

"In addition to that, I just discovered that George snuck into my shop the night before the murder," I went on, by now unable to resist the impulse to talk faster and faster. "The way he managed that is that he was wearing a pink shirt, which people on the set assumed was the same shirt that Lickety Splits' employees wear. The fact that he was here during the setup for the shoot means he could easily have put poison in the ice cream dish that Savannah was going to be eating out of the following morning, and—"

A shrill beep told me that my time had run out. All I could do was hope that Detective Stoltz called me back right away.

In the meantime, I had another important call to make. One that was related to the new realization that was throbbing in my head like a migraine headache: my grandmother was dating a murderer.

It took four rings before anyone at the house answered.

"Come on, come on . . . ," I whispered, ready to jump out of my skin as I listened to what seemed like endless rings.

It was Emma who finally picked up, greeting me with a cheerful, "Hey, Kate!"

"Put Grams on," I demanded.

"She's not here," she replied, the tone of her voice immediately changing. "Kate, what's wrong?"

"Where is she?" I asked, not wanting to take the time to explain.

"She went to the high school gym," Emma said. "She said she planned to meet George there nice and early this morning because they still had a lot to get done on—"

My sense of urgency had instantly escalated into near-panic mode.

"I'll call her there."

"What's going on?" Emma demanded.

I ended the call without answering her question. Then, with shaking hands, I pressed the keys required to call Grams's cell phone.

It rang and rang, my frustration practically making me

jump up and down. Finally, I heard the beginning of her taped message: "Hi! This is Caroline! I can't answer the phone right now—"

"I have to leave," I told Chelsea. She was still sitting opposite me, her expression a combination of confusion, astonishment, and alarm. "Just pull the door closed after you."

I grabbed my jacket and my purse, fumbling for my keys as I dashed out of my shop.

At this very moment, Grams was alone at the gym with a murderer. Which meant I had to get there fast.

I grabbed my jacket and purse, dashed out of Lickety Splits, jumped into my truck, and careened toward the high school. This was one time that I hoped going over the speed limit would attract the attention of Pete Bonano or some other local cop. I could have used the help.

There were hardly any cars in the section of the school parking lot that was closest to the gym. I wasn't surprised, given that it was still early on a Sunday morning. In fact, the only two cars I saw were Grams's gray Corolla and, three or four spaces away, George's black sports car.

I raced around the school building, trying three different doors before I finally found one that opened. Once inside, I ran through the corridors, glad that I still knew my way around the building.

When I neared the gym's double doors, I slowed down. My heart was pounding, and my mouth was dry. As I grabbed one of the handles, I paused to take a few deep breaths.

Finally, I opened the door cautiously and peered inside. I had expected to find the gym in the same condition as the last time I'd been here: a busy, brightly lit space filled with activity.

Instead, the gym was strangely dark. Glancing up, I saw that the windows high above the bleachers had been covered with black paper.

I blinked hard several times, trying to get my eyes to adjust to my dimly lit surroundings. Gradually, I was able to see that there were spots of light in the cavernous space: candles flickering in the windows of the haunted house, pale lights behind the grotesque grins of the jack-o'-lanterns scattered across the fake lawn, strings of orange, pumpkin-shaped lights draped throughout the room.

I had already decided that my strategy should be to start out acting as if nothing was wrong.

"Grams, are you here?" I called gaily. "It's me, Kate. I thought I'd stop by to see how Halloween Hollow is shaping up!"

"Stop right there!" I heard George's voice reply. "I've got your grandmother. And I've got a gun! Don't come any closer or you'll both be sorry!"

Chapter 17

The Joy Ice Cream Cone Company was founded
in 1918 by a Lebanese immigrant named Albert
George when he and members of his family
bought second-hand cone-baking machines and
started the George & Thomas Cone Company.
Today it is the world's largest ice cream cone company. It produces over 1.5 billion cones a year.

—https://www.joycone.com/about-us

It took me a few seconds to locate him. I could barely make
out his silhouette, since he was standing behind one of the
gnarled trees at the side of the haunted house, half-hidden by
shadows. I could also see part of someone else's head, close
to his shoulder as if he was grasping that person with one
arm.

Grams.

I felt sick. I knew I had to react, to do something. But I still
didn't know enough about what was going on to know what
that should be.

"What's going on, George?" I asked, trying to sound as
calm as I could. "It seems there's been some kind of misunderstanding—"

"There's no misunderstanding," he interrupted, his voice
seething with anger. "I know all about everything you've been

up to. I've been tracking every move you've made over the past week, ever since you showed up at Alpha."

I gasped. "How did you know about that?"

His response was a cold laugh. "I know everything that goes on there," he replied. "I had my company's offices outfitted with the best security system in the world. I watched you show up there myself, in real time. Frankly, I was astonished when your face appeared on my computer screen."

The man tracks the comings and goings of everyone who works at his company, I marveled. He even monitors every outsider who comes in—including me.

"I immediately got a bad feeling about what you were up to," he went on. "Why else would you be poking around the place where Savannah Crane worked? And when I came to Caroline's house for dinner, you were totally up front about taking it upon yourself to play the role of amateur sleuth.

"So I started paying even closer attention," he continued, "not only to you, but also to everything else that was going on at Alpha. Which is how I happened to catch Cornelia Jameson sneaking around the offices yesterday, going through files. Even *my* files! As if I'd be foolish enough to leave a paper trail, especially after the way all this has played out! But that woman has crossed a line. I can assure you that she'll be fired first thing tomorrow."

She might not want to work there anymore anyway, I was thinking. That is, if Alpha Industries even *exists* after all this comes out . . .

"And, of course, I heard the phone conversations the two of you had about Hudson Hideaways," George declared.

"You bugged her cell phone?" I asked, aghast.

"I don't need to bug anyone's phones," he jeered. "Not when I can already hear every word that's spoken within the walls of my company."

But before I had a chance to reconstruct our conversations

in my mind, he added, "I also know that you've been stalking my son. He told me you showed up at his place in Cold Spring the day after Savannah Crane died. He said he also caught you sneaking around his property on Friday night. He thought he heard a prowler, and when he looked out the window, he saw you driving away in your truck."

I noticed that George had referred to the Cold Spring house as Timothy's place.

"That house doesn't belong to your son," I insisted. "It's Savannah's."

Another icy laugh. "Who do you think financed their little love nest, back when it looked as if the two of them were going to be together forever?" Speaking more to himself than to me, he added, "As if that little fool could have afforded a house on her own! She never was someone who understood the importance of money."

"But your son did," I said as matter-of-factly as I could. "He was certainly helpful with the Hudson Hideaways development."

"My son had nothing to do with that project!" George insisted, sounding offended. "Aside from getting a few people to invest in it, that is. He even invested in it himself. He had no idea about the, shall we say, *complications* that surrounded it."

So George knew I'd learned about his shady Hudson Hideaways deal. I was wondering whether he also knew that I'd identified him as Savannah's killer when he said, "Since you found out about Hudson Hideaways in such short order, I knew it was only a question of time before you figured out why that vile woman had to die—and whose job it was to make sure that happened. Then I drove by your shop this morning and saw that person from the film crew walking in, the one who seemed to be running things. I knew you were on the verge of figuring out who the extra Lickety Splits employee was. And that you'd be running to the police as fast as you could, determined to be a hero.

"But what happened to Savannah was her own fault," he continued. "She was on the verge of becoming a big movie star, someone the press would have listened to. Someone all her fans would have been willing to support in whatever she did. She knew that as well as I did. If she'd only agreed to keep her mouth shut, all I'd have had to deal with were a few local tree huggers that my lawyers could have taken care of. And she could have gone on to become the big movie star she wanted to be. But she wouldn't listen. She was determined to use her new star status to blow this up into a national story.

"That stupid girl intended to ruin me!" George cried, spitting out his words. "Going public with what she considered the scandal of the century! She was too naïve to understand that what I was doing was merely business as usual. Alpha has done hundreds of development projects, and believe me, this isn't the first time we've cut some corners. That's simply the way things are done in property development. Hardworking, forward-thinking people like me work together with other like-minded people, sometimes behind the scenes, to accomplish things that some folks in the community might not appreciate until they've actually been achieved. And if people like me can make a little money that way, then good for us.

"And that idiotic actress had no idea how many people—good people—would have been decimated if she'd opened her big mouth," he continued. "Not only me, either. She probably would have destroyed my son's reputation. Then there are all the local officials who had enough vision to be willing to, shall we say, break a few rules in order to make my beautiful new development become a reality."

"Did you move to the Hudson Valley just to make sure Savannah Crane didn't ruin your development deal—and your reputation?" I asked.

"I've had ties to this area for years," he replied. "When I decided to cut back on hours—go into semi-retirement, in a way—this was the obvious place to settle. Then I met your grandmother and, through her, met you and found out that the movie Savannah was making was being filmed in your shop. The perfect opportunity had just fallen into my lap. How could I *not* take advantage of it?"

With a self-satisfied chuckle, he added, "And I've managed to commit what's commonly known as the perfect crime. No one would have ever suspected me. That is, until you came along."

I swallowed hard. "So what happens now?"

He laughed coldly. "You're about to have an unfortunate accident. One that involves a fatal fall." He paused, then said, "And the fact that I'm holding a gun on your beloved grandmother means you're going to do everything I tell you to do so that can happen."

By that point, I was feeling light-headed. Panic was starting to get the best of me.

Stay calm! I instructed myself, taking deep breaths. You need to think your way out of this. Not only for your own sake, either. He's got Grams!

"And we'll start by you going inside the haunted house," George said.

"Inside?" I repeated, the fear I'd been trying to fight off gripping me more ferociously than ever.

"I want you to walk through it, all the way to the back," he said. "And I'd suggest that you step it up. Your grandmother here is starting to look a little pale."

"Whatever you say," I said.

But I had a sense of what his plan was. And I was already hatching a plan of my own.

Walking through the gym toward the haunted house took

me past a disorganized mishmash of supplies. The haphazard pile included building materials, fabric, paper streamers, and several cardboard cartons. One of those cartons, I knew, contained the ingredients for the ice cream sundae station that I'd dropped off a week earlier.

I spotted the box as I walked by the heap. When I was about a foot away from it, I allowed my purse to slide off my shoulder, pretending it was accidental. Quickly I dipped down to grab it. As I did, I picked up something else as well.

And then I had no choice but to go inside the haunted house.

I shuddered as I passed beneath the skull that was hanging over the front door.

It's fake, I reminded myself, noticing that it was glowing in the dim light. Don't even look at it.

As soon as I opened the door, I saw that it was dark enough inside the house that I was going to have difficulty making out my surroundings. My eyes still hadn't adjusted as I stepped inside.

Immediately something white and ghostlike swooshed in front of me, brushing against my face.

"Agh-h-h-h!" I yelled, feeling my pulse triple.

Also not real, I told myself, taking more of those deep breaths. I vaguely remembered George mentioning that he was trying to figure out how to create an effect like that. He'd clearly figured it out.

I assumed that the place was rigged up to be motion sensitive because as I took a few more steps, a strobe light suddenly came on. The effect of the quickly blinking light was jarring. Especially because the room immediately began filling up with puffs of white fog.

The fog machine, I reminded myself. It's nothing more than a silly effect, one that's right out of a Grade B horror movie.

Somehow, it was very effective.

And then I heard strange sounds, soft at first, but quickly growing louder and louder. Low, eerie moans that sounded as if they were coming from something that wasn't quite human. And then, abruptly, the almost hypnotic sound was interrupted by the clanking of chains. I let out a yelp.

"Keep going!" I heard George yell. "Caroline and I are coming into the house right behind you. I've still got a gun on her!"

I hesitated, wondering if I was making a mistake by walking right into the trap that George had obviously set for me. But I didn't have much choice, since he was holding my grandmother at gunpoint. And I was still hoping that I could outsmart him.

I took a few more steps. And felt something brush against my face once again.

But this time it wasn't silky, like the ghost. This was rubbery and cold and—

Spiders! Dozens of spiders were dangling in front of me, the strobe light making them look as if they were swarming around me like bees.

I let out a shriek.

"You're taking too long!" George called to me, his voice angrier than before.

"I'm doing my best," I called back to him weakly.

I did begin to move more quickly, largely to get away from the chilling cloud of spiders brushing against my face and my neck and shoulders. I passed into a second room.

At least there was no strobe light in this one. The light in here was dim, though, just bright enough for me to make out an elaborate chandelier dripping with cobwebs. One wall was mirrors behind a line of life-size skeletons and ghouls and other creepy beings. They stood in pairs on small, rotating platforms that made it appear that they were dancing in front of it. Their dressy evening clothes were tattered, their hair was wild, and their expressions crazed. Soft music played in the background, just off-key enough to sound unpleasant.

And then I felt someone touch me.

I let out another cry, automatically jumping away. It was only then that I saw it was a dry, shriveled hand that jutted out of the wall and was rigged up to grasp whoever walked by.

By that point, I was more than ready to get out of there.

"Where are you?" I demanded. "And where's Grams?"

"We're right behind you," George replied. "Keep going. You're almost there."

I hurried through the ballroom, taking care not to step on the boney feet of the skeleton that was whirling around in front of me, the shreds of its pink skirt dragging on the floor.

Finally, I spotted a door and rushed toward it. As soon as I stepped through it, I encountered a wooden staircase.

I glanced up and saw that it led to the top of the foam pit.

Just as I'd anticipated, this was where George expected me to have my fatal fall.

"Go up the stairs," George commanded.

I began to climb the stairs, every muscle in my body as tense as a tightrope. My mouth was dry, my stomach knotted, and my heart was pounding with sickening force. As I neared the top, I loosened the top of the small bottle I'd grabbed from my box of ice cream ingredients. I desperately hoped I could manage to pull off what I'd planned. But there was one major problem: I didn't know how I could accomplish it without putting Grams at risk.

When I reached the top of the staircase, I found myself standing on the ledge that surrounded the foam pit, just as I'd expected. The deep wooden bowl was still only partly constructed. It was also in the exact condition I'd been anticipating: completely empty.

The gaping hole below me was only half painted, with the boxes of foam rubber that would eventually fill it still stacked up on the ledge that encircled it. Planks of wood jutted out from the sides treacherously. The people who were building this foam pit clearly had a lot of work to do before it would be safe for anyone to use.

I could hear George coming up the stairs. When he reached the top, I saw that he was alone.

"Where's Grams?" I demanded. "What have you done with her?"

He laughed. "She's not here."

I blinked. "But I saw her—"

"What you saw was one of those ridiculous dummies your niece made," he countered gruffly. "That woman hasn't been here the whole time. She's off in some other part of the building, doing an errand I sent her off on."

So he had lied about Grams being held at gunpoint. I was greatly relieved.

I was also relieved that he didn't appear to have a gun after all.

"Here's the plan," he went on, his mouth twisting into an evil grin. "That unfortunate accident I mentioned? You're going to lose your balance and fall into this pit. It'll be a pretty big fall, and the wooden surface is hard. But it won't be enough to kill you. What's going to accomplish that is you getting hit in the head as you go down by one of those two-by-four pieces of wood jutting out." His grin widened as he added, "At least that's what it will look like. What will really happen is that I'm going to give this process a little help."

And then he lunged toward me. He was still at least ten feet away, which gave me just enough time to screw off the lid of the bottle in my hand and spill out dozens of tiny sugar pearls, each one a perfectly round little ball.

George was either too distracted to notice what I'd done or too confused to figure out what it meant, because he kept coming toward me. In the second or two he was in motion, I noticed that he was wearing the same shiny black loafers I'd seen him wear before.

Loafers that no doubt had a slick leather bottom.

Which turned out to be extremely advantageous, since once he was almost close enough to grab me, he instead began slipping and sliding as those smooth soles encountered what amounted to a sheet of treacherous little BBs.

The way his arms flailed around as he tried to regain his balance was almost comical, making him look like a character in a Looney Tunes cartoon. He was also making a noise that made him sound like one: "Who-o-o-oa!"

And then, just as I'd hoped, he slid off the ledge and down into the pit. His head didn't make contact with the wooden planks, the scenario he'd had in mind for me. But when he finally hit the bottom, his leg was twisted in a grotesque way that told me he had most likely broken it.

"Ow-w-w-w!" he yelled. "Help me! I can't get up! Get me out of here!"

But I was too busy dialing 911.

I'd just been assured that both the police and an ambulance were on their way when I heard Grams's voice call, "Katydid? Are you all right? What on earth is going on?"

I saw her standing in the doorway to the gym, holding an armful of construction paper and glue and other supplies. The expression on her face was one of total confusion.

"Is George still here?" she asked. "And for heaven's sake, what are you doing up there? You should come down immediately before you get hurt!"

I had no problem with doing exactly that.

Fifteen minutes later, Grams and I were standing together with our arms around each other, watching two EMTs transport George Vernon Scott out of the gym on a gurney. Officer Pete Bonano had handcuffed him to the edge even though it didn't look like he was going anywhere, given how twisted his leg was.

"He's going to be fine, once he gets that leg taken care of," Pete Bonano said as he strolled over to us. "He'll certainly be in good enough shape to stand trial."

And then someone else came over to us, someone who had showed up at the gym mere minutes after I'd called 911.

"I'm not sure whether or not to thank you," Detective Stoltz told me begrudgingly. "The good news is that you figured out who poisoned Savannah Crane and then managed to catch the killer. The bad news is that you almost got killed yourself in the process."

"But that didn't happen," I pointed out. Trying to add a little levity to the occasion, I added, "And once again, my passion for ice cream saved the day. Can you imagine that there are some people who don't understand how important the regular consumption of ice cream can be to a person's health and safety?"

Detective Stoltz didn't look the least bit amused. In fact, he just sort of grunted. Then he turned and walked away.

But when he had almost reached the double doors, he stopped and turned back. "Good job, Ms. McKay," he called. And then he left.

Once Grams and I were alone, she seemed to crumple, her shoulders sagging as she covered her face with her hands.

"Oh, Kate, I feel like such a fool!" she wailed. "How could I have ever been silly enough to fall for a man like that?"

"George is someone who's very good at covering up who he really is," I assured her. "He's been deceiving a lot of people for a very long time."

Sadly, I added, "Unfortunately, Savannah Crane was one of the few people who *wasn't* deceived. And in the end, it cost her her life."

We were both silent for a while, still thinking about the

horrific events of the past week and a half. Finally, I took a deep breath and slung my arm around Grams's shoulders.

"Come on, Grams," I said. "Let's go home."

Grams looked astonished. "Go home? When there's still so much to do? I've got my painting crew coming any minute now, and I have to be around to tell them which walls to make black and which ones to make gray. Then there's Arnie, a crackerjack bingo player who happens to be a retired electrician. He's going to help put in more lighting. And Marilou is a top-notch seamstress, and she's going to be making costumes for some of the other volunteers to wear . . ."

I started to protest, then stopped myself. My grandmother, I could see, was as unstoppable as I was.

I held up my hands. "I've got an extra pair of these, in case you need them," I told her.

"I can always use more help," Grams replied, smiling. "Any chance you're as handy with a paintbrush as you are with an ice cream scoop?"

"Maybe I'm good with an ice cream scoop," I told her, "but that's nothing compared to what I can do with a few sprinkles."

Chapter 18

In Ireland and Scotland, ice cream cones are called
pokes. In other parts of Britain, they are called
cornets.

—en.wikipedia.org/wiki/Ice_cream_cone

Halloween had never seemed less scary. Or more fun.
The high school gym was swarming with elementary-
school–age kids, laughing and chattering away so enthusiastically that the noise level was nearly ear-shattering. All of
them were wearing costumes. I spotted clowns, pirates, prin-
cesses, mummies, ghosts, Disney characters, and at least six
different versions of Superman, all with a red cape. Some of
the parents, sitting on the bleachers or standing in clusters,
were also wearing costumes, or at least funny wigs or makeup.

I was pleased to see that there was a big crowd of children
around my do-it-yourself ice cream sundae station. It had
been clear from the moment the doors opened that it was
going to be a huge success. Not surprisingly, the fake eyeballs
and the gummy centipedes were turning out to be even more
popular than the M&Ms and Skittles. As for the volunteers
from the senior center who were helping the kids make the
craziest concoctions imaginable, they appeared to be having
even more fun than the little ones.

And the centerpiece for all the Halloween high jinks was
the glorious haunted house. Grams's brainchild was magnifi-

cent, somehow both cute and eerie at the same time. Every element had come out perfectly, from the glowing jack-o'-lanterns to the fake graveyard with its funny sayings. Even the foam pit behind the house looked enticing, thanks to the strings of pumpkin-shaped lights all around it. It was filled to the top with chunks of cushiony foam, and I could hear the children's laughter as they jumped into it—safely.

The schoolchildren weren't the only ones in disguise today. Emma had made good on her promise to whip up some fabulous costumes. She and I were both dressed as witches, wearing the classic, long black dresses they're known to favor. We also had tall black hats, rustic-looking brooms, and enough green makeup on our faces that the two of us were barely recognizable. I turned out to be excellent at cackling, a natural talent I'd never known I possessed. Emma wasn't bad, either.

As for Willow, she had gone the princess route. She had found, at a local thrift store, a shimmery floor-length blue dress with a full skirt. Emma had made it more princess-worthy by cutting the neckline more deeply, making the sleeves really puffy, and sewing twinkly silver sequins along the neckline and hem. Like us, Willow was barely recognizable, thanks to the long blond wig she wore over her pixie cut. Her silver tiara from a costume shop was the perfect finishing touch.

Grams had made her own costume. After all, the woman was undoubtedly the source of Emma's creativity genes. She had decided to come as Raggedy Ann, complete with a starched white apron, red-and-white-striped stockings, and a wig made of bright red yarn.

"This is so much fun!" Emma exclaimed as we stood by the front door, greeting the children as they came in and handing them each a goodie bag filled with toys and sweet treats. "And the kids really seem to be enjoying themselves!"

"They all look so cute in their costumes, too," Willow added. "Check out that pirate over there. He can't be more than six years old. He doesn't look very scary, does he?"

I looked over at the little boy she was talking about. Not only did he not look the least bit threatening, thanks to his mop of curly, orange-red hair and freckled cheeks; he was clearly miserable over the patch he was wearing on one eye, which kept slipping down. He finally grabbed it, yanked it off, and angrily stuffed it into his goodie bag.

"I guess he's more into the treats than the tricks," I said, laughing.

"I just know he's going to love the gummy centipedes," Willow added.

I turned to Grams. "You've really put together something amazing," I told her. "This was such a great idea. But now you'll have to do it every year!"

"It did come out well, didn't it?" she said.

She immediately grew silent. I had a feeling I knew why.

As much fun as the day was turning out to be, it couldn't help but be overshadowed by the events of the previous weeks. Especially by George Vernon. Or George Vernon Scott, to be more accurate.

Willow must have been reading my mind. "I've been meaning to ask you something," she said, nervously looking from me to Grams and back to me again. "How is that man doing? The one who—you know?"

"He's still in the hospital," I said. "But the doctors say he's going to be fine once his broken leg heals."

"He'll certainly be in good enough shape to go straight to jail as soon as he's on his feet again," Emma added. "He's been charged with the first-degree murder of Savannah Crane, the attempted murder of Kate, bribing public officials, breaking land-use laws, and a whole list of other things. It looks like he's going to be spending the rest of his life in jail.

"And he's not the only one who's in trouble," she added. "So are all the local politicians who were involved in this scam. But the best news is that they've already started taking down that horrible Hudson Hideaways project. The land is going back to being preserved, even though it'll take a long time for it to get back to its original state."

Turning to me, Willow said, "Kate, you deserve an award for solving this mystery. The others you've been involved in investigating on your own, too. They should build a statue of you in the Mashawam Preserve."

"I'm just glad this case is finally closed," I said. "Chelsea Atkins is, too. She flew back home to California as soon as Detective Stoltz told her it was okay to leave."

"What about Savannah's boyfriend?" Emma asked. "Is he going to get in trouble?"

"The authorities are definitely looking into the role he played in the Hudson Hideaways project," I told her. More to myself than to anyone else, I muttered, "I wonder if Amanda will still find Timothy attractive once he's been slammed with a bunch of felony charges."

"It sounds as if every last piece of the puzzle has been put in place, thanks to you," Emma said with a sigh. "Thank goodness that ugliness is behind us. Now we can all breathe freely."

"Here, here," Willow agreed.

Grams still looked troubled, however. I knew she was continuing to wrestle with the fact that she had actually been developing feelings for a man who turned out to be completely different from the person he appeared to be.

Talk about a Halloween disguise.

I had a feeling that it would be some time before Grams allowed herself to take another risk. But I was hoping that I'd be able to help her with that.

After all, I had come up with a decision of my own. One

that was very closely related since it involved the possibility of a broken heart.

At practically the same moment I had that thought, Sir Lancelot came through the door. That is, Sir Lancelot with Jake Pratt's face.

He was wearing a suit of armor, or at least pants and a shirt made out of shimmery silver fabric. He had on a head-piece, too, kind of a skullcap thing with silvery mesh hanging around the sides.

The finishing touch was a shield and a sword. Given their flimsy appearance, neither of them looked as if they'd serve him very well in a serious fight, not to mention a joust. Fortunately, it didn't look as if there were any possible challengers around, aside from a little boy of about seven I spotted who was also dressed as a knight. And he didn't look like he was about to challenge anyone. He was too busy pouring about a pint of caramel sauce over a baseball-size scoop of vanilla ice cream that was studded with eyeballs.

As Jake came over to us, he struck a knight-like pose, holding out his shield and raising his sword into the air.

"A knight?" I said, laughing. "Really?"

"Hey, I'm not just *any* knight," he countered, pretending to be offended. "I'm a knight in shining armor."

"Too bad I'm not in need of a rescuer at the moment," I commented.

"I've said this before, and I'll say it again," Jake replied seriously. "I've never thought of you as someone who needs rescuing, Kate."

He thought for a few seconds, then added, "Although you might do well to accept a little assistance whenever you're confronting a killer. By yourself. In a deserted place."

His voice thickened. "If anything ever happened to you, Kate, I don't know what I would do."

The intense look in his blue eyes made me feel as if he really was a knight in shining armor.

I guess Emma picked up on that vibe, because she abruptly said, "Grams, I think we should go check on the candy corn over at the ice cream table. It looks as if they're about to run out. Willow, could you please help us?"

"Certainly!" Willow quickly agreed, gathering up her voluminous blue skirt and skittering after them.

"That was subtle," Jake said, grinning.

"The members of my family aren't exactly known for their subtlety," I commented. I took a deep breath before adding, "Which is why I'm going to come right out and tell you what I've been thinking."

"Okay," Jake said nervously. I could tell from his expression that he didn't expect this to be good news.

"I think your plan to open the roadside stand is a great idea," I told him. "I have no doubt that it's going to do well. But I've decided that I don't want to be your business partner."

He thought for a few seconds. "I guess I'm not surprised," he finally said. "I was hoping for a different answer, of course, but—"

"There's more," I interrupted. "I haven't told you the reason."

He looked at me expectantly as I paused to take another deep breath. "It's because I want to try being your partner . . . in a *different* way."

The tension in his face immediately dissolved. But I wasn't sure I'd made myself clear.

"What I mean is—"

"I know what you mean," he said softly. "I know *exactly* what you mean."

And right there, in the middle of the high school gym, with

a couple of hundred little kids surrounding us, he took me in his arms and kissed me.

"Eww!" I heard a little girl cry. "That knight is kissing a witch! Those two don't belong together!"

I, however, thought the two of us made a fine pair.

Affogato

Affogato, an Italian word that means "drowned," combines two heavenly ingredients: ice cream and espresso. It sounds simple (and it is), but this basic recipe leaves plenty of room for creativity.

While chocolate, vanilla, and coffee are popular flavors for the ice cream, you can use any flavor that you think pairs well with coffee. You can also add Grand Marnier or Amaretto or another flavored liquor, top it off with berries, nuts, amaretti biscuits, or chocolate shavings, or add whatever else suits your fancy. (Chocolate-covered coffee beans, anyone?) You'll soon find yourself saying *"arrivederci"* to more ordinary desserts!

To make four servings:

1 pint of ice cream or gelato
4 shots (about 8 tablespoons) of hot espresso (regular or decaf)
whipping cream
sugar

Beat the whipping cream, adding sugar to taste. Scoop the ice cream into attractive serving dishes, pour the hot espresso over it, top with whipped cream and other add-ons, and serve immediately.

Baked Alaska

Baked Alaska is a fun dessert consisting of cold ice cream encased in a warm crust made of either pastry or, more commonly, meringue. It is also known as an *omelette à la norvégienne* or "Norwegian omelette," because Norway, like

Alaska, is cold in the winter. Other names are omelette surprise and *glace au four*.

There are many stories about how it got its name. A popular one is that Charles Ranhofer, chef at the legendary New York City restaurant Delmonico's, named his version Alaska, Florida in 1894 because of its combination of cold and hot.

While the dessert is wonderfully dramatic, it's also easy to make. The most important thing is to keep the ice cream and the cake as cold as possible. One trick is to make the cake base in advance, wrap it up tightly, and freeze it.

4 egg whites
⅛ teaspoon of cream of tartar
½ cup of sugar
1 quart of hard ice cream (you can use more than one flavor)
8-inch-wide, round layer of pound cake, brownies, or other cake, preferably frozen

Beat the egg whites until they are very stiff, gradually adding the cream of tartar and sugar.

Cover the cake layer with the ice cream, arranging it to get the shape you want. One option is to press the ice cream into a bowl and freeze it, creating a dome-shaped ice cream layer.

Cover the ice cream and the side of the cake with the meringue. Sprinkle the meringue with chopped nuts or coconut, if desired.

Bake at 500 degrees Fahrenheit for 5 to 10 minutes, until the tips of the meringue begin to brown. Be sure to keep an eye on it! Serve immediately.

Please turn the page for an exciting sneak peek of
Cynthia Baxter's next
Lickety Splits mystery
GAME OF CONES
coming soon wherever print and e-books are sold!

Chapter 1

In August 1850, the women's magazine *Godey's Lady Book* said that a party without ice cream would be like "breakfast without bread or a dinner without a roast."

— *Daniel Joseph Boorstin,* The Americans: The National Experience

"This isn't exactly my idea of a romantic getaway," Jake mumbled, peering out the rain-splattered window of my truck.

I leaned closer to the steering wheel, struggling to focus on the curving road ahead of me. Given the sheeting rain, the ominously dark afternoon sky, the *Wizard of Oz*-style wind, and the thick mist that was threatening to turn into serious fog, I had to agree that this certainly wasn't what either of us had expected.

The idea of spending a long weekend at the Mohawk Mountain Resort, an old-fashioned lakeside hideaway nestled in the Catskill Mountains just thirty miles away from our hometown, had sounded positively idyllic when I'd first gotten an email from the resort's general manager a few months earlier. Growing up in the Hudson Valley, I had heard plenty about the historic hotel that had been a popular retreat since the mid-1800s. Yet I'd never actually had a chance to stay at the sprawling resort, enjoying its unique style of rustic luxury and pretending that I was living in another era.

True, when I was a teenager I'd hiked around the 30,000-acre property a few times. I had had the pleasure of tromping through the woods and across clearings and over ridges, making my way along trails with colorful names like Pine Needle Walk and Mountain Vista Ridge and Rocky Road—a name which these days, as an ice cream empress, I found especially endearing.

But that was just the grounds that surrounded Mohawk. The glorious stone and wood building that constituted the actual resort, perched high atop a mountain as if it was the preserve's centerpiece, had merely served as a distant backdrop during my day trips. After all, while the outdoor area was open to the public, the 250-room hotel and its reported Old World luxury had been reserved for guests only. And those aforementioned guests were required to have some pretty impressive credit card limits in order to bask in its splendors.

So when I'd unexpectedly received an invitation from the hotel's general manager, Merle Moody, I had literally whooped with joy. In fact, I had decided to say yes even before I'd read her entire email.

In her note, she had explained that Mohawk frequently conducted theme weekends as a way of attracting visitors during the off-season. Past theme weekends had ranged from jazz workshops to yoga-and-meditation retreats to storytelling marathons. She told me that she was getting in touch with me because she knew I had an ice cream emporium, the Lickety Splits Ice Cream Shoppe, located nearby. In mid-November, she was interested in having Mohawk host a weekend of lectures, demonstrations, and hands-on workshops built around the theme of ice cream. Payment would be minimal, but the gig would give me a chance to combine work and play in a scenic spot.

The general manager went on to say she wanted to call this theme weekend "We All Scream for Ice Cream." She hoped I'd offer classes on topics like Making Exotic Ice Cream Flavors at Home and Thirty-Three Toppings to Make Your Ice Cream Sensational. Ms. Moody noted that mid-November was a particularly slow time, so she was anxious to offer something exceptionally upbeat.

I wasn't surprised that business at the resort was sluggish at this time of the year. My ice cream shop had also been experiencing a dramatic slowdown. And all I had to do was look out the window to understand why.

"Think of it this way," I told Jake as we chugged along in my red pickup truck. "You and I will be tucked away inside a cozy mountain retreat, sipping hot chocolate and eating ice cream in front of a roaring fireplace. We won't care at all about the storm raging outside."

"I was hoping to do some hiking," Jake said. As I glanced over at him, I saw that he was squinting as he gazed out the window. I got the impression he was wondering if somehow he could will the rain away. "And according to the website you can go canoeing on the lake. They have rowboats and paddleboats and kayaks, too. And paddle boarding, which is something I always thought would be great to try, since you actually stand up as you skim the surface of the water. Then there's swimming in the lake. And fishing, of course . . ."

He let out a deep sigh. I knew exactly what that sigh meant: that given the storm raging all around us, none of those options was going to be even close to feasible.

Even though I was already pretty bummed out over the weather being so horrid, Jake's dismay over the way it was ruining our plans was making me feel even worse. While his purpose in tagging along was supposedly to serve as my "assistant" over the course of the weekend, there was a lot more behind my decision to bring him with me.

He and I had recently rekindled our old romance, one that had started when we were back in high school. While our relationship had been rudely interrupted by fifteen years of having no contact whatsoever, fate seemed to have brought us together once again. The two of us were still feeling our way, trying to decide whether or not we could make a go of it now that we had been given another chance.

My sense was that Jake had few doubts about the two of us being a couple once again. In fact, he had been the one who'd pushed for it. Not long after he and I had accidentally run into each other after our long separation, he had made it clear that he'd be happy to pick up where we'd left off. And I had finally agreed that our relationship deserved another chance.

Now that we were actually back in that relationship, however, I continued to wrestle with uncertainty about whether or not I had made the right choice. I thought I had forgiven him for the painful and abrupt way our high school romance had ended. But deep down, I still wasn't one hundred percent convinced.

But there was more to it. I wasn't sure about whether or not I even *wanted* to become involved with anyone at this stage of my life. I was working long, exhausting hours as I struggled to get my own business off the ground. Lickety Splits was still brand new, having opened only six months earlier. Running a retail store that specialized in home-made gourmet ice cream was a huge change from working at a public relations firm in New York City. And while I loved being my own boss, the demands of running my fledgling enterprise practically single-handedly were turning out to be a lot more daunting than I'd ever dreamed.

There had been plenty of other huge changes in my life,

too. After a decade and a half of being pretty much on my own, I was back in my hometown, Wolfert's Roost, living under my grandmother's roof. While this was the house that I'd pretty much grown up in, a wonderful Victorian that I truly loved, being back there was still a major adjustment. Cohabitating with my grandmother as an adult, rather than as a child, gave me delightful companionship but less independence. And because I'd moved back so I could help Grams as she aged, it also meant that I'd taken on more responsibility.

Then there was the fact that suddenly I was also looking after my eighteen-year-old niece, Emma, who had moved in with Grams and me unexpectedly. She was lively and strong and very much her own person, but it was still my job to serve as a sort of mother figure to her.

I'm not saying that I was unhappy about my new situation. It was just, well, *different*—not to mention demanding, complicated, absorbing, taxing, and at times absolutely exhausting. And the idea of adding Jake Pratt into the mix sometimes struck me as one challenge too many.

But as I drove along, I reminded myself that this wasn't the best time to be thinking about my ambivalence about my relationship with the man sitting beside me.

"The weather can't be this bad the whole time we're there, can it?" I said.

I had just turned off the main road onto a considerably narrower one. It was marked by a rather crude wooden sign with the hand-painted words "Mohawk Mountain Resort" and a big arrow. But I already knew the answer to my own question. I'd been checking the ten-day forecast all week. Not only was rain predicted for the entire weekend ahead. The torrential rain, fog, and wind that already surrounded us had been labeled a nor'easter, a serious storm that's almost as bad as a hurricane.

As if to answer the question I'd just asked, at that very moment a tree branch flew into the windshield with a loud bang, making me jump. Instantly my heart leaped into high gear as adrenaline coursed through my body.

"Whoa!" Jake cried. "This is going from bad to worse! Hey, you don't suppose they'll cancel the workshop, do you?"

I shook my head, meanwhile making sure to keep my eyes glued to the road ahead. By this point I was pretty sure the mist could officially be called fog. That was because I could only see about ten feet in front of me.

"I got an email from Merle Moody early this morning," I told him. "You remember me mentioning her, don't you? She's the general manager of the resort and the person I've been in contact with all along. She said that Mohawk hasn't ever shut down, or even cancelled a program, since the day it first opened in 1868 as a simple tavern with four guest rooms."

"It was nice of her to check in with you," Jake commented.

"Actually," I said, "from the tone of her email, I got the feeling she wasn't trying to reassure me as much as she was making it clear that *I'd* better not be thinking of cancelling."

Or maybe I was just being too sensitive, I thought. The wording of the general manager's email had struck me as crisp. Cold, even. But I told myself that the feeling I got, that she was ordering me to show up rather than simply being matter-of-fact, was probably related more to my own apprehensions about the weekend ahead than anything else.

Jake and I were both silent as we continued up a road that was quickly becoming steeper, narrower, and more twisting. We were already surrounded by a dense growth of trees, mighty maples and white-barked birches and towering evergreens so dense that they practically formed a barricade. The fog was growing thicker with every turn in the road. Yet even through the hovering mist's dense grayness, I could make out signs printed with warnings about deer, and then wild turkeys, crossing the road.

"Funny, I don't recall this road being so scary," I finally remarked, hoping I wouldn't encounter any wildlife along the way. "Then again, the last time I was here was when I was about sixteen. Willow and I drove up on a Saturday in October. I was so excited to be spending the entire day with my best friend! It was positively thrilling that the two of us were going off on an adventure all by ourselves.

"I remember that the air was brisk and the leaves were absolutely gorgeous," I went on, feeling as if I was actually going back in time. "They were blazing with color, bright red and orange and gold . . . it was one of those perfect autumn days that make you glad you live in the Hudson Valley. Willow and I spent the whole day hiking and taking pictures. I also remember that we brought along a fabulous picnic lunch that Grams had packed up for us. She made the best chicken salad, with walnuts and grapes and celery. And she'd baked tiny chocolate chip cookies that were so much fun to eat . . ."

"That sounds really nice," Jake commented. From his wistful tone, I got the feeling that the rest of that sentence, best left unspoken, was something along the lines of "unlike now."

We drove on, my teeth clenched so hard that my jaw started to ache as I slowly veered around one treacherous turn after another. At least there were no deer or wild turkeys flinging themselves into the road. Unlike us, they were apparently much too smart to venture outside on a day like today.

Jake and I traveled higher and higher up into the mountains, with clouds of fog still drifting past. At times we could see just how perilous the road was, while at other times we could scarcely see what was in front of us at all. Frankly, I didn't know which was worse.

And then the fog suddenly cleared. In the distance I could see the resort's expansive main building looming up ahead of us like a mirage.

In all the photographs I'd seen, as well as in my own memory, Mohawk had seemed like paradise. The hotel, with its jaw-dropping backdrop of mountains and forests and a gigantic lake, had looked palatial. The resort was huge, a jumble of half a dozen different wings and extensions jutting off the original wood and stone building that stood at the center. The newer parts were painted a muted shade of apple green that blended in with the natural setting. As for the oldest section, it remained dark brown, with the same rough-hewn wooden shingles and craggy gray stone walls it had always had. The wooden porch that lined the original building, overlooking the lake and the mountains beyond, had been duplicated in the newer sections as well, creating a cohesive look to what might otherwise appear a bit chaotic.

In the photographs, the lake was invariably sparkling in the bright midday sun. Happy guests in canoes and rowboats cheerfully waved to each other. Other guests, also smiling, strolled along the trails, looking as if there was no place else in the entire world they would rather be.

Today, however, Mohawk reminded me of a haunted house. Hill House, perhaps, the eerie mansion that was featured in the classic black-and-white horror film *The Haunting*. That's the movie in which the actress Julie Harris sees throbbing walls with eyes and hears children crying until she's driven to near insanity, rushing out onto a road where she's accidentally run over by—

Stop! I told myself. There's nothing the least bit creepy about the Mohawk Mountain Resort! It's a luxurious, historic hotel with a fine reputation and a top chef and a fireplace in every room. And you're going to enjoy every single minute you're there.

Three seconds later, I heard a tremendous boom and felt the earth shake.

"What was that?" I shrieked, stomping down on the brake and bringing my truck to a complete stop with a jolt.

Jake had already turned around in his seat, trying to see out the back window. "It sounds like it was behind us," he said, "but I can't see anything from here. I'll have to get out."

"Don't get out!" I cried. I had visions of never seeing him again. I figured that like Julie Harris, he'd meet up with some terrible fate, perhaps one that involved evil deer or malicious wild turkeys.

"I'll just take a quick look around." He had already opened the door and was climbing out of the truck, pulling up his hood in a feeble attempt at protecting himself from the pelting rain.

A few seconds later, he was back, hurling himself into the truck and splattering me with so much water that I might as well have gone outside with him. His light brown hair was soaked. So were his shirt, his pants, and from the looks of things everything else he had on as well.

"A tree fell," he announced grumpily.

"Is *that* all," I replied, relieved.

"You don't understand," he said. "A *big* tree. A *really* big tree. With a thick trunk. Like a five-foot-wide trunk. And it fell right across the road."

I'd barely had a chance to digest his words before he turned to me and explained, "From the looks of things, nobody's getting in or out of here for a very long time."

"You mean we're *stuck* up here?" I cried. Suddenly, the idea of spending a few days in a lovely but remote mountain resort struck me as terrifying. I tried to remind myself that nothing much had changed, that this had been the plan all along. But somehow, having no choice in the matter put a very different cast on the situation.

"Maybe it's not that bad," Jake said. "If a work crew came in here with some electric saws, they could probably clear the road. If they worked on it for a while, anyway."

I tried to believe him. But I definitely got the feeling that he was just trying to make me feel better.

I started driving again, my heart even heavier than before as we continued on our way. Whatever enthusiasm about the weekend ahead that had lingered even after the horrendous weather had put such a damper on things—pun entirely intended—had by now fizzled out completely.

As the big house got closer, I wondered how many people would manage to make it up the mountain for the theme weekend.

Jake must have been thinking the same thing. "Even if they have to cancel the ice cream workshops," he said with forced cheerfulness, "we can still have that romantic getaway we've been planning."

I looked over at him and forced myself to smile. "Candlelit dinners, cuddling in front of a roaring fire . . . yes, we certainly can."

I tried to hold on to that thought as I drove into the circular driveway in front of Mohawk, the uneven cobblestones that paved it making for a strangely bumpy ride.

While the scale of the building was truly grand, the façade was anything but. The rough-hewn wooden shingles were faded and in some spots missing. As for the front porch, up close it looked pretty dilapidated, as if a serious gust of wind could knock it over. The windows that ran along the front as far as I could see were dark, almost like eyes that were staring out at us dully. On a dreary day like this one, I would have expected the entire place to be lit up in an attempt at making it look at least a little bit inviting. Yet it almost looked as if no one else was here.

The main entrance, an imposing wooden front door, was

marked only by a small sign. I pulled my truck up in front of it, expecting a bellman to appear. Jake and I were going to need some serious help to unload. It wasn't our suitcases that were the problem. It was all the paraphernalia I'd brought along for the workshops I'd be leading. My demonstrations on how to make ice cream and all kinds of assorted related concoctions, for example, required multitudes of bowls, spoons, machinery, and of course lots of ingredients. But as we sat in the truck, staring at the front door, we still didn't spot any signs of life.

Jake and I exchanged nervous looks.

"Should I honk?" I asked, my voice cracking.

Before he had a chance to answer, the big wooden door opened. Slowly. In fact, the only reason I even noticed it was opening at all was because of a dim light that was on inside, a striking contrast to the grim gloominess all around us.

But rather than a perky bellman leaping out, a thin, slightly stooped woman eased her way through the door. She stood on the porch for a few seconds, studying the two of us as we continued sitting in the cabin of my red truck.

My first impression of her was that she was stern. The serious expression on her face was a good match to her simple gray dress, navy blue cardigan, and practical black shoes. Somehow she managed to emanate an air of gloom, as if she was a member of the Addams Family. She reminded me of someone, but I couldn't quite place who that was.

Jake and I climbed out of the truck, each of us grabbing one of our suitcases.

"You must be Katherine McKay," the woman called to me from the porch. It almost sounded like an accusation.

"That's me," I replied. "But please call me Kate. And you must be Merle."

"Mrs. Moody," she corrected me sharply. "I prefer to be addressed as Mrs. Moody."

It was then it clicked. I finally figured out who she re-minded me of: creepy Mrs. Danvers from the Daphne du Maurier classic novel *Rebecca*. Somber, disapproving, and as cold as the icy rain that was dripping down the back of my neck.

Jake and I exchanged another look. *Oh, boy,* it said.